TEA SHOP FOR TWO

LOVE ON BELMONT
BOOK ONE

LORI WOLF-HEFFNER

HEAD IN THE GROUND PUBLISHING

Editing by Susan Fish and Jennifer Dinsmore

Cover design by Fresh Design

Kitchener Blizzard used with permission

Cover photographs from Shutterstock

Print ISBN: 978-1-989465-27-1

Ebook ISBN: 978-1-989465-28-8

Head in the Ground Publishing

Waterloo, Ontario, Canada

headintheground.com

 Created with Vellum

To Jeff Hyslop, whose performances lifted my spirits when life was getting me down.

CHAPTER 1

*P*auline was drenched in sweat. She took a swig of Belmont Blizzard iced tea.

"A little team spirit, Derek!" She'd normally do a handstand or aerial for her handler to perk up his mood, but she needed her energy for the after-game crowd of almost twenty thousand fans.

And she also needed her hip.

"You're not going to tell Ben about that, are you?" Derek pointed to the ice pack on it.

"No. And neither are you. If our grumpy PR manager isn't going to let me tell my family what I do for a living, he can live with a few secrets himself."

"Fair enough." Derek indicated her thermos. "I can smell your tea from here. You drink it all the time. Why doesn't your mom just call it 'black tea with peppermint, cranberry, and ginger'?"

Pauline smiled. "Nothing my mom does is without meaning. Belmont is the name of the street where her store is, and blizzard after me." She took another swig. "Because she says I can never sit still."

Derek smiled. "That's why you do what you do."

Pauline held her thermos up in a toast. It was true. Pauline loved her job. In fact, she loved her whole career.

The sound of a collective groan from the arena spilled into the changeroom. She glanced up at the monitor, which showed a missed goal by Toronto Peregrines centre Evanoff. Derek and Pauline threw their fists in the air and shouted, "Nooo!!!" The score was tied and only four minutes remained in the game. If Evanoff had scored, the Peregrines could have won their first North American Hockey Association Cup in fifty years.

Derek shook his head. "He's going to be so mad at himself."

The game broke for commercial.

Benjamin Landry, the team's PR manager, came barging in. The image of perfection, at least in public, he was dressed in an expensive suit and polished shoes and wore glasses Pauline figured cost as much as her condo. His face was red.

"Why aren't you out there?!"

In private, "less than perfect" didn't begin to describe his people skills.

Pauline looked down at him from her height—the skates added another four inches to her six feet. "No one wants a blocked view of the winning shot. Besides, you wanted me in skates for photos." She lifted a foot. "I can't exactly walk on concrete in them."

"Then at least finish getting dressed!"

Why did he always have to have the last word?

"I've got easily ten minutes, Ben, and as much as I love my job, I enjoy breaks from breathing my own breath. I'll be ready. You know that."

"I don't need to remind you that no matter what happens in

the next five minutes—" Ben's phone rang. He answered, turned on his heel, and strutted out the door.

Pauline and Derek shook their heads in disbelief.

"I guess he didn't need to remind us," Derek said.

The game resumed, and thirty seconds after the puck dropped, the Peregrines got a penalty for high sticking.

Pauline and Derek could hear Ben swear in the corridor.

Derek's phone rang.

"A family's looking to get a photo with Perry before the crowds leave the stadium," he reported to Pauline. "They've got young kids."

Pauline put her drink and ice pack on a table. "Say no more."

She lifted Perry's head off the small fan that dried out the inside, and turned on the tiny fan inside the head that helped circulate air and keep the mask from getting too stuffy.

She stood in front of the full-length mirror and lifted Perry's head over her own. Perry was grey fleece from head to toe, with a peregrine falcon's tail protruding from his lower back, and narrow wings from his arms. He wore the red-and-white home uniform of the Peregrines and red skating boots, with Pauline's real skate blades protruding from underneath. His expression was one of courage and motivation.

Pauline fastened the chin strap, and Derek handed her Perry's three-fingered gloves.

Once fully dressed, Pauline flexed her arms, clapped her hands, and motioned for Derek to follow her out. In costume, Pauline didn't speak—it would break the magic of the character.

If the Peregrines won the cup in the next few minutes, it would be the pinnacle of her career as a mascot performer.

Part of her wanted to stare at the monitor and wait for that goal, but children were waiting for Perry, and that was far more important to Pauline.

~

RICHARD COVERED the microphone on his phone. "I promise: she's a really wonderful person, Todd." He uncovered it again. "Pauline, I know about the cup win last night. It's just for a few days, honey."

She's a Peregrines fan? Todd thought. *Great.*

Nothing like starting a new job—heck, a new career—and needing to bring in the owner's daughter. It was mortifying to say the least, after being at the pinnacle of his last career before the curtain closed on him faster than he'd expected it.

"But isn't there someone else who can help whoever plays Perry?"

Did Pauline actually *work* for the Toronto hockey team? This was topping the Worst First Days on the Job list.

"Can't that Ben guy help just for once?" Richard paused. "Well, what if you do some of your work from here? It's just that your sister can't leave her work and family in Vancouver, I still have to run my brokerage—summer's the busy season—and take care of Mom now, and Todd just started today of all days."

Magnificent. So not only did Pauline work for the Peregrines, but she could step in because she had no family or business of her own to care for, and so she was free enough to babysit forty-three-year-old Todd.

This couldn't get any more embarrassing. All this over tea?

"The paramedics said your mom just dislocated her knee. She should be fine to train Todd from a chair by Monday. We're really desperate, Pauline, or we wouldn't be asking you for this."

Am I really that hopeless of a cause?

"Thanks for considering it, sweetheart. This would mean a lot to us, but especially to your mother." Richard hung up and tucked his phone back into its holster on his hip.

"And?" Todd tried to sound hopeful.

PAULINE RUBBED her eyes as she dragged herself to the bathroom. How could she talk to her father like that?

"That's what you get for not turning your phone off last night," she said to herself.

To accept the biggest role of her career, Pauline had had to sign a non-disclosure agreement: she wasn't allowed to tell anyone she played Perry. Although normal in the pro mascot industry, most performers at least told their innermost circles. But Ben had made it clear when Pauline signed on that she couldn't even tell her family.

Which led to moments like these, where Richard and Claire believed Pauline had a nine-to-five desk job. Since her official title was community engagement manger, they had no reason to believe otherwise.

It wasn't that Pauline had been out partying after last night's win. She could no longer afford that kind of time off if she wanted to do what she loved most about her job: the real community engagement. After every home game, she came straight to her condo, soaked in an ice bath for fifteen minutes, then lay on her couch while she drank a rehydrating solution followed by a calming tisane to bring her adrenalin down. Only then did she go to bed, often not until two or three in the morning. Normally, she turned off her phone, but in the excitement of the win, she'd forgotten.

Hence her angry first response to her father's request.

But all of this was temporary: at forty-seven, she could only perform at this level for a few more years. And now with the win, for those next few years, she'd be performing to sold-out audiences, and Perry's popularity would soar. She'd be able to help so many organizations raise awareness, and therefore money, for their causes. In fact, they had a huge fundraiser planned for the Toronto children's hospital at the end of the month, and this win was going to make that so much more successful. She could feel it!

"But first things first. Once I'm fully awake, I'll call Dad and apologize." Of course she'd ask for a few days off to help her family. This was normally the time when she'd visit them, anyway. With the school year ending, school visits were down, and she deliberately booked fewer community events. But the team's unexpected success in the playoffs had changed that this year.

The problem was that Ben didn't like surprises. He had made it clear that if they won, she might not have time off until just before the next season began: he wanted her on the summer tour with the cup.

But being a mascot involved taking risks. Pauline had jumped through flaming hoops and rappelled from stadium ceilings. Surely she could ask her manager for a few days off.

PART OF TODD hoped that Richard's and Claire's daughter could help him for a few days—he'd never worked a day of retail in his life. The other part hoped she couldn't. He wanted a fresh start: bringing in someone from Toronto risked the possibility he'd be recognized.

Richard shook his head. "I hope your years of teaching prepared you for today. I'm so sorry, Todd. Pauline works in community engagement with the Peregrines, so the earliest she can come is tomorrow, if she can get the time off at all. She accompanies Perry, their mascot, so he doesn't get accosted by the public. Today they have to do a hospital visit, and those visits take a lot out of the actor. Pauline spent a few years working in theme parks in Florida, so she can help the actor deal with it."

At least Pauline *sounded* like a nice person.

Richard continued. "She's good at her job—when you meet her, you'll see what I mean. But her manager's a control freak; he's the reason she lives only an hour away and has rarely come home these past few years. Normally, she'd be free this time of year, but with the playoffs and now the win, I guess her schedule's packed."

Richard wrote down two phone numbers on a piece of paper and slid them to Todd. "Here's Pauline's number and mine." He shook Todd's hand. "We're so glad to have you. If you hadn't been here, I don't know how long Claire would've been on the floor before someone found her—Mondays are super quiet. If there are any emergencies, call me. But if you have any questions about tea, try Pauline. She's hard to get a hold of, but she is helpful." Richard checked his watch. "I'd better get to the hospital."

Todd thanked Richard, and a moment later found himself alone.

It was a comfortable place to be, despite the unfortunate circumstances. The quiet tea shop, with its subdued colours and lights, was a calming contrast to the bright lights and ever-changing scenes of his previous profession. And although he knew Claire expected him to learn a lot, this learning didn't rely on his body any longer. Also a bonus.

He pulled out the notes he'd taken before Claire's accident. He felt guilty. Could he have insisted she not step onto that chair to dust those photos? But Claire had said it was her weekly ritual. The photos were of important moments with family, friends, and customers. Dusting them was her way of thanking them for all the years of happy memories and of reminding herself why she sold tea.

Could I have thought of a different way to help her accomplish the same goal?

He added that to his notes and continued reading.

"Right. She said I could take home three samples a day. I guess I should try something." Claire had suggested starting with the basics, like a Darjeeling, Assam, or Keemun.

Being forced to retire at his age from a profession he loved was painful beyond words. That it had happened so publicly only added to the hurt. Fortunately, Claire had hired him on the spot, but if he couldn't keep this job, he'd have to continue applying to more, increasing the chances of being recognized. Those chances were slim in Kitchener, but still.

He returned to the counter and stared at the wall of several hundred jars of tea. His eyes practically jumped out of his head as he counted twenty-six Darjeeling, six Keemun, and nineteen Assam teas. Learn something new indeed! How was he supposed to pick?

"Just start with the first of each," he said to himself.

He opened each jar to take a whiff. Claire had said she could identify most teas just by their aroma.

But after inhaling each half a dozen times, he couldn't discern any difference: they all smelled like…well, like tea.

This was not a good start. He definitely needed help if he wasn't going to lose Claire business.

And therefore lose his job.

CHAPTER 2

*a*n hour-long jog, second breakfast, two cups of Earl Claire, and a hot shower later, Pauline was standing outside the Peregrines office.

Every mascot performer understood that you sacrificed your personal life for your work. But everyone she knew could take time off for family emergencies when needed. Could Pauline? She was about to find out.

"Hey, Pauline!" Sarah, the receptionist said.

Pauline waved but didn't stop to chat because she saw Ben come out of a meeting with the CEO. She was on a mission.

"Ben, I need to talk to you—now."

He didn't even look at her. "You've only got a few minutes and it had better help me get promoted."

Great.

"There's been an accident at home…"

"No." Ben continued walking.

"You don't even know if anyone's seriously hurt!"

"You're a mascot, Pauline. Your job is to grab my attention

with the strongest thing you've got, and all you've got is 'There's been an accident.' Still no."

For the love of all things holy. He could really see through anyone. "Ben, please. I haven't asked for extra time off in three years."

"We've never won. Now we have. You're too important to the Peregrines' image, Pauline. It's why you get six figures." He continued past the visitors' seating area.

Pauline jumped over a couch and landed in front of Ben, surprising him.

"Derek said he can step into the costume and do the two community photo ops with the cup this week. My mom dislocated her knee, so nothing serious, but serious enough that she needs my help."

"Still no."

The nerve of him! "I'll just be in Kitchener for a few days!"

"And risk losing the best mascot in the league to an industrial-leftover city?"

Pauline threw her hands in the air. "Ben, this is my mother's *tea shop* we're talking about. I promise you, I'll have cabin fever by day two. And you know how much I love the community work you're letting me do. I very well can't do that glued to a counter passing out bags of tea. But my family's important to me, and legally, you have to give me time off."

Ben began to walk to his office. "Legally," he said over his shoulder, "your time off is when I say it is, and that's after the cup's tour and before the season begins."

Pauline let out a grunt of frustration and ran after Ben. "I can manage Perry's social media accounts and book community events from Kitchener. You really don't need me this week."

"What's going on?"

Pauline turned around and found the CEO behind her. Before Ben could spin his charismatic magic, she blurted out her plea like a team of hockey players scrambling for the puck. "My mom dislocated her knee and needs me to help out for the rest of the week. I'm just trying to get some time off."

The CEO smiled. "That shouldn't be a problem. Pauline's done an outstanding job with Perry." He checked his phone. "Nope, no appearances this week that require her special skill set. You're okay with that, right, Ben?"

Ben smiled his PR manager smile. "No problem at all. We'll be absolutely fine. Derek can step in."

"Great idea, Ben. That's thinking like a director of marketing."

So that was the promotion he was hoping for. Pauline was about to explode like a kettle filled with too much boiling water.

Ben raised his fist for a fist bump, and Pauline responded in kind only because the CEO was standing behind her.

"Enjoy your few days off," Ben said. "We'll see you Sunday to prep for the victory parade on Monday."

The CEO patted Ben as he passed him. "Great find with her." He stopped and turned back to face Pauline. "By the way, that video that went viral? The 'Chicken Dance' with those three guys? Fantastic idea."

Pauline smiled. Compliments from the CEO were genuine.

Once the CEO closed the door to his office, Ben's smile turned to a scowl.

Pauline dropped her smile, too. "You need a heart, Ben."

"Mine beats just fine."

Satisfied she got her wish, though, Pauline said nothing more. But now she faced her next challenge: how to lie to her parents for the rest of the week about her real job.

≈

THE INFORMATION in the huge binder before him had begun to dance in his mind. Claire had said there was a tea for every emotion, problem, and celebration, and she had written it all out in this binder and expected him to memorize it. Todd could memorize the language of movement in two seconds. The last time he'd needed to memorize words was in high school.

He rubbed his temples. An hour had passed and still no customers. He was grateful—he'd survived one hour alone without embarrassing himself or his employer—but if business was this slow, how was Claire going to afford to keep him?

His phone beeped, pulling him out of his worries: it was a video text from his dad.

What now?

Todd looked to the storefront door. No one was coming.

He hit play.

"Oh my god…" he muttered aloud.

Todd's dad and brothers, Mark and Tim, were dressed head to toe—complete with makeup—in Peregrines paraphernalia and were covered in string confetti. They had clearly been at last night's final and were doing the "Chicken Dance" with Perry.

That Perry.

"Wish you were here!" they shouted in unison at the camera.

The message accompanying the video read, *Hope you're doing well, son, wherever you are. Call me when you have a moment. Worried about you.*

Was something wrong? Todd wasn't used to that much emotion from his dad. He texted back that everything was good, but that prompted an immediate phone call.

"Dad, listen, I'm at work, so I really shouldn't talk…"

"You got a regular job? That's wonderful!"

Even after over two decades in his past career, Todd still

couldn't get his father to acknowledge that he'd had a regular career. "Are you okay, Dad?"

"Yes, yes, I'm fine."

"Then I really need to go. I started today. I can't be caught on the phone." Not that anyone was walking through that door to catch him.

"Listen. Your brothers and I are in Toronto. Any chance you're nearby? We'd love to visit. It'd be nice to see you. You don't have to go through this alone."

"Has anyone from the media called you?"

"Well, yes…"

"I want you to be honestly able to tell them you don't know where I am."

In all his years of fame, Todd had never asked his family to lie for him, especially because his father was well-known across the country in his own right. Fans gossiped, especially on social media.

"Suit yourself then."

He could hear the hurt in Michael's voice. "Dad, I just need some privacy to sort things out."

"You could come into the family business."

"Hardly private." Someone approached the door. "I have to go. Someone's coming in."

However, as soon as Todd and his father hung up, the person at the door waved to another person, and the pair walked off.

Kitchener was only an hour away from Toronto, but when it came to the performing arts, it was like moving to the middle of nowhere. Kitchener and the neighbouring cities of Waterloo and Cambridge had an active arts scene to be sure, but nothing compared to Toronto. For starters, Todd could have never made a career for himself in Kitchener, because no such company existed. In fact, when Todd had performed at Kitchener's two-thousand-seat theatre several years ago for one night, ticket sales didn't even fill the orchestra section. In Toronto? He performed in a sold-out four-thousand-seat theatre two weeks in a row, several times a year.

Moving here let him hide because no one here cared about who he was or what he did.

Almost no one. He still had to be careful.

Was there a tea for how he felt right now? Rejected and depressed? Todd leaned on the counter and paged through the binder again. He stopped at a tea circled in red called Earl Claire. *For feeling angry, sad, depressed, and hopeful all at once*, read the description. That would work.

He brewed himself a cup and found, to his surprise, that it did indeed offer help. The lavender was calming. The vanilla made him think of desserts he'd tasted on his travels. The citrus flavour of the bergamot refreshed him, like a glass of orange juice for breakfast. And the gentle whiff and taste of rose...yes, it did give him hope, but for what? The description didn't say hope for anything specific, just hope.

"Hope it is."

Hopefully, Pauline—if she came—would help him make sense of all this tea. Because if she couldn't, he'd surely cost Claire business, Claire would fire him, and he'd have one more colossal failure under his cap.

Then his new life would be over before it had really begun.

He had to have hope.

CHAPTER 3

The twelve-year-old boy's eyes opened wide as Pauline gave him a hockey card signed by Evanoff. He flexed both his arms like Perry, and Pauline replied in kind. His mother thanked her as she and her son headed off down the platform at the Kitchener bus station.

Richard opened his arms to his daughter for a hug. "You never stop thinking about others, do you?"

Pauline blushed as she wrapped her arms around her dad. "Except when my dad calls me to help out with the store." There was nothing like the loving hug of a father to make you feel even guiltier for acting so selfishly. "I'm so sorry again about the way I answered yesterday."

Richard took her suitcase. "This win is huge. Your mother feels bad for asking you to come at such a time."

They passed through the doors, and in two seconds were in the parking lot. Things were a lot smaller in Kitchener.

"How's Mom?"

Richard laughed. "A little loopy. They had to operate, unfortunately."

"What? Why didn't you tell me?"

"We thought it best to give you time to pack up and finish whatever work you had to do. One of her ligaments tore. She's good now, just on some strong pain meds."

When they reached the car, Richard asked if Pauline wouldn't mind loading her own suitcase into the trunk. "What happened to your mother has got me scared about my own abilities!"

Richard's words struck a chord of sadness in Pauline, and she noticed she was now a smidge taller than her father. His hairline had receded a little, too, and his wrinkles seemed deeper. He looked no less distinguished, just older. As sad as she was for Claire's injury, she was thankful it gave her an excuse to come home for a few days.

"Anyway," Richard continued, "they're going to release her later today."

"That's good to hear."

As she sat down in the passenger seat, Pauline winced. Her hip again.

"You okay?"

"Just some stiff muscles. I don't do well sitting for long periods of time. You know me." But her father's expression told her he didn't buy her lie. He didn't say anything, though. Instead, he commanded his phone to dial Claire.

"My Darjeeling, Pauline's in the car."

"Hi, Mom."

Richard pulled out of the parking lot.

"Oh my goodness, I never thought I'd hear your voice. I was so scared that Ben fellow would keep you in Toronto."

"He wanted to. It actually took the CEO to give me the rest of the week off. I have to get back to Toronto on Sunday."

"I can't believe you have a desk job that's so demanding you can't visit us more often. I'm so happy you're here. So, so happy, Pauline."

"Me too, Mom."

Pauline looked out the window as the trees of Victoria Park passed. She wished she could explain to her parents why she couldn't come, how long she now took to heal after every performance — both physically and emotionally. Any day off was a day on the couch accompanied by any of several teas and tisanes from her mother's tea shop. Two days off? A day on the couch plus a day running errands. Only if she had a third day off could she visit family, and that rarely happened.

But she couldn't explain any of that. "So, any last-minute tips?"

"Oh, of course! You'll want to know who you're working with. His name is Todd. He's a retired teacher."

"Retired?"

"Just because he's retired doesn't make him old, Pauline. But he drinks *bagged* tea, so make sure he doesn't tell customers that. He'll be amazing at teaching people about tea once he's learned about it. Teach him everything you know. He's very nice. You'll like him."

Richard leaned over and whispered, "She's not herself. The medications."

They would reach the store in a few minutes. Nestled between Glasgow Street to the south and Union Boulevard to the north, Belmont Village was in an older part of town, between working-class Belmont neighbourhood to the east and upscale Westmount neighbourhood to the west. The first houses had been built almost one hundred years ago, but the shops in Belmont Village were a mix of buildings from the fifties, sixties, and seventies, with façades as recent as this decade. Pauline loved the character of the entire area: so much individuality living together.

But time was running out; they were almost there.

She repeated her earlier question. "Mom? Last-minute tips?"

"Oh!" Claire's voice was suddenly loud and high pitched. "I didn't get a chance to tell him that today's the summer sale. And I forgot to make signs. He doesn't know."

"Mother!" Pauline slapped a hand to her forehead. "There's probably a line-up and he'll have no idea why!"

"Oh, he'll be fine. He's a teacher. He can handle thirty people at once. It'll be just like when he was at school."

"But not thirty regulars of Claire's Tea Shop who know exactly when your sales are and are expecting to see you behind the counter and not some strange man."

"Sorry? Oh, yes, of course. My Darjeeling, honey, I need to go. They're taking my blood. Bye!" Claire hung up.

Richard was laughing. "Yup, loopy. And not used to having to communicate her plans to someone else. Explains why no one was there yesterday, apart from it being a Monday. Poor guy was probably wondering why Claire hired him."

He turned right onto Belmont Avenue.

Pauline's heart beat faster than it did before a game, but for the life her she couldn't imagine why. Although it had been a year since she'd last helped in the shop, she'd grown up there. Yes, she'd be a bit rusty in some respects, but keeping an arena of thousands of fans entertained was a lot harder than selling tea to a few dozen people.

Richard stopped the car in front of the shop. All the parking spots were filled, and the lineup went out the door.

"Oh my god, he needs help," Pauline said.

"I'll have to park farther down. I'll bring your laptop in for you and take your luggage to the house later."

Pauline sprang out of the car and squeezed her way through

the crowd, receiving a few scowls and angry comments. Although younger people certainly shopped at Claire's Tea Shop, to be a "regular" you had to be over sixty, ideally with a deceased parent who had shopped at Claire's first. The biggest part about Claire's sales wasn't the twenty-five percent price drop, it was the new blend release. Pauline hoped her mother had at least pre-packaged it on the weekend.

Pauline couldn't see past the crowd inside despite her height; the counter was set back too far. But the store was packed, tempers were running too high for what should've been a group of polite tea drinkers, and behind this crowd was some poor old schmuck who had no clue what was going on.

Pauline had to take control of the situation quickly. She moved through the crowd and jumped up onto the empty side counter. Her stunt worked: all eyes were staring at her.

But not at Perry. She could actually *see* all eyes on *her*. Now she had to say something. She hadn't thought that far ahead. She couldn't very well mime her message. That would look ridiculous. But she wasn't exactly a practised public speaker. The room fell quiet.

She had to say something.

"Um, hello, everyone? I'm, um, Pauline? Robinson? Claire's daughter?"

She sounded like she didn't know who she was. Who else would she be? But the introduction worked. Murmurs of recognition travelled through the crowd. Pauline continued, her voice flowing a little freer now. "We're really sorry for the chaos today. My mom had an accident and dislocated her knee yesterday."

The atmosphere in the room changed immediately. Pauline could see her father outside. She relaxed, her confidence now returned.

"This is—" She gestured toward the man behind the till, and almost fell off the counter. Expecting a balding, overweight, sixty-plus-year-old, she found instead a man with a warm smile and grey temples who was extremely fit. He was clearly in his forties.

How could he be a retired anything?

CHAPTER 4

She must have had nerves of steel to command attention that way. Todd didn't have the guts to jump on a counter like that, even if he'd owned the business.

He found her stature unique and intriguing, but her gumption intrigued him the most.

She bent over to talk with him, and her cheeks turned bright red. "This is embarrassing," she said. "I'm sorry, what's your name again?"

"Todd." He swallowed his sigh of relief. She hadn't recognized him.

She stood back up. "Todd started yesterday, so he's just learning. He's an excellent teacher, but you all know only Mom really knows her system of teas. However, she wouldn't want anyone leaving today without her new blend, and that's why you're all here. Plus whatever else you'd like to buy today. As you can see"—she gestured to the wall of tea—"we're stocked. We'll move as fast as possible. Thank you all for your patience." She beckoned to Richard, who was still standing outside, and the crowd let him in.

Pauline jumped down from the counter. She was actually two inches taller than Todd, wore her hair short, had broad shoulders...*Get your head in the show, Todd Parsons*, he thought. *You're here to work, remember?*

"Can you do cash?" she asked as she wiped down where she'd stood with a bleach solution.

Todd nodded. At least he hoped so. With no customers yesterday, he had only rehearsed different scenarios on the POS system.

"Great. I'll look after teas."

Richard approached the front, smiling and shaking his head. "We won't tell your mother you did that." He looked at Todd. "It's a thing, Pauline and countertops." He rubbed his hands together. "How can I help?"

Todd loved how this family helped one another. His mother, when she was alive, had helped wherever she believed she was needed, including with Todd's career.

"Can you go to the back room and package some of the new blend?" Pauline asked her father. "I have a feeling Mom was going to do most of that yesterday. These are Mom's regulars, so one-hundred-gram bags should be good for now. Even if you help for just an hour to get us ahead, that would be amazing."

"Sure thing. I'll leave your bag back there, too." Richard disappeared into the back room.

Pauline returned her attention to Todd. "Mom probably didn't show you how to do discounts, right?"

Todd shook his head. This woman was just a little intimidating. She appeared to function at a breakneck pace.

She quickly showed him how to enter discounts and then began taking orders, deftly pulling down jars from the shelves, weighing and packaging tea on the fly. She took sandwiches and snacks from the glass counter and wrapped them up for each customer who asked. Customers introduced themselves to her, and Pauline smiled as she appeared to remember who they were.

Todd did his best to stay focused on his sole task, and he believed he did it well given his minimal training. But two thoughts kept pushing into his mind. First, in all his travels, he'd never met a woman like Pauline. Confident—except apparently in public speaking, but then she was endearing—professional, muscular, athletic, ready to *literally* jump in and help out. Second, why would Claire hire someone like Todd when her daughter could obviously run this place as though she'd worked here her whole life?

GREAT, Pauline thought as her leg bounced while she sat in the back room. *Only five hours in and I'm already getting cabin fever.* They'd served maybe seventy customers, which for Claire was a lot, but for Pauline was peanuts. Poor Todd, though, looked frazzled.

She pulled out her phone and checked Perry's social media accounts to make sure Ben didn't think she was neglecting her work.

"Was not expecting that after yesterday," said Todd. "Hope I didn't embarrass you or your mother."

"No, you look good." Pauline held her breath as she caught her Freudian slip. *Oops.* "Once everyone knew you were new, they understood. Mom's regulars are used to Mom." Pauline texted a few replies to fans. "Sorry," she said, as much about the unannounced crush of customers as about her texting while talking. "Mom keeps day-old sandwiches in the fridge. We should refuel and package more of the new blend. There's an after-work crowd, too. Will start at around four-thirty. Some fifty-gram bags would be a good idea this time."

"Right. Can I get you a sandwich?"

"I'll take two, actually," she said. "Whatever's got the most meat." He returned with two tuna sandwiches for her and one for himself.

They ate in silence while Pauline continued replying to comments.

"Sorry," she said, her mouth full. "Trying to appease my boss."

Todd waited until his mouth was empty. "No problem."

The door chimes jingled and Todd immediately set his sandwich down and left to help. Pauline took this as a good sign, but a minute later he returned.

"I'm really sorry to bug you." Todd ran his hand through his hair as he explained the customer's request. "I don't really know what to recommend."

He looked so lost. Pauline was getting the sense he was out of his element and that it scared him.

"It's not a bother at all. I'm happy to help." She was, but she wondered why her mother hired him and not someone more knowledgeable about tea. Seventy such people had walked through those doors today so far.

She greeted the customer: a man likely in his thirties, so not a regular.

"I'm looking for something for my best buddy, as he's getting a new job out west in forestry. Loves to travel, has the most amazing garden. We both got into tea after a trip to China last year."

Pauline smiled. Although it was certainly not uncommon for men to drink tea, she had to admit, most of her mother's customers were older women. It was nice to see a younger, male customer.

"I'd recommend a Wuyi rock oolong. It reminds me of the

forest floor. Just a moment." She pulled the jar of tea down from the shelf, opened it, and offered it to the man to smell.

His eyes lit up. "You're not kidding! Yeah, I'll take a hundred grams. He'll love it."

"Wonderful." She handed the jar to Todd. "Do you want to package it?"

Todd took the jar from her. "Sure."

"I'd love to work in a tea shop someday—when I retire," the customer said. "Feels like it'd be so relaxing."

Pauline smiled, hoping her smile came across as genuine, because relaxing was the last word she'd use to describe working at her mom's shop. Confining, stressful, restrictive... those were more applicable. She could feel her leg wanting to bounce.

Once the customer left, Todd and Pauline returned to the back to finish their lunch.

"So, where are you from?" she asked him between bites of a third sandwich.

"Vancouver."

"My sister's out there."

Another uncomfortable silence followed. How did Claire think he was going to teach people about tea when he clearly didn't know the first thing about it, or seem to want to talk much about anything?

"So, Mom says you're a retired teacher? What did you teach?"

"Ballet."

"Oh, that's..." But she couldn't come up with anything to say about it. She'd never seen a show in her life. Ballet was the antithesis of sports: slow, choreographed, quiet.

"No worries," Todd said. "You wouldn't be the first person who finds it boring."

Pauline was certain her cheeks turned redder than the Peregrines' uniform.

To try to relieve the awkward atmosphere she had created, she asked why he wanted to work for Claire.

He shrugged. "Just trying to figure out the next steps in a new career, and this was the first step available."

Pauline's conversation attempts weren't helping. If anything they were confirming her initial suspicions: Claire had made the worst possible decision in hiring this man. How on earth was Pauline going to train him in a few days?

Swallowing the last of her sandwich, she fell back on what she'd learned as a mascot: if she couldn't change the atmosphere, then she had to get out of the situation.

"I'd better take a look around. It's been a while since I've been here."

Claire had last renovated ten years ago, in time for a major Christmas sale. Although Perry was Pauline's first major league gig, she'd been performing as a pro sports mascot since shortly after that sale, thanks to her mother's push to finally take the risk and audition for a women's basketball team mascot. It didn't pay much, but it let her dive deep into community engagement.

The café still had the same deep brown, metallic bistro chairs with cream cushions and matching tables. The walls were painted a rich cream, too.

"You know," she said to Todd as he followed her to the front, "Mom painted those walls so it would be easier to decorate at Christmas. This renovation was a huge change from how it was when I was a kid." She laughed. "It was so eighties it wasn't funny. She even had the glass tabletops on brass legs. She *hated* cleaning them."

Todd smiled, and Pauline's skin tingled. "Actually, my dad still has ours in the living room," he said. "Mom had a love-hate relationship with it also because of the cleaning, but he keeps it because it reminds him of her."

"She passed away?"

"Two years ago."

"I'm sorry."

Pauline walked back to the lounge area, which had a large cream couch and matching chairs around a coffee table. A few stains dotted the furniture. She lifted the cushion and found a colony of crumbs.

"Looks like it's been a while since Mom deep-cleaned this place."

"Anything I can do?" Todd asked.

"I just want to vacuum these crumbs up while it's quiet."

"I really don't mind helping. I can do pretty much anything: cleaning, minor repairs…"

He really seemed to need this job. "We'll put a plan together, but let's just get through today."

When she returned with the hand vac, he was lifting the cushions off the couch, his shirt tight against his back muscles.

Yes, she was having a hard time ignoring how his physique filled out his clothing. And she had a thing for grey temples like his. Then there was that smile he'd given her a few minutes ago… She took a deep breath to slow down her racing thoughts. Besides, she'd be returning to Toronto in a few days. Victory parade on Monday, more community events in the coming weeks, and she'd be leaving for the cup tour at the end of the month. She lived for her work and had no time for a relationship.

She hit the on switch, and the hand vac roared to action.

Then it whimpered to silence.

"I guess she needs a new one," Pauline said.

The shop wasn't irreparably run down, but its age was showing.

"I don't recall seeing these problems when I was last here. But then, maybe I wasn't paying attention. Why don't you study Mom's bible of teas for now," Pauline said. "I'll start writing up a list of things that need fixing."

"I guess it's no secret that I'm new to the world of tea."

It certainly wasn't.

Todd brought the binder back out and stood in front of Claire's assortment, evidently trying to match what was on the wall with Claire's notes.

Why did Pauline find him so attractive? Fine, he was in shape, but so was the hockey team. Most of the players were in their twenties, although a few were closer in age to her. But someone close in age to her who was polite and didn't try to make a move on her…

Not all professional athletes were jerks, of course. But once you filtered them out by age, that didn't leave many in their forties who were professional, polite, unmarried, straight, and took an interest in tea.

TODD TRIED hard to concentrate on what he was reading and avoid eye contact with Pauline. After learning yesterday morning that she wasn't keen on coming to town, Todd had been certain he didn't want to meet her. But his opinion changed the moment he saw her jump into action. Yes, she was attractive—unique didn't begin to describe what he thought about her body—but his physical attraction was already expanding into something more.

Was she staring at him because he was doing something wrong? Or because she was thinking the same thing?

If he wanted to recommend Pauline a tea, which one would he choose?

CHAPTER 5

*T*odd closed the binder and headed to the back room.

Oh, lord. I was just staring at him, wasn't I? Pauline clapped her hand to her eyes.

The chimes above the door jingled, and a voice asked cautiously, "Pauline?"

Pauline looked toward the door. She gasped and immediately jumped over the counter, ignoring the sudden pain in her hip when she landed.

"Oh my god oh my god oh my god! Tracy Tschirhart!" She ran to the woman, and the two hugged so tight they almost fell over. "It is *so* good to see you!"

"You're going to break my ribs!"

Pauline pulled away immediately. "Are you okay?"

Tracy laughed. "Of course, I am." She squeezed Pauline's upper arm. "You're huge!"

Pauline flexed her arm. "Still working out."

Tracy flexed hers and then jiggled the flesh that hung below. "Still not."

They hugged again, but this time Pauline caught sight of an

angry teen boy almost as tall as her saunter in behind them. His hair was unkempt, and he had dark circles under his eyes. His wrinkled T-shirt hung over his blue jeans. Underneath it, Pauline could make out a fit physique like Todd's, and despite the teen's slouched entrance, a certain grace to his movements.

Pauline pulled out of the embrace. "Oh my god, Tracy, is this Austin?"

Tracy's demeanour darkened. "It is. He's sixteen now if you can believe it."

Pauline smiled at him, expecting the teen to look up at the mention of his name, but Austin stayed glued to his phone, a far cry from the happy-go-lucky kid she remembered from that Christmas sale ten years ago. That kid who had danced so freely to *The Nutcracker* and dreamed of being a ballet star. What had happened?

"Is everything all right?" Pauline gestured to the couch in the lounge, a little away from Austin, who had already sat at a table in the front, still staring at his phone.

The women sat down.

Tracy stared at her hands and lowered her voice. "To be honest, no, it's not. Austin has epilepsy. He's not dancing anymore."

Epilepsy could be a devastating diagnosis. Pauline put a comforting hand on Tracy's shoulder.

"I don't know if you remember, but Austin used to stare into space a lot," Tracy said.

Pauline shook her head. She'd never noticed.

"We always thought it was daydreaming, because he snapped out of it really fast. But during his last year at ballet school, these bouts of staring started happening while he was dancing, including while he was lifting girls."

Pauline's hand flew to her mouth.

"He dropped a girl a few times during practice, and he's…"

Tracy glanced over her shoulder. "He was one of the most caring people you've ever met. But when he dropped a girl during the recital last year…he was so humiliated, Pauline, that he literally walked off the stage and refused to return."

Pauline shook her head in sympathy. Some children had felt embarrassed having seizures in front of her characters, and she'd left notes with the nurses for those children to make sure they understood they were still loved.

"Anyway, we returned to town to live close to my parents, because it made no sense to stay so far away anymore. We got the diagnosis last fall. The neurologist said we were lucky we caught it before he started driving. If he had a seizure behind the wheel…" Tracy dabbed at her eyes. "He said the excessive caffeine Austin had been consuming had affected his sleep and exacerbated his seizures. That's why we hadn't noticed them earlier."

What Pauline wouldn't give for her costume right now—it gave her privacy to let her emotions flow, confidence to know how to act, and freedom to comfort without the cumbersome need to find words. As she let the news sink in, she realized with growing guilt, that last fall Tracy had sent her a few texts, but she hadn't taken time to respond.

"Medication?"

Tracy shook her head. "We tried one. It left him like a zombie, and he's refused to try any others."

"And he really can't dance?"

"He doesn't believe he can be a ballet dancer if he can't lift girls."

Pauline glanced in Austin's direction. He was hunched over his phone, anger spewing out of every pore in his body. "Dance was his main form of expression. Like gymnastics is…was mine." She had to watch her words. "I bet he feels completely trapped and has no way of letting his feelings out."

Tracy nodded as she dabbed at her eyes again.

Pauline had to do something. "Can I send home a package of green tea with chamomile and lavender? That might help calm your nerves a bit but also give you a little energy to help you through your days."

Tracy nodded. "You're so like your mother. Sure."

Pauline walked to the counter and called Todd.

"I don't know if you've met Todd yet," she explained to Tracy and Austin. "He used to teach ballet. Mom thought his teaching background would help him teach new customers about tea." To Todd, she said, "Austin used to take ballet lessons."

Austin's eyes opened wide.

Todd's breath caught.

"Could you package Calming Plains? One hundred grams?"

Todd nodded, without saying another word, and Austin returned his attention to his phone, though his energy changed from angry boredom to engrossed frenzy.

"How are your siblings?" Pauline asked Tracy.

"They're too far away to see as often as I'd like, and Austin doesn't want to visit anyone. Even getting him to school every morning is a fight."

Austin banged his hand on the table and stood up. "We're leaving! I'm not some Face—" He stopped, staring into space.

"That's a seizure," Tracy said. "He has them anywhere from twenty to forty times a day, maybe even more for all we know. He's not always aware of what he was saying when he comes out of them."

Midway through Tracy's sentence, Austin indeed appeared aware of what Tracy was saying.

"Stop studying me like I'm a lab rat. And yes, I know what I was going to say: I'm not some Facebook post to update your friends with all the time!"

Tracy explained further. "And he can—"

"Just stop it!"

Pauline's heart broke. She understood her friend's need to talk to someone, and although Tracy didn't know this about Pauline anymore, Pauline had spent half her career listening to parents when no one else would. But Austin's world had been turned upside down by this diagnosis, and he appeared to be caught between needing to talk to someone and burying his own ugly journey deep in the ground.

Todd brought the package of tea from behind the counter. "Can I help at all?" His voice was gentle.

"You're the last person I need help from!" Austin replied.

"I'm sorry."

Sorry about what?

Todd handed the bag of tea to Tracy and retreated to the back room.

"Austin!" Tracy admonished her son. "You don't talk to people like that!"

Austin's anger was consuming him, but words weren't going to help. Would he let Pauline put a comforting arm around him? It was a risk. In costume, Pauline knew immediately if someone would welcome it or not: They either approached her or stood far away as soon as she entered a room. But something had to pierce Austin's anger before it turned to rage.

She stepped into his personal space to see if he would step back. Anger shot out of his eyes, frightening her. She wasn't used to making eye contact like this. But Austin froze again for several seconds.

"Another seizure," Tracy explained.

When he came out of it, he stormed out the door.

Tracy unlocked the car using her fob. "I've tried all sorts of psychotherapy with him. Nothing. His father walked out on us shortly after the diagnosis, which makes this all worse."

"Oh my god, Tracy, no..."

She nodded. "Our marriage was shaky already. The move out of province for ballet school several years ago...we gave up everything for Austin's dream, and now that dream's been taken away from him. Pauline, my son barely speaks to me. And the worst part is, these are mild seizures. They'll probably either stay like this or turn into those seizures you associate with epilepsy—the ones where they fall to the ground and start shaking. How can he live a life when his brain takes over like that? Can he get a job? Will he find a husband? Have a family?"

Pauline hugged her friend one more time. She had to do something for Tracy. The bag of tea wasn't enough. Her mind raced through a million ideas, but all of them involved the costume packed in Toronto. Would Austin remember Pauline as the reindeer from that Christmas sale and therefore still love interacting with a life-sized stuffed toy? Or had he grown into someone who'd lost the ability to play?

She'd find a way to make Tracy and Austin happy, even if it was only for a few moments. Maybe they could start to see possibilities again. Pauline didn't know what those possibilities were; she just knew they existed. All she had to do was find those few moments of happiness to open the door.

But would a few days be enough time?

TODD HELD a fist to his mouth in concentration. He had overheard everything. That poor boy. Austin had recognized him, but when Todd had offered his help the teenager's rebuke had felt like a pointe shoe in the face.

And what if Austin told his friends where Todd was now? But the more Todd thought about it, the less probable that was. From the sounds of it, Austin would be too embarrassed to contact his friends from his former ballet school. *And I don't think he has any friends here.*

What kind of life was that for a teen?

"You have to try again, Todd Parsons," he told himself. "That kid is all alone. For once, do something useful with your career."

But when he heard Tracy and Pauline say their goodbyes, he realized it was too late. He'd have to get Tracy's number from Pauline.

He got up from the desk and headed into the front of the shop, but instead of finding the confident athlete he was expecting, he saw a sagging Pauline, sitting at a table, wiping away her tears.

He passed her a serviette. "Maybe I can help you?"

Pauline gave him a weak smile, stood up as she dried her face, then walked behind the counter to throw out the serviette.

"Tracy tried contacting me around the time of Austin's diagnosis, and I didn't even take half an hour to call her." She pulled another serviette from the dispenser; the tears didn't stop, though Pauline was trying hard to hold them back.

She leaned over the counter, propping herself up on her elbows. "Tracy's not normally that blunt with people like she was with Austin at the end there. She's one of the world's best executive assistants. She knows how to be discreet. But she's at her wits' end with him. Happens to a lot of parents when their lives have been turned upside down with a diagnosis like that."

This was the first personal detail Pauline had shared with Todd since she'd arrived this morning. "You've done a lot of work with families like Tracy's?"

Pauline hesitated before answering.

Have I overstepped professional boundaries? She broached the subject. I was only trying to make conversation.

"You could say that."

What if I shared more about myself? Would that ease the atmosphere?

"I've taught at some of the best ballet schools in the country and around the world. I've seen things like this before. It's heartbreaking to watch. Do you have Tracy's number? Maybe I can talk to Austin."

Pauline shook her head. "And I can't search for the messages Tracy sent me because I didn't realize, for the longest time, that I had messages set to save for only thirty days. I get tons of messages." To underscore her point, her phone dinged several times.

She wiped the last tears from her eyes. "Thanks for listening, and sorry to dump all this on you."

Todd gave Pauline's shoulder a squeeze. "No need to apologize. I'm happy to listen."

Everyone in Todd's previous career was physically close; you couldn't dance without being comfortable that way. So giving Pauline a comforting squeeze wasn't unusual for him. What was unusual was the heat he felt when he touched her. He pulled his hand back. *No, this can't happen. Not now. I need this job.* He hoped she hadn't felt it, too, but he had already learned one thing about Pauline that day: she couldn't keep her feelings hidden. She had inhaled quickly with his touch.

Her phone dinged several times to remind her of her messages. She pointed to the back room. "I'd, um, better check what that's about."

THREE TEXTS FROM BEN. She sighed loudly as Todd came into the back room.

"Everything okay?"

"Ever worked for someone who doesn't trust you to do your job?"

"Can't say that I have."

"Consider yourself lucky. It's only Tuesday and he doesn't need an answer till Saturday."

"For what?"

"My thoughts on the Peregrines' victory parade."

"Oh."

Todd's lack of enthusiasm for the Peregrines was refreshing only because he was a kind of anti-Ben. "You're not a fan, eh?"

"Sorry. Not really."

"No need to apologize."

She responded to Ben: *I'll reply by 11:59PM.*

"Your boss?"

"More an entire thorn bush in my side than my boss, but yeah." She sighed. "The only nightmare in my otherwise dream job." She threw her phone back into her bag and turned to face him, not realizing just how close he was standing to her. Would he mind if she ran her fingers through his hair?

She glued her hands behind her back. "Okay. Right. The basics of tea. Let's get you strained, um, trained. My mom calls my dad Keemun, and he calls her Darjeeling."

Oops. Not those kinds of basics.

CHAPTER 6

*H*olding a bouquet of flowers she'd just bought in Belmont Village, Pauline had to settle for the fifteen-minute walk home instead of a much-needed two-hour jog through the Westmount and Belmont neighbourhoods before seeing her mother for the first time in months. She wasn't sure what was worse: creating excuses about why she rarely visited or reporting that Todd was a bad hire. How was she going to train him by the end of the week?

But she smiled when she remembered his descriptions of some of the black teas: a Keemun he'd tried tasted "lower" and a Darjeeling tasted "higher." She had no idea what he meant by either, but the descriptions sounded sweet.

Like his grey temples and the way he double-checked that his sleeves were rolled properly when he got embarrassed or nervous.

You already don't have time for your family, she reminded herself. *How would you have time for a relationship?*

She passed by the homes that made up Westmount, each one different from the next. Some would have been stately mansions in their day, built by rich business owners on large properties. Others were bungalows, but just as beautiful. When she crossed the street, she found it refreshing to not have to watch out for daredevil cyclists weaving in and out of several lanes of traffic.

Pauline held her breath and paused. She'd arrived at her family home: a brown two-storey set back from the street, with a neatly manicured lawn. Beautiful flowers, ornamental trees, and trimmed bushes adorned the front of the property. She had no issue rappelling from stadium ceilings, but it appeared she was developing a thing with entering buildings: first the Peregrines offices and now here. She let out her breath and shook out her free hand before ringing the doorbell.

Richard answered. "How'd it go?"

She stepped inside and looked around. "Okay." Nothing had changed. Everything was neat and orderly, contemporary with a nod to tradition, just like Claire's Tea Shop.

"Everything all right, honey?" Richard asked.

Honey was her parents' nickname for her. They called Dawn *sugar*. Given that it was a tea-loving family, though, Pauline and Dawn took comfort in the fact that their nicknames weren't *oolong* and *pu-erh*.

Pauline took off her shoes and set her bag to the side. "Yup. Just nice to be home."

"Is that Pauline?" Claire called. "Come up and let me see you!"

Richard lowered his voice. "She's back to her old self."

Was that good news or bad news? After her embarrassing moments with Todd today, she had to do her best to conceal her emotions. When she entered the room, she hoped her smile hid what she was really feeling: surprise and worry at her mother's appearance. Claire's white, shoulder-length hair was matted to her head, while her usually made-up face was pale as snow.

Despite it being June and the warm breeze blowing in from an open window, Claire had blankets pulled up to her underarms.

Her smile, though, was as Pauline knew it: warm, inviting.

And somehow still intimidating.

"Hi, Mom." She handed the bouquet of flowers to her.

Claire's smile brightened. "Oh, Pauline, are these from the Village?"

Her mother's reaction took thirty years off Pauline's forty-seven, turning her into a teenage girl wanting to impress her mom. How did that happen?

"They're so lovely. Thank you." Claire inhaled their scent. "They remind me a little of Garden Gnomes, the tea I used to sell to Mr. Shoemaker."

Pauline tried to remember who that was.

"You didn't know him," Claire said. "He passed away when you were still very young. He was a quiet man, so I never knew much about him. I guess he fought in the First World War before immigrating to Canada from Romania. He only ever saw his wife and children once in the forty years he lived here."

"Seriously?"

Claire nodded. "He visited them sometime in the sixties…"

Richard had come into the room. He reached for Claire's hand. "You and I hadn't started dating yet."

"That's right. I gave him a canister of Garden Gnomes for himself, and one for his wife. Whenever she wrote him a letter or read his, she could brew herself a cup, and he could do the same. The aroma from the tea would remind them of each other and bring them pleasant memories."

How does Mom think of things like this?

"My goodness," Claire said. "That was exactly fifty years ago." She passed the flowers to Richard. "Do you mind putting these into a vase for me, my Keemun?"

Richard gave Claire a peck on the cheek before he disappeared into the kitchen. Pauline was worried. Today was Tuesday. If Claire couldn't even get out of bed, how was she going to manage from a chair by next Monday?

Claire took hold of Pauline's hand. Her grip was weaker than Pauline remembered it. "It's so good to have you home, honey."

"It's nice to be home. How are you feeling?"

"I'll be doing physiotherapy for the rest of the summer, at least."

And running her shop? With Todd—who knew nothing? Claire's had hundreds of teas. Pauline had learned about them over decades. How was Todd going to learn about them in such a short period of time?

More importantly, how was her mother going to handle all this from a chair? She was going to drive the poor man out the door. And then what?

"It's good you're getting the help you need, Mom. But why didn't you let Todd dust those pictures? I know it's important to thank your past customers and all, but..." She gestured to her mom's knee. "There's got to be a different way."

Claire sighed, and Pauline immediately regretted how strongly she'd come on. But several of her mother's recent decisions didn't make sense to her. Her independent streak had gone a little too far.

"Speaking of Todd," Claire said, "how's he doing?"

Where was a flaming hoop to jump through when Pauline needed one? But she had to say something: Claire didn't appreciate it when people avoided answering her.

"He's learning."

"Good. I knew he would."

There was no way her mother was going to be back in the shop in a week. That left Pauline with only one option.

~

"YOU'RE JOKING, PAULINE. A MONTH?"

Pauline was lying on her bed in her childhood bedroom, which was still decked out in sports memorabilia. "I'm not, Ben. You know me. I'm dedicated—"

"Blah, blah, blah. I know the drill. Do you know how often someone says they're dedicated to their job and then they leave?"

Pauline imagined throwing popcorn in Ben's face. Or maybe blindfolding him and leaving him standing in the middle of the ice while hockey players shot pucks around him.

"You said one week, Pauline. You *promised* one week."

"That was before I knew they'd operated on Mom's knee. I can run a lot of my work from here."

"Let me get this straight. You probably earn more money playing dress-up in a quarter than your mother makes selling tea in a year, and you want to help for a few weeks and risk getting fired?"

If anything angered Pauline about her job, it was people accusing her of "playing dress-up." That'd been half the problem with Gary, her ex-almost-fiancé.

"I don't play dress-up, and you know it. If you want to take the credit for my skits and stunts so you can get your promotion even though I'm the one literally risking my neck out there, fine. Why don't you try getting in front of thousands of people knowing that if you screw up, the brand you represent will be all over social media in a minute? Or, no, you know what you should do? Put that costume on and hold a dying child's hand. You want proof that I'm dedicated to my job? After the win on Monday, a drunk woman grabbed my crotch—in front of her husband and all the kids there—and whispered her phone number to me. I couldn't very well push her back. And she's not the only one to do it to me—happens all the time. So don't tell me I play dress-up! I'm the best thing to happen to your marketing since the PR disaster from the last guy, and you know it! And it's because I put families first! So please, for the love of god, let me put my family in second—no—in third place, after planning the cup tour and taking care of Perry's social media, and let me help my mother out!"

There. Rant over. But hopefully she hadn't been so loud that her parents heard. If he said no, she had to listen to him, and she didn't want to get her parents' hopes up. But Claire needed Pauline's help. If Ben didn't listen to her, could she make a formal complaint about not getting the vacation time she was legally owed? She would find out. The truth was that Pauline cared about the kids and families she helped through her work. Sticking with being a child psychologist would have meant regular hours and less physical pain, not to mention fewer concerns about workplace safety—child psychologists didn't tend to do backflips off ladders, for example—but there was something healing in connecting anonymously without words.

"Listen, I don't need to stay here all the time. I'll obviously be in Toronto for the parade, and we'll still schedule a few events. But I'd like to spend some time here to help Mom."

And Tracy and Austin. But they were none of Ben's business.

"I'll make sure you have better security at the parade," Ben said. "For now, help your mom, keep Perry's social media going, try to arrange some Peregrines publicity so we're not paying you for nothing. We'll see you Sunday for parade prep and talk about the tour after the parade on Monday."

He hung up.

Pauline stared at her phone. Was he just saying something nice to her and he'd fire her on Monday? She was used to being groped—it happened to all mascot performers. In fact, the men joked she was lucky she didn't have an extra appendage *down there*. Nothing for kids to accidentally crush when they came running at her.

"What do male ballet dancers wear down there?" she asked herself. She shook her head. "Pauline, get your head out of the gutter. Ben just gave you a month. Whatever happens don't disappoint him, or you'll lose the best job of your life."

CHAPTER 7

"The last customer left twenty minutes ago, and your leg's been bouncing ever since," Todd said when they finally took a break for lunch the next day. "I'm going to start calling you Hungry, Hungry Hippo."

Pauline smiled. "I need to burn my energy off somehow." She swallowed the last bite of her sandwich. He'd never seen anyone eat so fast. "Do you mind if I go outside for a few minutes? Mom would be mortified if I served customers hopping around like a rabbit."

No sooner did Pauline leave through the back door than a customer walked in the front door. Todd straightened out his shirt and took a deep breath before entering the shop with the same amount of concentration and nerves as if he were about to begin a solo in front of four thousand people.

The woman looked like Claire—about the same age and dressed to the nines—but furrowed her brow when she saw Todd.

"Where's Claire?"

A regular. No different from the seasoned patrons at the

theatre who had extremely high expectations. But that usually came with a good dose of empathy if you knew how to uncover it. Over twenty years of performing had taught him how to disarm this customer's outer shell within moments.

The instant he turned on a muted stage smile, the woman's furrow softened a little. "Claire had an accident on Monday and dislocated her knee. It was my first day on the job, unfortunately, so I'm afraid you're stuck with the new hire. I used to teach ballet." Even though few here cared for ballet, the older crowd usually held it in high esteem—the kind of "it must be very special because I don't understand it" high esteem. He wished people wouldn't see ballet as something needing extra education to understand, but the woman did change in expression from frustration to surprise.

"Please tell Claire that Doris passes on her best wishes for a full recovery."

"I will, Doris." Using names helped, too. He didn't want to manipulate anyone, but after being bullied as a kid, he had always had low tolerance for any kind of mean behaviour, even if it was someone as harmless as Doris. Any tactic he could use to bring out a person's nice side was fair game.

The elderly woman gave Todd her order, which was thankfully simple. Pauline returned just as Doris was waving to him on her way out the door.

Pauline shot him a playful look. "Doris is a tough cookie. Are you like this with all the older women?"

Todd smiled and shrugged. "I like making people happy."

Pauline's eyes brightened, and Todd loved the light in her eyes.

"I'm just glad she asked for something simple. I don't know if I'll ever be able to replace your mom."

Pauline wagged a finger at him. "Oh, no, no, no. No one can replace Claire Robinson. That's why this is called *Claire's* Tea

Shop." She clapped him on the shoulder, startling him. "You'll learn," she continued. "But even my mom can't really have a tea for *every* emotion, problem, and celebration. There was this one time when I ran up a ramp, jumped on a trampoline, and was supposed to do a flip over seven mascots and land on a mat. Instead, I landed on the seventh mascot."

Todd's jaw dropped. "What?"

"Thankfully, he had a lot of padding. The sixth one didn't. I don't think Mom would have a tea for that."

Todd laughed so hard he worried he'd split open.

Pauline finished her story. "You just have to get up again. And never search YouTube for 'biggest mascot failures.' It's on there."

Todd made a mental note to search exactly that. He didn't want to laugh at her, just learn more about her. But would she look him up online? Hopefully not. If she had any desire to learn more about him, whatever she found would squash it like she would have squashed that sixth actor.

The front door opened again, and Pauline immediately ran around the counter to hug the elderly woman who walked in.

"Jan!"

Jan's hair was coloured brown and blonde, and pinned in an up-do. She wore a flowing, floral summer dress that reached to just above her ankles, a large, brightly coloured beaded neck-lace, and bright sandals.

"Todd, this is Jan Brubacher, Tracy's mom. Jan and my mom have been best friends for, I don't know, how long, Jan?"

Jan grinned from ear to ear. "Since long before either of you were even a thought! Nice to meet you, Todd. Claire told me she'd hired a new assistant. And good thing, too. Looks like you saved the day."

Todd's cheeks heated at the compliment. "Nice to you meet you, too, Jan."

Jan's smile grew even warmer. She grasped Pauline's hand and they approached the counter. "How are you doing?" she asked Pauline. "Claire says you're staying for a month? She was so overjoyed!"

Todd tried to look busy behind the counter—this was clearly another reunion—but he wanted to hear anything he could about the woman who'd become his temporary boss. His attraction to her was growing, and therefore, too, his curiosity.

"I'm okay. Worried about Mom, but she'll pull through. She always does." Pauline came back around the counter. "I'm just trying to figure out the most important things to help her with."

"Knowing you're here will ease her mind," Jan said.

"It's not enough, but I'll figure it out. But now you have to fill me in on Tracy and Austin," Pauline said. "Tracy told me a lot, but I want everything."

Sensing the topic of conversation might be personal, Todd excused himself to dust the stereo equipment and television on the other side of the room, but he couldn't help but overhear them.

"She has nowhere left to turn," Jan said. "Sedrick and I have tried everything, too, but that boy is so filled with anger."

"She told me about his diagnosis and his father leaving them, but is that it? I know these things can be hard, but something tells me she didn't share everything with me. She's a mom —sometimes moms don't share..." Pauline hesitated, as though she were struggling to find the right words. "Sometimes they don't share when they feel they're failing their child."

Jan didn't answer right away. Was it because she didn't want to betray her daughter's trust? Or because what she had to say was too painful? Todd couldn't tell.

"Kids at school are bullying him again, but anytime anyone asks Austin about it he leaves the room. These bullies do it where no one can see them, so the teachers have no proof of anything, not even names. It's no different than before he left for ballet school. Oh, Pauline, you should've seen him at that school. Sedrick and I flew there every year for his show. He was such a different person: open, happy, alive. I swear his jumps went higher by at least a foot."

The anger in Todd came up too fast for him to stop himself from interrupting the conversation. "He was being bullied for his love of ballet?"

"And for being gay. It was horrible, just horrible. And now, it's worse: he won't tell anyone what's happening."

Todd's grip on the duster tightened. This happened all over the world and was the main reason many boys didn't even try ballet. Regardless of why Todd was in Kitchener, he knew his former celebrity status might help.

"I used to teach ballet," Todd said slowly. "Maybe it would help if I talked to Austin." There. He had said it. If he had to ask them to keep his secret, he would. He couldn't let a boy live with that much pain.

"Oh my goodness, would you really? That would be simply wonderful." Jan pulled out a slip of paper and pen from her purse, wrote down Tracy's number, and passed it to Todd. "You know," she said, "I once saw Nureyev in Toronto with the National Ballet of Canada. He was magnificent."

"In *The Sleeping Beauty*?"

"Yes, with Karen Kain."

"I'm jealous. I grew up in Vancouver. Did you know he choreographed that? If it weren't for him, the National wouldn't be where it is today. I always looked up to him. But when I saw Baryshnikov as a kid, that sealed the deal for me."

Pauline stared at them. "Who are you talking about?"

They stared back at her.

She shrugged. "What? I find ballet boring." Her hand flew to her mouth and her cheeks turned red. "Sorry."

"Pauline," Jan said, her tone friendly, "you really should be careful with what you say."

"I know. I'm working on it, I promise."

If Pauline worked in community engagement, wouldn't she be practised at watching what she said in front of others? And Todd believed she would enjoy ballet if she gave it a chance. Ballet didn't have to tell a classical tale, like *The Sleeping Beauty* or *Swan Lake*. As far as he was concerned, audience members could make up whatever story they wanted to. Or no story at all. People needed only to let the movement and music touch them and see what their own imaginations conjured up.

"I've got an idea. I think there's something you'd like." He disappeared for a moment into the back room and reappeared with his phone. "You'll like Nureyev in this. It's called 'Swine Lake.'"

SHE HAD no idea what to expect, but Todd looked so excited it was cute. But given her unfiltered comment about ballet just now, Pauline worried she'd let the truth about her real work with the Peregrines slip before she finished her month at Claire's Tea Shop. She hadn't meant to hurt Todd's feelings. Her comment just flew out of her mouth. But if she divulged her real job, she could be on the hook for a million dollars. That could be a very expensive mistake.

Turned out it was a classic Muppets' skit, starring the guy whose name she'd already forgotten and a performer fully encased in a pig costume wearing a tutu. The skit was full of classic Muppets' slapstick, and although Pauline knew she was supposed to be amazed by What's-His-Name, she was enthralled by the dancer moving gracefully in how many pounds of foam rubber. The pig even got up on her toes!

The whole piece was brilliant, and Pauline laughed the entire time.

"Okay, you got me," she said when it finished.

TODD GAVE himself an imaginary pat on the back. Pauline had laughed and smiled throughout the whole skit.

"How did she get on her toes like that?" she asked.

"Actually," Todd said, "it was a man. Graham Fletcher. It's rare to see a man *en pointe*, though it's becoming more popular these days. But it takes a lot of practice. I don't have the training, so I'll never attempt it. I'd like to be able to walk into old age."

He unplugged his phone, and Jan frowned.

"Too bad," she said. "We could've watched the skit where Miss Piggy comes on to Nureyev in the sauna."

Todd and Jan laughed at Pauline's confused look.

"I'll show you later," Todd said. "I should probably get back to work."

"Speaking of coming on," Jan said, wiggling an eyebrow, "I have something planned for Sedrick tonight, so I came to get some more of my tea."

Pauline scrunched up her face. "TMI, Jan! You and Sedrick are like a second set of parents to me, and I already know what my parents do!" Pauline packed black tea with rose petals. Todd made a mental note: black tea with rose petals clearly meant romance. That connection was obvious.

"I have an idea. You wanted to know how to help your mother?" Jan said. "Spruce up this place a little. Nothing deadens your mother's spirits more than the thought of another renovation. She's a strong woman, my Claire, but she can no longer run this place by herself." She patted Todd on the hand. "But I have a good feeling about you. I think Claire does, too."

Todd hadn't received so many compliments in a day nor been surrounded by so many caring people in a while.

"Your mother's been talking about renovations for over a year. She just doesn't have the energy to do it." Jan paid for her tea and headed for the door. "If you need anything, Pauline, just call." She winked. "But not tonight."

After Jan left, Pauline returned the jar of black tea and rose petals to its spot. "The number of times I've walked in on my parents after closing…" She shuddered.

Todd's cheeks heated up. "That's not exactly something I need to know about my employer."

Pauline patted him on the shoulder again. "Would you rather hear it from me or accidentally walk in on them when you're grabbing your jacket at the end of the day?"

"Point taken."

Pauline leaned against the back counter. "But Jan's idea… what do you think about the interior of this place? I suppose it could use a fresh coat of paint, but I've grown up here, and you're totally new. What are your thoughts?"

Todd looked around and began to think about the possibilities. When he offered a few suggestions, to his surprise, she immediately began recording his ideas on a piece of scrap paper. Feeling encouraged, he continued.

They kept brainstorming between customers. At one point, Pauline was so engrossed in getting her own ideas down that a lock of her hair fell forward. Without thinking, Todd tucked it behind her ear.

Pauline glanced up, and the look in her eyes made it clear that something between them was brewing. He wished he could turn off the heat.

He couldn't handle any more regret right now.

CHAPTER 8

*P*auline sat in Claire's home office, sipping on a rooibos tea blend with lavender and red currants. Her mother was already asleep, but Pauline hadn't adjusted to "store owner time" yet; she was still on "hockey game time."

After spending an hour finding renovation inspiration on Pinterest, Pauline switched to Claire's online presence, which sadly only took ten minutes to analyze. All her mother did was announce sales and post a few photos of tea. Pauline could certainly improve upon that.

Next came Claire's financials. Finding what Pauline needed was easy: Claire had always been organized that way. As she began digging, she found Claire's first error in judgment.

Why so much on newspaper ads? she thought. *Social media ads are cheaper.*

After further digging, she discovered a line of credit that was half-used. Claire had been making payments against it, but she was losing a lot to interest.

A knock on the door startled Pauline.

Richard shot her a weary smile. "You're a ball of energy no matter what time of day."

"You look wiped," Pauline said. "A tea? A black tea with ginger to ground you a little? Or would you prefer something without caffeine?" She gestured toward the Goddess of Tea as Claire called the collection of seventy or eighty tea tins in her office.

"Black tea with ginger sounds great."

Pauline filled the kettle with water from the water cooler.

"One of my regulars wouldn't buy a house without me looking after the deal." Richard sighed then indicated toward the desktop cluttered with paperwork. "What do you think about the shop? And I want the truth, Pauline. It's been dripping money for a long time, but Claire's so independent. Hiring Todd was the first time she's accepted any serious help in ages."

Pauline placed a strainer over a tea cup and measured the dried leaves. He'd asked for the truth, so she might as well give it to him.

"He's really nice—he even charmed Doris—but he knows nothing about tea, Dad. Like, really nothing. I don't know how he's going to help Mom."

She set a timer on her phone. Her father preferred his black teas steeped for four minutes.

Richard inhaled deeply. "I can already smell it from here. Part of the problem was that Claire could never find the right people. For so many years, she used family and friends—you and your sister when you were younger, occasionally Jan, even Tracy. I always helped if I could spare a few hours here and there. But she couldn't find anyone who cared like we did."

"So, Todd just said the right words?" Although as soon as she asked her question, Pauline realized that was impossible. Todd wasn't exactly a conversationalist.

Richard shook his head. "He understood emotion, story, and

people. Your mom's eyes lit up the more we all talked. It was pure magic. And the way he carried himself—he understood presentation. Yes, he's a man, and your mother has always wanted to support women, but—between you and me—I think she hopes some of the ladies will flirt with him and therefore buy more tea."

"Dad!"

A glint of mischief shone in Richard's eye. "Why do you think she had me behind the counter once in a while? When I was younger, at least?" He winked at Pauline.

Pauline smiled. She had to agree—Todd had sold tea to Doris, who usually scared employees away. "Okay. So he has the right heart, and I'll teach him what I can this month. But then there's the marketing: she's running newspaper ads like it's the eighties."

Richard shook his head. "I know, I know. I offered her my marketing strategist's help, but…" He shrugged.

Pauline threw her hands up in frustration. "Why is she like that?"

Her phone beeped, and she pulled the strainer out of the teacup. She passed the tea to her father, who lifted the cup to his nose and inhaled again, releasing the tension from his shoulders as he exhaled.

"Your mom won't want me telling you this, but you should know."

He took a cautious sip.

"What do you mean? Is this the part where you tell me that we have another sibling or something?"

Richard shook his head. "It's not that earth-shattering, but it could have been. Your mother is the way she is because of a man she married before me."

A previous husband? Pauline picked up her cup of rooibos, letting its warmth help her focus her thoughts. In all the years she and Dawn had snooped through their parents' stuff—because that's what kids did—they had never come across anything that even hinted at a previous marriage.

"He died in a car accident. Your mother's only spoken about him once or twice to me, but I think more out of honesty before we got married than anything else. I know he believed women should be seen and not heard. Her choice to not talk about him is her way of making him just as invisible."

Pauline set the cup back on Claire's desk before she dropped it. "That's why the store name, the need to do everything her way…she wanted to be heard."

Richard nodded.

It hit her like a shipping container full of tea.

And whatever changes Pauline made to the shop, she had to make them with her mother's full approval. Period. That meant planning everything very closely with Claire.

It gave her another reason to lie to Claire about her real job. Ben wasn't Claire's first husband, and Pauline had willingly signed on the dotted line to have her dream job, but Claire would see similarities.

But if Pauline planned things with as much forethought as she did her skits and community engagement, she could set Claire up to live her dream for at least another ten years. If Pauline excelled at one thing, it was making people happy. Maybe she had neglected to make her family and closest friends happy, but now she had her chance to rectify that.

She shared her plans with her father and showed him some of her and Todd's ideas.

Richard's face brightened. "That sounds amazing. Let me make a few calls tomorrow. I should at least be able to get us some decent pricing."

Pauline was going to leave her mother with a renewed store that would engage the community, excite people when they dropped by, and generate more income so Claire's Tea Shop would again operate in the black.

Excitement in her rose like steam out of a pot filled with an exquisite, jasmine-scented green tea. Pauline loved planning to create happiness. Maybe Claire and Richard were right about Todd: he had the heart needed to work at Claire's Tea Shop. He just lacked the knowledge.

It was up to her to fix that.

CHAPTER 9

S o much for starting on the right foot.

Pauline hadn't fallen asleep until two in the morning: her mind wouldn't stop oscillating between questions about her mother's first husband and ideas for Todd. She woke up an hour before the store opened and realized she desperately needed to exercise.

Then Ben had texted her with Peregrines work.

She called Todd to ask him to look after the store until one in the afternoon.

Pauline had begun collecting her ideas in a binder so Claire wouldn't have to fumble with a computer. Whereas Richard had kept up with technology, Claire used it only when necessary, hence the scanty social media presence.

Pauline filtered her ten pages of ideas down to five, but that would still take too long and cost too much to complete. She wanted Todd's input so she wouldn't look stupid in front of her mother when she pitched her the plan. Her parents' interior décor gene had skipped Pauline and gone to Dawn.

When she entered the shop, a few customers were finishing

tea and sandwiches, and Todd was wiping a table. Pauline was drawn to the grace in his arm as it glided from side to side, his muscles rippling through the back of his shirt.

Do all male ballet teachers move like that? Hello.

He turned to face her before her thoughts could return to Earth, and caught her staring at him. He smiled and nodded.

"Hey." Her cheeks heated up like two kettles.

He collected dishes from another table and carried them to the sink in the back room. By the time he'd returned, she had cooled down to the water temperature needed for delicate teas and opened the binder.

"Can I get your input on some things?" she asked.

Why did he look surprised? She had noticed the same reaction yesterday when she had asked for his opinion. For the next couple of hours, they discussed changes to the tea shop in between taking care of customers. Then a group of women in their thirties entered. They wore business casual, and the woman who appeared to lead the pack explained they were on a half-hour break from a business conference and had heard this was *the* place to go for tea and desserts.

She eyed Todd up and down. "This is apparently the right place to go. You look like a hockey player. I like hockey players, especially sweet ones. Wanna come play this evening?"

Where was Evanoff when you needed his slapshot right between someone's eyes? To Pauline, inappropriate comments and groping were the same disgusting thing. But she had to remain professional to avoid the customer leaving a bad review online.

Todd also retained his professional demeanour. "I'm afraid we don't serve pucks, only teas from around the world and desserts and sandwiches from various bakeries here in Belmont Village."

Deflected like a professional goalie.

The women giggled. Pauline couldn't help but notice that Todd seemed oddly comfortable with the situation, like many of the male athletes she'd been around who had to deal with women draping themselves all over them.

"What would you like?" Todd gestured to the wall of teas.

"Besides you?" the woman replied. She leaned forward on the counter. "What would you recommend?"

Although she couldn't usher this woman out of the shop the way security could drag drunken fans away from Perry, she could make sure this woman knew Pauline was still standing there. She cleared her throat. "I recommend a fruit-infused white tea for the afternoon. It's not the same jolt as coffee, but the flavour is refreshing and the L-theanine helps counter the adrenalin rush of the caffeine, so you'll get a slow release of energy."

The woman stood up and frowned. "I asked *him* for a recommendation."

Todd retained his composure. "I only started on Monday. Pauline is the owner's daughter and practically grew up here. I'd definitely recommend what she does."

The woman huffed but agreed. "And for dessert? Or can't you recommend that either?"

Wow. Just wow. With everything Pauline had seen over the years, people like this still amazed her because she couldn't understand why they would get so upset over such a slight.

Everyone has their story, she reminded herself. To get this insulted over not getting a tea recommendation from a hot guy must mean this woman carried a lot of pain inside her.

I just called him a hot guy, too, she realized. But at least she treated him with more respect. *Like saying his passion was boring.*

Okay. Maybe not. Pauline made a mental note to change that immediately. But she did try to support him against this woman.

Todd recommended the lemon lavender cake, and the women agreed to a piece for each of them. But the moment the woman lifted her phone to take a photo, Todd deftly turned his back to prepare their tea.

Pauline stepped in front of the camera. "You can take a photo of me, if you'd like." She smiled.

The woman snapped the photo. "I'm leaving a bad review on Howl."

What Pauline wouldn't have given to dump the tea on her head, like she had been tempted to dump pop or beer on a belligerent visiting fan's head many times. But instead, Pauline smiled. "Have a seat wherever you'd like, and we'll bring your tea and food to you shortly." This was her mom's store, not a hockey arena.

The women paid without saying thank you and sat as far away from the counter as possible.

Pauline helped Todd set mugs on trays. "For someone in the performing arts, you're oddly camera shy. I'll keep that in mind with future customers."

Todd shrugged. "Not a fan of social media."

"Wasn't part of our childhoods, was it? Back then we just had locker pin-ups." She pressed her lips together. Would he think she was calling him a locker pin-up? And would he be wrong? She had to keep talking. "I was totally into Patrick Swayze back then."

Todd raised an eyebrow and the corner of his mouth curled up. "I have a hard time believing you'd let me call you Baby."

She washed her hands in the small sink as much for food safety reasons as for the hope that it would cool her down while Todd pulled the desserts from the display case. Pauline poured the water into the tea pots and then added a little cold water to bring it to the temperature needed for white tea.

While the women were eating, Pauline couldn't help but notice Todd's continuing unease.

"What's bugging you? The hockey comment or fear of social media?"

Todd wiped down the counter. "Dad forced me to spend a year taking hockey lessons before Mom convinced him to let me take ballet. My brothers continued with hockey. It's a bit of a sore spot, I guess."

So that could explain why he wasn't nuts about the Peregrines: probably any hockey team reminded him of his father's lack of support for what Todd had apparently felt drawn to as a child.

How sad to not have the support of the people you love.

PAULINE LEFT to share their ideas with Claire. She said she would make sure that Todd got credit, too, which he appreciated.

Todd shook his head at her honesty and chuckled to himself. Pauline probably didn't know that Patrick Swayze was a classically trained ballet dancer.

He comfortably handled any other patrons who entered the store, but by three o'clock, the store had emptied again, so Todd sat down to study Claire's bible. He hadn't gotten very far, though, when a timid Austin entered the shop. The boy carried a backpack over both shoulders, tucked his hands into his jeans pockets, and avoided eye contact with Todd. He was the opposite to the dishevelled, angry storm Todd had met two days before and looked more like a ballet student with this relaxed but clean appearance. Austin's anger and accusation—*You're the last person I need help from!*—were the reasons Todd hadn't drummed up the courage to call the Tschirharts yet.

"You are Todd Parsons, aren't you? Like, *the* Todd Parsons?"

"Yeah, I am."

Austin raised his gaze and stared in awe at Todd for a full minute. This kind of treatment didn't bother Todd, but after Austin's outburst on Tuesday he wasn't sure what to expect.

"I'm really sorry about Tuesday," Austin said. "I was so angry with my mom for dra—"

Austin stopped talking and stared.

"Um…wait, what was I saying? This is really embarrassing. I hate this." He covered his face with his hands, then looked up again. "I'm standing in front of you, and I had to have a seizure. I probably looked pretty stupid, didn't I?"

"I wouldn't say that…" What was Todd supposed to say?

"No, seriously, just be honest. How stupid does it look when someone just randomly stares into space? I mean, my mom points it out to people all the time, like she did in front of Pauline. And then to see you here, and I was also angry with you for disappearing like that months ago, but then you're here, just like that, and I obviously didn't expect it, and I really needed you…and now I'm blubbering everything out in one go and embarrassing myself even more." Austin took a deep breath and stared again for a few seconds before continuing. "I'm sorry."

Did that mean he was aware of his seizures? Todd didn't want to ask. The poor kid was already going through so much, the last thing he needed was personal questions from Todd.

"Can I make you a tea?" It was the only thing Todd could think of to ease the awkwardness.

Austin shook his head. He closed his eyes, clenched his fists, and took several more deep breaths, which appeared to cause another seizure. Was deep breathing connected to them?

"It's okay," Todd said. "There's no one else here."

"No, no, you don't get it." Austin opened his eyes. "I've revered you most of my life and you're the only connection I've kept to ballet since my diagnosis. My mom doesn't know, because, well, the last thing I need is for her to have anything to connect with me over. But when people raked you over the coals for *Don Quixote* last fall and *The Nutcracker* at Christmas… and I thought your *Gilgamesh* was absolutely brilliant choreography, but apparently most people didn't…and then this stupid disease…but you're, like, here, in this tiny tea shop in *Kitchener*…"

Part of Todd was embarrassed to have his last year splayed out like a terrible newspaper review, but part of him was touched that this boy, going through a painful transition of his own, had actually paid attention to Todd's life.

"I mean, they thought you were bad because your jumps went from six feet to five!" Austin continued. "Five! Like that —" Austin stared into space for a few seconds. "You're not talking, which means I was saying something, wasn't I?"

Todd nodded. "Was that another seizure?" He wanted to understand.

Austin stared at the floor. "Yeah. Sorry about that."

Why would Austin apologize for something he had no control over? What should Todd say? He'd never met anyone with this disease. Would Pauline know? It sounded like she had experience helping kids with this kind of thing.

"Listen," Todd said, "words aren't my strength. It's why I danced. So I hope I'm not saying the wrong thing here. But please don't be embarrassed in front of me, Austin. That you even called *Gilgamesh* brilliant is already touching." He smiled. "Just for that, you can talk to me anytime you want to."

"You didn't think it was brilliant?"

Todd shrugged. "The critics and most audience members didn't."

Austin's eyes popped out of his head. "How couldn't they? It was so beautiful! Why did you listen to them? Why did you give up?"

The question hurt. Here was a troubled young man opening himself up to Todd when he'd closed himself off from his family. Todd guessed that if he didn't offer a similar gesture in kind, he would also hurt this boy who was already going through a difficult journey. The opportunity to help was here: Todd had to seize it, even if it meant opening his own wounds a little more.

"I couldn't do it anymore. The criticism, the harassment on social media, the critics. I danced to make others happy, and I felt like I wasn't doing that anymore."

The look of disappointment on Austin's face broke Todd's heart. "It just made me feel that if you couldn't take what life was throwing at you, then neither could I. Seeing you dance again would make me happy, that's for sure." Austin slumped down into a chair.

Todd sat in the chair opposite him. "I wouldn't exactly sell out the theatre here in Kitchener." Todd hoped Austin would react to the light dig.

Austin's face relaxed. "Because only dance students are interested in ballet. When you performed here six years ago, on November twenty-third, two thousand and eleven, they closed off the balcony, mezzanine, and back third of the orchestra because they couldn't sell tickets."

"You were there?"

"Hello? Seeing you live made me want to dance for a living."

Todd's eyes widened. "Really?"

Austin nodded.

Todd remembered something and snapped his fingers. "Were you that kid standing by the tour bus who wanted me to sign six or seven programs that night?"

Austin's face turned bright red. "I still have them. I wanted backups."

Both laughed.

"I honestly couldn't believe the difference to Toronto the next night," Todd said. "Four thousand seats sold out three nights in a row. Dozens lined up for autographs afterwards. And only an hour down the 401. That's when I knew I wanted to stay in Toronto for the last years of my career. I just thought I had more years left than I apparently did."

Would Austin open up to Todd about the bullying? No. Not yet. After decades as a dancer, he had an excellent feel for the space between two bodies. A wall still stood between Austin and Todd. Now was not the time to ask.

But Todd did have to ask one thing.

"I need a big favour from you, Austin. Everyone here thinks I'm a retired ballet teacher."

Austin snorted. "And they're buying it? What ballet teacher retires at forty-three?"

Sheesh. The kid even knows my age. "Only non-dancers would believe me, and thankfully, I've landed among a sea of them. Pauline didn't even know who Nureyev was."

Austin's jaw dropped.

"I think she's just been so involved in sports that she never opened her eyes to ballet."

They both heard the back door open.

Austin leaned in and whispered, "This'll be the most fun I've had in a year. Your secret is safe with me."

As Todd and Austin exchanged phone numbers Pauline bounced in, as excited as an amusement park mascot.

"Mom agreed to our plans!" she announced.

"Congratulations," Todd replied.

"What plans?" Austin asked.

Todd enjoyed watching Pauline become tongue-tied again.

"Hi Austin," Pauline said, noticing him. "Renovation plans for this place. We're going to make some changes."

"Can I help?"

Pauline looked surprised but she regrouped quickly. "As long as your mom's okay with it."

While Austin texted his mother, Pauline shot Todd a questioning look, and Todd mouthed back, "Later."

But seeing these moments of uncertainty in the six-foot, muscular, jumping bean of an athlete made her even more endearing to him.

Austin's eyes lit up a moment later. "She said yes!"

CHAPTER 10

*P*auline couldn't wait to ask Tracy what had changed in Austin. Only two days had passed and he already seemed like he was back to the teenaged version of the boy she remembered. Incredible.

She sipped on a calming white-and-green tea blend with chamomile, mint, rosebuds, and lemon balm while working on Peregrines tasks in the back room. One thing she enjoyed about tea was that its depth of flavour gave her something to focus on, which in turn helped her mind focus on the task at hand.

Unfortunately, it didn't help her leg, which wouldn't stop bouncing. She'd need at least an hour workout for it.

"Or an evening in the arena," she said to herself.

She finished an email confirming Perry's appearance at a community skate in Scarborough after Monday's victory parade and then opened Perry's Twitter account. She shot back at a few fans from other teams, added hearts to comments from Peregrines fans, and shared photos that were still making the rounds from the win.

"Hey, Pauline."

She slammed her laptop shut. "Hey, Todd." Where did he come from? Oh, right, he worked here.

"Sorry to startle you like that."

"No worries." Could he maybe keep rolling those sleeves up so she could see his upper arms?

"When do you think you'll start renovations? I've got some plans coming up and want to make sure I can help out a bit."

Would he wear a T-shirt to help with renovations? Then she could see those upper arms…

"That's really nice, but it's not necessary. You've already got a lot to learn with the tea and such."

You're returning to Toronto, Pauline.

"Actually, I'm more confident with a hammer than I am with tea. I grew up in a DIY family."

That would involve a T-shirt…

"Really? That would be great, then. We're closed Sunday, and I'm gone until Tuesday evening, so nothing until at least Wednesday. Oh…that leaves you alone two days—I hope that's okay?"

Todd chuckled. "Any more sales I should know about?"

His smile was so warm.

"Next one's not until Christmastime. Now that word has gotten around about Mom and that she's hired help, the regulars will certainly be nicer to you. And you're learning Mom's system slowly but surely."

"It's so complex. You learned as you worked here?"

"I guess you could say I was *steeped* in it."

Todd groaned at the pun and Pauline laughed with him. He leaned against the doorframe, and Pauline's internal temperature jumped.

"Is there any science behind what she recommends?"

Pauline stood up to head to the front of the shop and do something useful. At least, that's what she told herself.

"For some of her blends, she follows the basics of herbal medicine. For example, the tea I'm drinking has chamomile and lemon balm in it for calming effects." She smiled at the irony of that statement.

"But it doesn't work on you."

"Not when I feel caged up like this. But everything else is based on her impressions of how tea hits her palate, or, if she knows the person well, how it hits theirs."

"Which is probably what I'm feeling when something feels 'high' or 'low.'"

Pauline snapped her fingers. "You're probably right, actually. You're feeling if it hits higher on your palate or lower. I've never thought of it that way. Then the rest of what Mom recommends is often based on the meaning of the ingredients to what the person is going through."

"Like that guy you sold the Wuyi rock oolong tea."

"Exactly. But that can get complicated."

Todd appeared to think through what Pauline had just told him. "So, she finds meaning in it, the way someone might have a fond memory of a food from their childhood. Only it's more intricate than that."

"Something like that." She headed toward the door, and Todd moved out of the way. "I'll look after the tea shop for a bit. Maybe now that you know a little more about how Mom approaches tea, her bible might make a little more sense."

When she passed him, though, he suddenly pressed one arm against his back and grabbed her arm for balance.

The feeling his touch shot between them was like skates gliding on ice.

~

WHY, in the name of all that is holy, did Todd's back have to spasm now? And couldn't he have grabbed on to something else besides Pauline? Especially after he had unintentionally sent her that look a few minutes before? But the energy that shot through them like a *grand jété* was too powerful to ignore.

And too inconvenient to act upon.

Plus, the last thing he needed was to give her a reason to doubt his physical fitness for the job. Heavy lifting was in the job description, and after decades of hoisting women over his head, he knew he could do it. But it had been precisely all those overhead lifts that had left him with an injured back.

Pauline's cheeks flushed. She'd felt the sensation, too.

She placed her hand on his back. "You okay?" For someone so strong, her touch was so gentle. How would her hand feel on his skin?

He couldn't bring himself to pull out his barre at his new apartment and develop a new dance practice every morning. The kind that used to keep his back spasms at bay.

"Just an old injury. I'll be fine, thanks. Forgot to do my exercises this morning." He didn't want her to believe her mother had hired a failure. Everyone deserved a second chance, right?

"There's an ice pack in the freezer and heating packs in the first-aid kit if you need them."

The chimes over the front door jingled, and Pauline left to take care of the customer.

Still massaging his back, Todd couldn't help but wonder what she'd been working on that was so secretive. Had she been looking him up? He hoped not. There was nothing good about him online anymore.

He looked down at the cover of her laptop, which was emblazoned with a large, familiar bird.

"Of course. Peregrines' logo."

He closed his eyes and massaged his back again. "You're here for a new life, Todd," he murmured to himself. "Leave your old one behind."

But when you had loved what you did since childhood, leaving it behind was easier said than done, especially when the woman you were falling for worked for the very team that had become the antithesis of your passion.

"Where's the tea for that?"

He casually flipped through Claire's binder and surprised himself when he found one.

SATURDAY EVENING, Todd locked up so that Pauline could head home early and prepare for Toronto. The air was warm and humid, normal for June. He wasn't ready to head home himself yet. He'd survived his first week at his first job outside of ballet. That deserved a little celebration, didn't it? Sort of like after a show, when he and the rest of the company would head to a bar for a drink.

As he came around the front of the plaza, the lights of the beer park across the street caught his eye. That would hit the spot: beer, burger, and fries. And, if he gained two pounds around his waist, it didn't matter anymore: he was no longer expected to dance half naked onstage.

He crossed Belmont Avenue and entered the small outdoor beer garden. He found a secluded table and a few minutes later was listening to beer recommendations from a young server. Todd settled on a craft beer from Collingwood, a tourist town not quite two hours north of Kitchener known for its skiing.

Skiing was another sport his dad and brothers had pushed Todd to join them in. But the risk of injury was too great.

Finally they had stopped asking him at all. It was just as well: Todd needed the time to practise.

Todd took a swig of his beer and enjoyed the flavour, but surveying the beer garden, he realized how alone he was. If this had been Toronto and he'd been with his ballet company, by now, someone would've shared a story about some onstage mistake they'd hoped no one had noticed, or Todd would've been ribbed about the number of kisses he'd gotten from adoring women. He pulled out his phone and scrolled through his company's website. Only his picture was missing among those of his friends. He shoved his phone back in his pocket.

He could have asked Pauline to join him. She had to eat, right? But given how infrequently she'd apparently visited these past three years, she probably would have wanted to eat with her parents.

What kind of tea would Pauline drink with a burger and fries? Or would she drink any tea at all with this meal? Or a different tea at each course? Could someone drink that much tea in a sitting?

But they probably serve bagged tea here, he thought. *She wouldn't go near it with a ten-foot pole.*

That answered that question. The Robinsons didn't drink bagged tea. In fact, one of the photos Claire had been trying to dust was of Richard dressed as a used tea bag one Halloween when Pauline and Dawn were teenagers. It was his penance for suggesting Claire sell pre-packaged tea to help increase sales.

If Pauline were sitting opposite him right now, he'd love to get her to stumble over her words again, an odd quirk for someone involved in community engagement. He bit into the burger, trying not to chuckle. A hyperactive athlete who could match a calming substance like tea to people. Talk about polar opposites. Pauline had to stand still long enough to listen to someone's story to find the right tea.

But actually…the longer Todd thought about it, the more sense it made to him. Performers like her improvised more than they performed choreographed routines. That involved paying attention to the environment around them and the people they were interacting with.

Maybe selling tea wasn't such an opposite to her previous work after all.

Todd finished his meal and paid the server. On his way out, though, he saw Tracy getting up from a table of friends and waving at him.

He noticed the look of recognition on her face.

What was he expecting? If Austin had figured it out, his mother wasn't going to be far behind. To his surprise, she motioned him off to the side.

He didn't wait for her to ask. "I asked Austin not to tell you, and I'm really sorry about that. I know things between you are already tense. I'm just on edge with everything that's happened in the past year."

"So you are *that* Todd. I'll admit, I thought you looked familiar when we walked in on Tuesday, but I was so focused on Austin, and quite frankly, Claire's Tea Shop is the last place I would have ever guessed to see you." She broke into a grin. "You have no idea how much your presence here has changed Austin already. He stopped talking about you after his diagnosis, but he had you…"

The words appeared to catch in her throat. Tracy flapped a hand as though trying to fan away tears. She eventually continued. "He used to have you plastered all over his room." She took a breath and her smile returned.

Used to. Based on Austin's words to him that first day, he could imagine why *used to*. But Austin was willing to move forward, and Todd was going to do everything he could to support the teen.

"I do need to ask you something," Todd began.

Tracy crossed her heart. "I'm used to respecting confidentiality. I wasn't angry that you asked Austin to not say anything. I think it actually gave him something special for a change." Her smile turned into a frown. "Now I have to break it to him that it's no longer his secret." She sighed. "The challenges of raising a teen."

As Todd walked home, a warm feeling emanated from his heart. Despite his colossal failures in the past year, he'd met some amazing people this week, including two who knew everything about him and still wanted to be friends.

Would Pauline feel the same way?

CHAPTER 11

The music vibrated through Pauline, beating in her chest as she danced on the float that led the parade. The cooling vest — a vest with numerous pockets, each carrying a small cooling pack — and the camel pack filled with rehydrating solution on her back under her costume limited what she could do, but they were necessary to prevent the dead bird memes that would circulate on social media if she collapsed from heat stroke. She was, after all, wearing the equivalent of an Arctic-grade snowsuit on a hot June day. A fan on the float helped cool her, too.

She had to admit she would never be this uncomfortable serving customers at Claire's Tea Shop. The small fan at the back of Perry's head wasn't enough to remove the stuffy air that accumulated in humid heat.

A new song distracted her. She jumped off the float to high-five fans and flex her arms for the kids, who returned the gesture while their parents took pictures. A few adults reached for her tail, but the extra security detail Ben had ordered pushed them away. She jumped back on the float to cool down in front of the fan and take sips from the camel pack, the straw of which she held in her mouth the entire time. Another uncomfortable aspect of the day.

"You're loving this, aren't you?" asked Derek, who stood on the float with her.

Pauline nodded as she began clapping overhead, getting the audience to join in and cheer, "Peregrines to victory!"

"I'm glad it's not me in there," he said. "Those two photo sessions were enough for me."

She patted him on the back to thank him for stepping in and took another sip. Even though she'd frozen a good amount of the rehydration solution into ice cubes, her drink was already warm. She could've brewed green tea in there, come to think of it.

"By the way, Ben just confirmed some good news over the system."

Pauline waved to the crowd in the other direction, but she was listening.

"When we get to the stage in Nathan Philips Square, the prime minister of Canada wants a photo op with you."

Pauline whipped her head to face Derek and her gloved hands flew to Perry's beak. She couldn't wait to tell…well, no one. But who cared that she couldn't tell anyone? This was the ultimate life, even if she lived it in a rotisserie oven. She pumped her arms in the air.

"VIP section coming up."

Pauline gave him a thumbs-up and followed him off the float.

This win would mean so much for her performance career and her community work. As much as she was enjoying the break at home, she couldn't wait to return full-time to Toronto. Sold-out games, hospital visits, anti-bullying rallies…a city the size of Toronto would have no limits now that the Peregrines were everyone's favourite team again.

She pumped her fists in the air as she approached the VIP section.

"Hey, Mark, Tim! It's Perry!"

Was Pauline already dehydrated? Or had she just found her "Chicken Dance" partners?

THE MORNING HAD BEEN quiet so far, as though half of Kitchener had driven to Toronto for the Peregrines parade. Todd for the life of him couldn't figure out why. They were expecting over a million spectators and for what? To see a bunch of men who chased a piece of rubber with sticks?

"Your issue isn't with them," he said to himself in the intimate, subdued space of the shop. "It's with your family." More specifically, with his dad and brothers.

His phone rang: another video call from his dad. That made two within a week. "Seriously?" Kitchener was supposed to be a retreat, a chance to regroup and re-evaluate his life. Had he instead invoked the wrath of evil fairy godmothers from ballets passed?

He opened the video call app to see his dad and brothers in their full Peregrines garb again. Standing in front of them waving was Perry.

"You guys should've asked me for a makeup artist recommendation. I would've even paid for it."

Michael shouted into the phone above the noise of the crowd. "Hey, Todd! Look who stopped by for a visit!"

The grey peregrine falcon in the team's red-and-white uniform waved at the phone's camera.

Mark pulled the phone over to him. "It's so freakin'

awesome here! We know you hate Perry and the Peregrines, but you'd love it here anyway!"

Michael pulled the phone back. "This is probably what you felt like when you got your first role as the Nutcracker Prince!"

Wait a minute. When was the last time Todd's father had ever tried to connect with him using ballet? With his first professional casting as the Nutcracker Prince, perhaps the most well-known male role in classical ballet, Todd had felt like a million people were celebrating with him, even though it was just family and close friends.

Michael stared into his phone "Wait…are you working in a tea shop, Todd?"

Ho. Ly. Su. Gar. This is Todd's family? In a crowd of a million? AND HE HATES ME?

Well, Perry, not Pauline, but when Pauline was in costume, she and her character were one and the same.

What were the chances?

Literally three in a million.

And why was Todd's family in the VIP section?

"Can we come and visit you?" Todd's father shouted into the phone. "Why won't you tell us where you are?"

Pauline couldn't hear Todd's answers through Perry's head. How bad were things if Todd didn't want to tell his father and brothers he was only an hour's drive down a highway?

Pauline motioned that she had to go.

"No, wait, Perry! One shot! We have a huge collection of photos of you in our Peregrines' nest out west!"

What was a Peregrines' nest? Regardless, she placed her hands on her beak in surprise and nodded in approval. They hung up on Todd to take the photo.

Really? *Really?!* Did they really just cut him off for a photo with Perry, when they already had "a collection"?

After the photo, Pauline high-fived each member of Todd's family and headed over to some kids. She flexed her arms, and the kids followed suit. She clapped overhead, and the adults began to cheer "Peregrines to victory!" The kids joined in.

Pauline ran to the middle of the street and spread out her arms as though she were about to take flight. Derek understood the signal to clear the area.

Once everyone was out of the way, he shouted, "You're clear, Perry!"

Pauline ran, did a cartwheel, a back handspring, and a back-flip. On her final landing, pain shot through her hip, and she clenched her teeth, almost breaking the straw in her mouth. But the children and the adults around them applauded while Pauline posed for photos. She'd deal with the pain later.

On the float again, she wiped Perry's brow and sat down. The adrenalin coursing through her veins made her ignore the heat and the disgusting lukewarm rehydration liquid.

What it couldn't hide, though, was a question: Why would Todd's family place Perry above him?

CHAPTER 12

Todd enjoyed the homemade lasagna at Tracy and Austin's. Although he cooked himself—you didn't make a living as a ballet dancer without knowing how to cook on the cheap—lasagna was something he usually bought packaged. He enjoyed cooking, but not *that* much.

Whether it was Tracy's efforts in the kitchen, or an unusually good day at school, Austin was relaxed and chatty. The few seizures Todd noticed seemed to go undetected by Austin: he would simply continue where he had left off. And Austin's starry-eyed stares were different from the unfocused stares of his seizures. They reminded Todd of the better parts of his former life, when he had once been admired for what he did.

Emphasis on *had been*.

Because he no longer was.

Tracy stood up and began collecting dishes, and Austin immediately went to the kitchen and returned with a can of highly caffeinated pop.

"Austin," Tracy said quietly, "the neurologist said that stuff is the worst thing you can drink, especially before bedtime."

Todd tried to act as though he hadn't heard, but that was irrelevant. Austin slammed the can onto the table.

"Stop embarrassing me in front of people! I'm n—" Austin stared into space.

Todd had read online that Austin's seizures were called absence seizures. Austin could be having dozens or even hundreds a day, often without being aware of them.

When Austin came out of this one, he balled his fists. "I hate this!" He stormed upstairs, and Tracy jumped when he slammed his bedroom door shut. A minute later, *The Nutcracker Suite* blared from his room.

Tracy avoided Todd's gaze while they continued collecting dishes from the dining room. Only once they'd loaded the dishwasher did she speak. "Please don't judge me for not going after him."

How could Todd judge her? He didn't have children, and had a hard enough time dealing with his own issues. Plus, he'd been Austin's age once, too. "I know teen boys sometimes need time alone to process."

Tracy scratched at a dried stain on the counter. "He started caffeinating to give him energy at ballet school. It affected his sleep and lowered his seizure threshold during the day. That's when we noticed that his seizures weren't just daydreaming—he wouldn't come out of them quickly. I've tried not buying pop, but then he buys it at school. Maybe if you talked to him? You have no idea how much he looked up to you."

Todd leaned against the wall and stuck his hands in his pockets. The pedestal of celebrity status. Humans weren't perfect, and he was as human as the next person.

Tracy wiped down the counters. "The one role he'd hoped to perform in his life was the Nutcracker Prince. Ever since he was a child. I don't know why. Maybe it was the thought of a toy coming alive. It's the only connection to ballet he's retained since…since this whole frightening journey began." She wiped away tears with the back of her hand.

Normally, the polite thing to do would have been to give the family privacy and leave, but he sensed Tracy needed someone to talk to. The awkward part about celebrity status was that there was no getting-to-know-each-other period: he wasn't a stranger to them, even though they were to him. But he'd begun a new life here, one that included new friendships.

And a new question whenever someone was upset.

"Can I make you a tea?"

Tracy wrung out the dish cloth. "Only at Claire's a week and you're already getting the hang of it."

Ten minutes later, they sat in the basement, sipping on the green tea blend Pauline had given Tracy last week.

"Pauline has her mother's gift," she said. "This is perfect."

It was perfect. The gentle green tea blend supported the lavender, which relaxed Todd, and the chamomile reminded him of his mother, who'd had a sea of the tiny flowers growing in their backyard every year. She never harvested the white-and-yellow flower heads—too much work, she'd always said, and boxed chamomile tea was easier to steep—but they'd reminded her of tiny suns.

Tracy shared Austin's journey, from his childhood love of dance, to his seeing Todd onstage in Kitchener—she couldn't remember when. She smiled. "I had to wait while he had you sign a program."

"Actually, it was a small stack."

"That's right," Tracy said, finally laughing. "He hoped to sell them someday to earn a little money."

Todd raised his eyebrows in surprise. "Is that so? He'd told me they were backups in case he lost one."

"I believe they were destined for eBay ten or twenty years into the future. But you see?" Tracy said. "That's my Austin:

fun, mischievous, also thinking ahead and obsessed with ballet. Once he moved to ballet school, the bullying stopped, and he felt free. We also noticed that these staring spells never happened while he danced..."

She paused to sip on her tea, and Todd didn't push her to continue.

Tracy finally spoke again. "Then he dropped his partner a few times. In practice...as you know, it can happen. But then it happened onstage when people used flashes on their phones, even though they weren't supposed to. It set off a seizure that actually lasted ten seconds. Todd, he was so humiliated...he just quit."

Todd's skin burned all over his body as he felt Austin's humiliation. The worst thing that could ever happen to a male dancer was to let something happen to his partner. It didn't matter if it wasn't his fault.

"But you said he never has them when he dances?" Todd just wanted clarification.

Tracy shook her head. "Until he started caffeinating."

"So, aside from lifting girls, dancing sounds like it's safe for him, for now?"

Tracy nodded as she grabbed a tissue from the coffee table in front of her.

Todd couldn't help wondering where Austin's father was in all of this. How could he just abandon the family and let his son and his son's mother—no matter his feelings toward her—go through this alone? Todd at least had to give his own father credit for trying to stay in touch, even if it was through a monthly text or two-minute phone call.

"And medication?" he asked. If he was going to help Austin, he needed the full picture.

"When they started the first drug, he was a zombie. I could hardly get him out of bed, he missed tons of school, his marks dropped, he practically missed Christmas, he lost interest in the few friends he had… He didn't even recognize your face when I showed him a photo. But we had to try it for six weeks to give his body a chance to get used to things because maybe the side effects would subside." She shook her head, as though trying to shake away memories she didn't want to remember. "We took him off the meds, but you can't just stop them, you have to wean. I wanted to try another kind, but Austin refused. He got back on caffeine the next semester to keep up with his school-work, one friend moved away, the others….he said they had no interest in him, but I think he also pushed them away. His seizures returned and got worse. Then the bullying started. I think they're from his old school because they bully him for being gay, stupid, and a dancer, and no one here knows he dances. But he won't talk to me, and there's nothing I can do about it."

Todd felt useless. Yes, he'd occasionally spoken out against bullying, but when his messages only went to his fans, he was preaching to the choir. What good was that?

"Is there anything I can do? I feel like tea's not enough."

Surprisingly, Tracy broke into a smile. "Besides telling Austin to stop it with the caffeine? Don't take this the wrong way, but I could really use Pauline's antics right now. She could always make me forget my worries. Sometimes, that's all I can ask for in my life."

Todd could see why Tracy would say that.

"When I was in high school, this guy dumped me. I swore he was the love of my life, of course. I was so depressed that I started skipping class. Pauline showed up after, I don't know, two days?" Tracy's face became animated. "I kid you not, Todd, she would walk on her hands *up the stairs*. She practically gave me a heart attack! Shocked the guy out of my system! A few days later, we'd heard that the guy who played the school mascot had quit, and I told her to ask about it. She wouldn't do it at first—she was too nervous—but she said when she saw the costume, she knew it was her calling."

She finished the tea in her cup, and Todd hurried to finish his: it would soon be time for him to go.

"Which is why I can't for the life of me imagine her in a desk job," Tracy finished. "She's an incredible entertainer. You should look her up." She gave Todd the names of Pauline's previous teams, and Todd committed them to memory. He would definitely search a few of her stunts online, including the one where she failed to clear all the poor performers lying on the floor when she flipped over them. Not to laugh at her, of course.

Okay. Yes, to laugh at her. But out of kindness.

Out of love?

No, Todd, not love. She'll be gone in a few weeks and then you'll never see her again.

Tracy stifled a yawn, and that was his cue to exit.

"I have to open tomorrow, and I still have lots of teas to study."

Tracy walked him upstairs to the door. "I should call Austin down."

Todd placed a comforting hand on her shoulder. "If he finds solace in Tchaikovsky, let's not interrupt him. But please tell him I said goodbye."

"I can't believe you're actually here. Everything has been going so wrong for us and then out of nowhere Todd Parsons shows up. Seriously, you're a dream come true. Thank you for coming. And…thanks for listening."

Once out on the sidewalk, Todd looked up at Austin's window, wondering if the boy would look out. The curtains were open.

The teen was dancing in his room.

So he did still dance. It was clear ballet was Austin's life: Todd could see the music cascade through his body.

Then Austin flopped onto his bed. Todd saw the door open and Tracy pop her head in. Only after the door closed, though, did Austin press his face against the window and see Todd. He waved, and Todd waved back.

Todd performed a little choreography from James Kudelka's staging of *The Nutcracker*. The National Ballet of Canada had invited him several years ago to perform at a few shows during their traditional Christmas run, and he guessed Austin would recognize it.

Todd was right: it brought a smile to Austin's face. Todd held his pinky finger and thumb to his ear, signalling to the teen he could call him whenever he'd like. Austin nodded. Todd did a triple *tour en l'air* but when he landed, pain shot through his knee. Jumping on concrete in loafers was not a good idea. Austin clapped, and Todd took a bow.

Should he try to mime a message to Austin about his caffeine intake?

He pretended to take a huge swig out of an imaginary can of pop, then wagged his finger at Austin, a stage-worthy angry expression on his face. Next, he laid both hands along his cheek and tilted his head toward one shoulder, the standard mime in ballet for sleep. Yes, it was early, especially for a teen, but Austin was clearly on edge, and rest, without caffeine, would do him good.

There. He'd spoken to Austin, but "in ballet."

Austin feigned a stage pout, to which Todd pulled his legs together and pretended to draw a sword, which he pointed at Austin, commanding him to listen. Austin crossed his arms, furrowed his brow so strongly it would have been seen all the way at the back of the Four Seasons Performing Arts Centre in Toronto, and shook his head.

Todd broke down, laughing. Austin joined in and they waved goodbye.

As Todd walked down the street toward his apartment, he also couldn't help thinking that the sooner Todd went to sleep himself, the sooner Pauline would be back in town.

He wondered how the parade had gone for her and her mascot.

CHAPTER 13

*R*elaxing on her couch after a fifteen-minute ice bath, Pauline reviewed an estimate from the flooring company her dad had recommended. But with her heat exhaustion she couldn't concentrate. She sipped on an iced Belmont Blizzard she'd prepared the night before. She loved her tea, hated this ritual.

"I have to treat myself like an Olympic athlete with this job, and I'm hardly one," she said aloud in her sports-cluttered condo.

What was the deal with Todd not telling his family his location? Then there was the comment that Todd getting his role as the Nutcracker Prince for the first time was just as big as this NAHA win. There was no way getting some role in a ballet was *this* big. Her thoughts flew to Austin and how he danced with abandon as a six-year-old to *The Nutcracker* at her mother's Christmas sale. What if Todd's father was referring to how Todd had *felt* when he won the role? As though it was a big break?

A big break in a career.

If he'd had a career, there would be an online trail.

But before she could even type a "T" for "Todd" into the search engine, Ben called. It was just as well. Why did she care about a ballet career? She didn't even know who What's-His-Face was in that Muppets skit, and neither Jan, Tracy, nor Austin recognized Todd, otherwise they would've said something. Some people got really happy with the smallest piece of good news, like Todd was happy working in a tea shop as his new career.

"Probably just a high school play," she said as she swiped her phone open. "Hey, Ben."

"Everyone loved you today, and Perry's social media feeds are on fire. Excellent work."

Ben wanted something. If he'd been a genuine human being, he'd have asked first how she was feeling. And if he was his usual self, he'd have taken credit for her performance today.

"Thanks. Community skate in Scarborough is a go for tomorrow afternoon, and I've got more events in the works. They should be confirmed by the end of the week. Ow." She pressed her hand to a throbbing spot on her head.

"What?"

"My head's still killing me from today."

"Make sure you enter everything into the PR calendar."

What a jerk. He really didn't care about his employees. That being said, it came with the territory. Like the groping. "It's all in there, Ben, even the tentative appointments."

There was a pause. "Mmm. But nothing in Kitchener."

"You've always said Kitchener's a waste of time, so I've been focusing on Toronto community events and social media."

"It was a waste of time to send you there when Toronto has millions of people and the largest school board in Ontario. But since you're in Kitchener, and Kitchener is one of three cities in Waterloo Region, which has a population of over six hundred thousand, that's lots of families for ticket sales next season. Find a school or two and do the anti-bullying rally. That should help capitalize on our positive public image right now, and it'll be a good rehearsal for the tour."

Because the actual message of the anti-bullying rally isn't important? Pauline's work boiled down to numbers for Ben. It was never about the people.

"You realize high schools are going into exams soon?" Pauline said.

"You promised you wouldn't let me down, so don't." Ben hung up without giving Pauline a chance to protest further.

Pauline loved performing in the anti-bullying rally: it motivated hundreds of students to treat each other with respect. As her anger at Ben's attitude toward the rally simmered, she felt embarrassed that she hadn't thought of the idea.

Austin. He went to her old high school. She could kill two birds with one stone. No pun intended.

"Why does Ben have to have good ideas?" It made it hard to hate him all the time.

She yawned. She had to get this flooring company booked and then go to bed. Perry resting in a chair tomorrow would not go over well with the children and their families. She filled out the company's contact form and sent it off, then visited the website for Eby Heights to look up the email address for the principal and send an inquiry.

She'd be back in Kitchener Tuesday night, which meant she'd see Todd soon.

The aches in her body eased up a little more.

BACK AT CLAIRE'S desk in the back room on Wednesday, Pauline kept backspacing in her email to the Peregrines' marketing coordinator: her fingers couldn't target the right keys accurately enough on the keyboard. The community skate had almost been as much fun as the parade, but in a different way. A kid had had a hard time with skating, and it had only been through Pauline's feigned tripping that the child had developed the courage to give it a go. Yes, meeting the prime minister would be one of the highlights of her career, but helping a child overcome a fear…that was the cherry on top.

Only…she couldn't tell anyone about it.

"Mind telling me what's making you smile?"

Todd's voice gave her goosebumps. Happy goosebumps.

"Nothing important. Just had a good time yesterday." The lie punched her in the gut. It was one thing to lie about her job, but to say that the change in a child wasn't important? That hurt. Yes, she could have said that she'd watched Perry help this child, but that would begin a slippery slope of lies, and she would eventually slip up.

She closed her laptop and lifted some upholstery samples out of her bag. "Ouch." She rubbed her shoulder. The sample binders were heavy. Her shoulder would probably take another day or two to calm down after Monday.

"You okay?"

"Weights again yesterday morning." What else was she going to say? Handsprings on asphalt along a sweltering three kilometres? At least her fleece gloves had protected her hands.

She carried the sample binders out to the café, which was empty yet again. Yes, it was a weekday morning, but Pauline remembered as a kid that stay-at-home moms would hang out here sometimes and chat after dropping the kids off at school. She hoped her social media plan, the renovations, and her public relations outreach would bolster sales past her time in Kitchener.

"I have no idea where to start. If I show Mom the wrong colours, she'll worry she's left her shop in the hands of a preschooler with Magic Markers, try to get out of bed on her own when Dad's at work, fall down the stairs, re-dislocate her knee, break a hip…" She threw her hands up in the air.

Todd laughed at her hyperboles. "You even worry on adrenalin."

"If I'm not careful, I can get myself tea drunk. Then watch out."

"Is that really a thing?"

Pauline explained what being tea drunk was. "It only happens when I'm having an existential crisis, though."

Todd shook his head in amazement. "I had no idea what I was getting myself into when I signed up for this."

Pauline laughed. "I'll bet you didn't. So, what tea would you recommend for me in this situation?"

Todd thought for a moment. "I believe your mom's bible suggests pu-erh, because it aids in bold decision-making."

"Under normal circumstances, you would be right. However, pu-erh isn't for everyone, and that's exactly the tea that I get drunk on."

"Noted. Then how about Kambaa tea, a bold, full-bodied, Kenyan cut-tear-curl tea? It steeps quickly. Recommended for impatient people."

Pauline feigned indignation. "You wouldn't be suggesting anything about my personality now, Mr. Parsons, would you?"

Todd shuddered. "Don't call me that. That's what everyone calls my dad." He got up to brew them both tea, but Pauline saw her opening.

"Your family must've been happy about the championship."

"Yeah."

"Did they watch the parade on Monday?"

Todd measured out tea into disposable tea bags for both of them. "Yup."

She paused, wondering if he'd say anything else, but he

didn't. *I can't force him to talk about it*, she thought and dropped the topic. As a mascot, she couldn't ask any questions. How was that different from now? People talked about what they wanted when they wanted. Just because she could speak now didn't change that.

"I was at Tracy's house for dinner on Monday."

Todd clearly didn't want to talk about his father since he was changing the topic. "Had a good time?"

"It was interesting."

Todd brought their teas over—he'd chosen a green tea infused with watermelon for himself. As they flipped through upholstery samples, Todd shared with Pauline the events of that evening, and Pauline shook her head in sadness.

"But I felt so torn," he said. "Tracy's lost because she can feel her son slipping away from her, but Austin's completely withdrawn from his mother because she can't stop 'helping' him, if you know what I mean. Granted, caffeine for anyone before bed isn't good, but I kind of get where he's coming from. To him, a pop is the least of his problems. She believes he's stopped dancing, but he was dancing in his bedroom last night. Probably the entire time we were talking. I know you don't know much about ballet, Pauline, but Tracy told me some of the previous teams you used to perform for. My jaw dropped when I watched some of your stunts. Austin can't do any of that, but can you imagine feeling like all you have left for your energy is a bedroom?"

He'd looked her up? Pauline's cheeks heated up at the compliment. But she understood what he meant with Austin. Even her mother's tea shop was too small for her. For people who didn't have the need to express themselves through their bodies, it was sometimes hard to explain what that kind of confinement felt like. The best example Pauline could come up with was covering half your face with a thick scarf all day: your eyes could see, but without the freedom to breathe openly through your nose and mouth, you felt gagged. For someone who used their entire body as a form of expression and as an outlet of energy, they needed space to "breathe" freely. Without the space to let that energy out, depression and anger could set in. In fact, depression was common among professional mascot performers when their season ended because they couldn't perform.

"I'll see what I can do," Pauline said. "And I promise I won't tell Tracy about Austin's dancing. He has to tell her. If we do, it'll betray his trust in us."

"I don't even know if he knows I know."

"The best way to help Austin right now is to maintain his trust, unless either of us thinks he's in imminent danger. But I'm glad they're both opening up to you. Maybe he'll tell you about the bullying, and then we can step in."

"I was hoping for that, too."

Pauline pointed to the upholstery samples. "But, in the meantime, you'll need to grace me with your flair for interior decorating."

Todd nodded as he flipped through the sample book. "This one. With the right paint colour, it'll give an inviting atmosphere in here."

How does he do that? Pauline wondered. She wrote the sample name down.

"That's so sad to hear about Austin, though," she said. "Ten years ago, Mom had this Christmas tea sale. Austin was six. Jan was looking after him, and they had to keep a *Nutcracker* CD in his bag in case he got upset."

Todd laughed. "With all the students I've taught, I don't think I've ever heard that before."

"I forget what happened, but he did get upset, so we put the CD in. You should've seen him dance. He was so free. I guess it was always his dream to perform in some starring role in that ballet?"

"The Nutcracker Prince. It was one of my favourite roles."

That's what Todd's dad had alluded to at the parade. "Must have been exciting the first time you got that role." Was that letting on too much?

"Funny. My dad said that to me the other day."

"Oh?"

But Todd said nothing more. She didn't press any further. As curious as she was, she didn't want to hurt him.

"Do you mind showing me a little?"

Todd raised his eyebrows. "Ballet?"

Pauline stood up, proving she was ready to learn.

"Um, okay. Why?"

Pauline shrugged. "I feel like I've been missing out." But a smile crept onto her face. "Okay, and if I ever do mascot work again, maybe I can use a little."

Todd crossed his arms. "So you can mock us?"

Pauline gave him a sheepish smile. "Only with the greatest respect."

Todd threw his head back in laughter. "That is the most creative request for teaching I've ever heard." He set his mug on the table and stood up. He turned his feet outwards nearly one hundred and eighty degrees, and Pauline's eyes popped out of her head. She tried to accomplish the same feat but he immediately admonished her.

"You're going to kill your knees if you do that. Turnout starts at the hips. But let's talk about posture first—ignore my feet. They turn out automatically. Bring yours parallel."

Pauline did as she was told.

"Stand up straight."

She did.

"Your lower back's sticking out. Try to feel like your tail bone is reaching to the ground, not the wall."

Pauline did her best to follow his instructions, but judging by the millions of metaphors Todd used to help her fix what felt like correct posture to her, she wasn't getting it.

"I guess all those years of gymnastics have left you with a warped sense of straight," he said, his voice gentle. "Do you mind if I use my hands to correct you? It's how I was taught. Ballet these days is hands-off, which makes students feel safer, but this will go faster if I can place my hands on you."

She agreed.

Todd gently placed one hand on her lower back and the other on her abdomen and nudged her tailbone down.

The steam in the room was rising.

CHAPTER 14

The day finally over, Todd shut off the lights and stepped outside. Pauline followed him and locked the back door. She threw her key into her shoulder bag.

Something in her body wanted to close the professional space between them, like hot water pulling out the flavours and colours of dried tea leaves. But to what end? To have a summer fling? She couldn't put her heart through that. Nor his.

"So, no major disasters while I was gone?"

Todd shook his head. "No major disasters. I even pleased Doris a second time."

Pauline raised an eyebrow. "Did you now?"

Todd laughed, clearly realizing how his statement sounded.

"Did you want to grab supper?" he asked.

He had to ask. Why did he have to ask? She had to say no.

"Um…maybe."

"I've read that Uptown Waterloo is nice, and I think it's only a ten or fifteen-minute walk from here? We could talk about the renovations. Strictly business, of course."

"Of course."

Aaand...she had just said yes. Something calming about him pulled her to him, like an antidote to her constant need for movement. But Pauline had realized something else about Todd since last week: he helped others with an open heart. Yes, he was sexy. Locker pin-up material for sure. But Pauline had spent years around many men who had the necessary looks. They lacked the heart she needed in a partner.

You don't have time for a partner, Pauline.

As they walked around the plaza and headed for the Iron Horse Trail, the walking trail that would lead them to the downtown area of Waterloo, she couldn't stop stealing side glances at his grey temples, his strong forearms, or the way he stood so straight.

Her eyes travelled down his muscular body and she noticed for the first time that he also walked with his toes turned out, though not to the almost one hundred and eighty degrees they had turned out to in the shop. She laughed, but she couldn't avert her gaze before he caught her.

"What?"

"It's just that your feet are..." Pauline stopped before she finished her sentence: Todd wasn't laughing with her. His shoulders tensed and he clenched his jaw. "Sorry." She looked straight ahead. "When I was in costume, I didn't have to worry about what showed up on my face. I never spoke, but I had to react right away to those around me. It's a really hard habit to break after three decades."

"Even after three years, eh?"

Pauline shrugged. "I guess everyone's used to me at work." *Curse you, Ben.* She imagined pummelling him with water balloons. Lots of water balloons. Filled with ice water. She needed to move the conversation to a different topic. "But this is relaxing. It's nice. I'm sorry. I really don't mean to make fun of you. Without a mask, my thoughts still have a voice."

Todd's shoulders relaxed. "My dad and brothers always teased me for my love of ballet. Including the turnout. I'm actually jealous of Austin. Except for his father's recent abandonment, from what I can gather, his parents supported his dreams. My father only ever saw me perform three times in my whole life."

Pauline stepped back. "What?"

Todd stuck his hands in his pockets. "Yeah. Three times in… if you count my student days, it'd also be just over thirty years."

Pauline continued walking. "I didn't mean to dredge up that kind of memory."

"You didn't know."

They walked a minute or two in silence, when Pauline realized something. "You performed often then? I thought you only taught."

Todd glanced at her, as though he were debating if he should share something. Her heart skipped a few beats.

"I did perform a little. I just omitted it from my resumé, because I didn't think it was relevant to selling tea. But I also taught. It wasn't a lie."

Pauline smiled at his honesty. "People who don't perform don't always understand the transferable skills we have. I get it. You didn't know you were applying to the mother of a former mascot actor."

"You have no idea how many times in my life people asked me when I'd get a 'real job.'" He used air quotes around "real job."

Pauline punched him in the arm. "I'll bet you I got asked that more often, *and* I'll bet you were never told it must be nice to be paid to play dress-up."

Todd held up a finger. "But can you twirl like this?" He formed a circle with his arms over his head but stuck his fingers to his scalp and twirled on his tiptoes.

"'Must be embarrassing to wear those costumes,'" Pauline added.

"'Must be easy to get a girlfriend.'"

Pauline raised an eyebrow. "Ah…so *that's* the real reason you went to ballet. You wanted to meet girls." She gently shouldered him to prove she was teasing.

The wrinkles around Todd's smiling eyes warmed her all over.

"I guess that's one thing we have in common," Pauline said. "I'm usually—I was usually—the only female performer in all the mascots of any sports association I performed in." She hoped he didn't pick up on her slip of the tongue. He was so easy to talk to. "But speaking of mascotting and ballet, it would be kind of fun to do that 'Swine Lake' duet you showed me. You'd be that Russian dancer and I'd be in the pig costume. Only, I wouldn't be as graceful. That much I can promise you. But I'd be very comfortable jumping off a trampoline and through a flaming hoop if we could work that in."

Todd hooked a finger around one of hers when he laughed. "Yes, that would be fun."

Pauline didn't pull her hand away. She felt so comfortable around him, and not just physically. There were so few people outside her family and professional circles where she could say something like that without them downright laughing at her.

You wouldn't believe the incredible day I had Monday, Todd. Over a million people! And the prime minister of Canada! And I've already met your father and brothers! I could've been on the menu at Swiss Chalet by the end of it, but it was just incredible! And then there was this kid on Tuesday at the community skate!

Of course, she could tell him and ask him not to say anything, but what if they broke up? She'd only known Todd all of a week, and as much as she'd love to fully trust him, Pauline couldn't know for sure how he'd act if they split. He could get angry, go online, share her identity, and she'd be out a million dollars and all the performance days that were still to come. She'd heard too many stories over the years of people gone nuts after a breakup.

Besides, would he really want to hear about her work as Perry? He knew she worked for the Peregrines, but the clues she had assembled so far suggested his father and brothers somehow placed more importance on the Peregrines and Perry than on Todd. And with what she'd just learned, maybe he really disliked her team and didn't want to say. Yet his father had called him, and Todd's family had been overjoyed to talk to him. She was missing something there.

Todd took her performing arts work seriously, unlike other men she'd dated. So, it wasn't her career he didn't like. In fact, to finally have someone understand her on this level, both athletically and artistically...even the athletes she'd dated didn't get the performing arts side of her career.

As they reached Uptown Waterloo, the old-fashioned street-lights against the beginning of dusk gave off a romantic mood. Pauline slipped her hand out of Todd's and slid it behind his waist. She could feel his breath quicken as he put his arm behind her. They arrived at a small shopping centre with a public square out front. A craft market was in full swing in the main area, but in one corner of the square stood a rusty bell sculpture.

"I have to admit," Todd said, "my body feels like that at times. Bent and out of shape."

She had always hated that sculpture, but looking at it from that perspective, she could identify with it, too.

They faced each other, and Pauline wanted nothing more now than to kiss Todd. Judging by the look in his eyes, he felt the same.

A guitar strum startled them and a band in the square began to play.

Todd held out his hand. "May I have this dance?"

Pauline's insides turned into a mishmash of butterflies and cocoon goo: she was so attracted to the man whose outstretched hand she wanted to accept, but she only felt comfortable dancing hidden inside a costume. Otherwise, she was as skittish as a silverfish in light.

"Let's start with the fact that you're a trained ballet dancer," she said over the music.

Todd took hold of her hand. "How often have you watched *Dirty Dancing*?"

"Uh…too often to count?"

He tugged her hand slightly to spin her in and she recognized the move from the main dance Patrick Swayze trained Jennifer Grey to perform in the movie. Well, Johnny Castle and Baby.

Details.

She spun out, her improvisation skills waking up despite the lack of a costume, but with the next spin in, they froze, their lips not even an inch apart.

Baby had to move on with her future, and Pauline would have to, as well. With the win of the NAHA cup, the pinnacle of Pauline's career had begun, and she'd already caught herself almost breaching her contract. She couldn't risk losing everything she'd worked so hard for to her body's desires.

She pulled back. "I'm sorry, Todd. I can't."

TODD COMBED his fingers through his hair. What on earth was he thinking? A relationship with his boss's daughter, who was returning to Toronto in a few weeks? "I'm really sorry, Pauline. I shouldn't have."

But having her arm around his waist had felt so right.

"Business meeting," she reminded him.

"Business meeting. Should we find a restaurant?"

Pauline glanced in the direction they'd come from. "No. I think I should get back."

She paced back and forth like a caged animal. Was she that scared of him? Or of their unmistakable attraction? Todd knew a relationship was a bad idea, too, but it saddened him more than frightened him. Had he not been trying to hide from the public, he would have accepted a relationship that involved constant travel to Toronto. It was only an hour away. But with the arts and culture scene so vibrant in Canada's largest city, he wouldn't last twenty-four hours without someone discovering him and hounding him about where he'd been, what his next plans were, why he believed *Gilgamesh* had flopped, why he no longer danced... He needed time away from all of that to find himself again, to find the Todd Parsons who had existed before fame in the world of ballet had struck. He wasn't ready to expose himself to all that yet.

But in Pauline's eyes he'd seen fear. Why?

"I'm just going to go," she said. Without waiting for him to respond, she ran off.

The craft market on the square looked inviting, but now that the magic of romance was rinsed out of Todd's system, all he could see was everyone's smartphones. His shoulders slouched, he stuck his hands in his pockets and walked home. He'd look up what tea Claire would recommend in such a situation: falling for the boss's daughter with no hope for a relationship.

CHAPTER 15

*T*he next day at Claire's Tea Shop couldn't end fast enough for Pauline, and she suspected the same for Todd, judging by how often he checked his sleeves. At the same time, she'd been caught staring at his lips at least three times—yes, she'd been counting—and she'd caught him staring at hers, too. The attraction was evident.

So was the realization that a relationship was impossible.

But it was already Thursday of the second week. Only two and a half weeks left. She could hold out.

When Tracy entered the shop, Pauline's apprehension vanished: they had their own date planned for the evening. But when she returned from the back room, her things in hand, she found Tracy and Todd talking in low voices, as though she wasn't supposed to hear the conversation.

No matter. She was an adult, they were adults. Only two and a half weeks, right? None of this mattered, whatever this was. For all she knew, they might have been discussing Austin. Tracy didn't have to tell Pauline anything—Pauline had to earn that friendship back. And maybe Austin simply trusted Todd more in a man-to-man sort of way.

"Ready to go, Pauline?"

"Yup!!" She pasted on her best happy-go-lucky smile. But when she passed Todd, she felt the pull of a bee to pollen. "You'll lock up, right?"

"Of course."

"Thanks."

"Sure."

See? Nothing awkward.

Once they were outside, Tracy asked, "What's going on between the two of you?"

Pauline evaded the question during the entire fifteen-minute ride by remarking on the changes in downtown Kitchener. It still had a seedy, industrial feel to it despite all the improvements.

Tracy parked beside a small white business building, and they took the stairs into the basement of a Greek restaurant that had always been their favourite haunt in this part of town.

"This place also hasn't changed," said Pauline. She had never stayed in one place longer than a few years, so returning to a restaurant like this was a treat.

Once they were seated, the server poured them some water and set the bottle on the table. After they ordered, Tracy began opening up about her struggles with Austin.

"I never thought I'd be raising a child with a neurological disease, Pauline, let alone by myself. Mom and Dad are helping where they can, but as I told you the other day, they're getting older, and my siblings don't live here. I thought moving back to town would let Austin be close to some family without being too far from important medical care, but he's so closed off we might as well have moved into the Canadian tundra."

Pauline reached across the table and held Tracy's hand. "And I owe you an apology."

"For what?"

"For not being there when you called. My schedule with the Peregrines has been so demanding that it's kept me from staying in touch with you when you did try to contact me. I've missed everyone so much, including you, and I'm sorry I haven't been there for you."

Tracy placed her hand on her heart. "Pauline, the fault's just as much mine. This story with Austin is only about a year and a half old and doesn't explain the last twenty-some-odd years."

Pauline took a deep breath. Of all the relationships she'd made in her career, how could she have ignored the people closest to her heart?

One server cleared the appetizers and another brought their main course, giving Pauline the distraction she needed to regroup.

"My goodness, Pauline, how do you eat all that and not gain a pound?"

Pauline had ordered the Greek platter, complete with stuffed grape leaves, rice, spanakopita, pita wedges, and hummus. Tracy had ordered souvlaki on a bed of lettuce.

"I stay active."

"Even with a desk job?"

Pauline nodded.

The women ate for a few minutes in silence, savouring their food.

"Okay," Tracy said, "out with it. What was that with Todd?"

"What do you mean?" But the moment Pauline's cheeks turned red, she knew her face had once again given her away.

"Oh my god, Pauline, you *do* like him!" Tracy's face lit up like it used to when they had swooned over celebrity crushes in high school. "I need some happy news in my life. Tell me *all*!" Tracy stuffed a piece of souvlaki in her mouth.

When Tracy got like that, Pauline had two options: insist there was nothing between her and Todd while her face got hotter, thereby leading Tracy to believe something indeed was going on between her and Todd…or just 'fess up.

"Okay, okay. Yeah, there's something."

Tracy pulled her shoulders up and cooed. "I knew it!"

Then Pauline thought about yesterday evening. That statement wasn't entirely correct. "Well, there was. We almost kissed yesterday, and then I pushed him away."

Tracy's jaw dropped. "What? Why?"

Pauline sighed and sat back in her chair. "With the NAHA cup tour this summer, and then all the sold-out games we're expecting… I won't have time for a relationship. I mean, look at my schedule already, Tracy. I couldn't even stay in touch with you and my family these past few years, and the Peregrines were losers the entire time!"

"Seriously? You've only just met the man and you're already predicting the end of your relationship?"

Dang that NDA, Pauline thought. How could she explain to Tracy why this wouldn't work without telling her more?

"So?" Pauline said once they'd reached Tracy's car at the end of the evening. "Can you forgive me for not being around?"

"Only if you can forgive me."

The women embraced, and Pauline allowed herself to believe that her best friend was back in her life.

Just then Pauline's phone rang. She didn't recognize the number, but she picked it up, anyway.

It was the principal from Eby Heights! "I'm so very sorry for calling at this hour and from my home," he said. "The end of the year is so busy, and I needed a few days to confirm scheduling. If the Peregrines are still available, we'd love to have you."

Pauline jumped in the air, surprising Tracy, but kept her voice calm on the phone. After settling a few details, she hung up and explained the anti-bullying rally to her best friend.

"This isn't until next week," Pauline said. "Any chance you have an appointment in Toronto? I have to get a few things for this now. I could drive, if you wanted, and you can for once, I don't know, sleep? Have someone to chat with? Or we could both keep Austin entertained?"

They got in the car. "Next Tuesday, actually, we're seeing the pediatric neurologist again. Austin just listens to music or sleeps, anyway, so if you're good to keep me company, I'd love to have you along."

Tracy turned on the ignition and checked her watch.

"Want to catch a movie?"

Pauline sighed. After all her regret about not dedicating enough time to those important to her, she had to decline. "I'd love to, but right now, I'm working two jobs. Rain check?"

Tracy smiled. "Absolutely. It's so good to see you back in town, Pauline."

Pauline couldn't help but feel the same.

PAULINE STARED at the ceiling in her bedroom, the only empty piece of real estate in it. Photos and posters plastered every other surface like wallpaper: of amateur and professional sports teams she'd loved over the years; herself in mascot costumes, sometimes holding the mascot's head in her arms, something she'd never do anymore (she didn't understand back then that it disrespected the character); herself as a gymnast in different poses and bodysuits; high school banners; her and Tracy acting goofy in shopping-mall photo booths.

Oh—and peeking through on her bulletin board was indeed an eighties pin-up of Patrick Swayze.

She loved her life. Everything in her bedroom proved to her that she'd dreamed of this goal ever since high school. She thought back to how in her teens, when she had been a babysitter, she'd watch kids' shows with the kids she was looking after. One show in particular involved a store mannequin, and if you said the magic words when he wore his magic hat, he'd come alive. But if the hat fell off, he'd become a mannequin again. It didn't take Pauline long for her to make a game out of that with the kids: they'd find one of their mom's hats, and she'd find herself frozen in the oddest positions, like hanging off the couch or halfway through a cartwheel. But she'd been told back in high school that children's entertainment wasn't a legitimate career. Plus, she couldn't sing to save her life. So, she'd studied psychology at university, planning to become a child psychologist, and of course volunteered as the varsity mascot. Luck of the draw led her to a theme park in Florida, where she'd realized she could marry her love of performance with her desire to help children into a single career.

Now, she'd reached the top of that career. Every picture and poster on her wall had culminated into this year. If she replaced the picture of Patrick Swayze with one of Todd Parsons, that's how Todd would feel: crowded out by everything she had worked toward and now achieved.

Someone knocked at the door.

"Come in."

The door opened, and Claire hobbled in on crutches.

"You're out of bed?" Pauline scrambled to stand up. "I could've come to you."

Claire sat down in Pauline's office chair and leaned the

crutches against the desk. "The physiotherapist said it was time I tried to move around a little. I can even try getting out of the house, but only an hour or so at a time. Nothing too long or too tiring." She rubbed at her underarm. "Wish I'd learned how to sew. Then I could make pads for those crutches."

Pauline made a mental note to order pads online and lay back down on her bed.

"Besides," Claire continued, "it's not often I get to talk to one of my daughters in her bedroom anymore." Claire studied the collection of photos on the hutch of Pauline's desk and pulled one down. "This was your first paid hockey gig, right? With the Kitchener Blizzard?" Pauline had performed as the local hockey team's mascot—which was a fox, complete with a heavy tail at the back. It attached to her via a belt and then stuck out through the costume.

"Yeah. Took me a few hours to get used to skating with so much weight. I didn't realize how much the tail would affect my balance."

Sadness shrouded Claire's features. "Why don't you do this anymore? You used to love it. You were so talented."

Pauline's stomach rose to her throat and she cursed Ben. "I love the job I have, Mom. Besides. The actor had a serious case of heat exhaustion after the parade on Monday."

Claire set the photo back on the shelf and drilled her gaze into Pauline's eyes. "Something like that never stopped you. You loved performing so much, you always found a way to make it work. You're hiding something from me, honey. Whenever we have our family conference calls, you always change the subject when we talk about your work. Is it this Ben? Is he that controlling?"

Pauline's stomach was about to fly out her mouth. She swallowed it back down.

"He's just trying to climb the marketing career ladder. He's like that with everyone." She didn't want to risk betraying her father's trust. And Ben really did treat everyone like that. Okay, everyone under him.

"That's still not right. He'd accomplish more if he managed from the heart instead of his ego."

Claire pulled another old photo off the shelf and smiled.

"I will always support your dreams," Claire said. "But I want to talk to you about another option in case you change your mind about work."

She set the photo back and became serious. Pauline's palms began to sweat. She wanted nothing more than to disappear inside Perry right now.

"Your father and I always supported your dreams and Dawn's, but I'd always hoped one of my daughters would take over the tea shop some day. Dawn, like your father, can work in her career past retirement age. But you, my honey, you've been so hard on your body that you would eventually have to retire from your work early."

Pauline's breath caught. Had Claire noticed the pain in her hip and shoulder?

"It's not that I *expect* you to take over the shop. Maybe you have other plans. And I know I can't offer you the thrills and excitement of a full stadium. But you know how to listen, you know tea, and you could run as many family events to perform at as you wanted to. It would be easier on you."

Claire pushed herself to her feet. Pauline jumped off her bed and helped her mother with her crutches, unable to speak.

"Anyway," Claire said, "I don't want to try to convince you of it. I just wanted to tell you it was an option you could consider. That was all."

Pauline had wondered what would become of Claire's Tea Shop when her mother finally decided to retire, and she remembered conversations long ago with Dawn about which of them would take over. But they'd both found their callings, and those conversations had been forgotten.

The look Claire gave Pauline said everything: regret, hope, and love. "I can tell you're not yourself and that your body is giving you pain. Even Todd's hiding pain of some kind. The two of you are too young to have broken bodies, but I guess that's what happens when your career is physically demanding. But I hope you'll be open with me, Pauline. I'm your mother. That's what I'm here for."

After Pauline closed the door behind her mother, she collapsed onto her bed and fought back tears. She should've been happy: that her mother would offer her the store was an honour.

But she couldn't accept it, not if she was going to work as a mascot for another few years.

And now she couldn't tell her mother why.

"Seriously, Ben," she said to the ceiling. "What harm is there in telling my family?" She mimicked his voice. "'Telling them would interfere with my promotion.'"

As though some torturous supreme being in the universe were out to get her, Pauline's phone dinged.

It was Ben.

You're going to be happy. Just secured a major sponsor. Your budget's been increased by 20%. Expecting more family events from you this summer on the tour.

Pauline's happiness shot to the moon. More free community skates! Basketball skirmishes! Could she retrain herself to do a somersault slam dunk off a trampoline? Maybe some gymnastics clubs would enjoy having Perry in their facilities! Would dance studios do it? She'd never thought of that before. Also worth a try! A whirlwind of ideas tore through her mind.

She felt guilty at how fast her job hijacked her attention, but that confirmed that running Claire's Tea Shop was not in the cards for her, at least not for now. Could Pauline renegotiate that clause with Ben? Then her mother could see that Pauline was truly happy. That in turn would help her focus on healing, and once Pauline and Todd had finished improvements to the shop, Claire's life could continue where it had left off before the accident.

She texted Ben her gratitude and promised herself to discuss it with him when she was next in Toronto. Everything might work out after all.

CHAPTER 16

"*I* think an Irish breakfast blend would be nice. It's robust in flavour. Will wake you up in the morning." Todd looked to Pauline for confirmation. She nodded.

The man standing before them at the counter agreed. He was another second-generation regular, somewhere in age between Pauline and Claire. The number of people who belonged to this group astounded Todd. It must have rivalled the number of season ticket holders at his previous company, but it came with people who shared story after story about Claire, and these stories sometimes reached decades into the past.

"So, what animal are you going to play at the reopening?" the man asked Pauline as she took his cash. He was referring to the big event they were planning after a week of renovations. "I'd love to bring my great-nieces—they're twins—and my great-nephew."

Todd enjoyed watching Pauline blush from the implied compliment.

"A dog. Dogs remind people of community." She handed the man his bag.

"I've always enjoyed watching you entertain the kids. Nice to see you home, even if for a bit. Give my regards to your mother."

"I will."

The man left. Todd wanted to congratulate himself for getting this recommendation right, but Pauline had helped him with the previous four. He was mastering the teas he had a strong opinion about. He didn't particularly like Irish breakfast tea himself, for example, but this man struck him as someone who would. But with several hundred teas to try, and Todd only able to try a few a day right now, it was slow going at best.

But I've travelled all over the world, learned entire ballets in six weeks, picked up new exercises in ballet class the first time they were introduced, and I can't for the life of me remember a list of ten tea recommendations. Todd wanted to bang his fist on something, but he couldn't show his frustration to Pauline. What if she told her mother?

Who was standing in front of the shop, waiting for Richard to open the door.

Oh, crap. I should've studied more.

Claire struggled with getting the crutches and herself over the threshold. Todd moved to come around the counter, but Pauline jumped it and beat him to Claire.

"Pauline!" Claire admonished her daughter with a smile on her face. "Some things will never change, will they?"

"Sometimes the fastest way is the best," Pauline responded.

Todd prepared a table by pulling out a chair. She looked a little unsteady on those crutches.

Claire grabbed Todd's hand. "I knew you were the right person to hire. How are you, Todd? I can't believe what happened on your first day."

What a charming family and friendly employer. He had enjoyed his last company until the new artistic director had been hired, and now only had a sour taste in his mouth when he thought about it. He couldn't have found a more welcoming place to bide his time as he attempted to heal from that and move forward.

"You have the sign on the door warning everyone that we close Monday." She laughed. "Much better communication than what I left you with last week. I'm so sorry."

"It's a good thing Pauline was able to *jump in*," Todd said, smiling at her.

Everyone groaned at the pun. Pauline laughed but averted her gaze.

I sent out signals, didn't I? He couldn't help it. He was attracted to her. Pauline was a remarkable woman. But he wouldn't expose himself by returning to the public eye right now, and she clearly wasn't staying in Kitchener.

Several people seated at the other tables greeted Claire, and Claire invited them to join her and Richard. What a small community despite the size of the region.

Once everyone was seated, Claire started talking. "You won't believe the beautiful ideas Pauline and Todd have come up with for this place. But I won't tell you—you'll have to wait and see. Pauline, come join us!"

Although the invitation for Pauline and not Todd to join them was completely understandable—he was the employee, Pauline the daughter—it scratched at Todd the way his former ballet company's website had, and the way his father and brothers did with all their hockey fandom. Another reminder he was an outsider.

"Can I get you and Richard something to eat or drink?" Todd asked, as much to do his job as to cover up any visible

118 | LORI WOLF-HEFFNER

discomfort. The other regulars already had their orders. "And you, Pauline?"

Claire ordered her Earl Claire and Richard a Keemun, but Pauline's eyes practically begged for an excuse to leave. She burst out of her chair to help him.

"I'll get my own tea, Todd, thank you!"

"But Pauline, everyone would love to talk to you," Claire said.

"I've already served everyone, so we've caught up. You can start without me." She smiled at the group. "Should I also get a selection of cakes? Not everyone ordered something to eat."

Claire's eyes lit up. "That would be lovely, honey."

Another regular entered the café—it was busy this morning—and immediately sat down with the group. Todd took her order and joined Pauline behind the counter.

"I wish I could hide." Pauline pulled a jar for that last order of tea from the shelf. "I know they're going to ask me more questions now that Mom's here."

"You really don't like talking about yourself, do you?"

Pauline washed her hands, pulled off the lid, and put on disposable gloves. "No. And if I sit there with Mom and her friends, they're going to ask me a million questions, like they're asking her right now, and especially about why I don't want to stay around. And there's nothing I can say that won't insult her."

Todd glanced over his shoulder, and indeed Claire's friends were doing just that. It was the verbal equivalent of hundreds of camera flashes. As much as he enjoyed his anonymity right now, he did miss being recognized; it let him know he was doing a good job. Sure, some people felt the need to tell him about some tiny mistake they'd noticed onstage, and he received the odd "stay away from my wife" warning from husbands. He didn't even know who these men were talking about, and he certainly wasn't the type to sleep around or even send out signals. Photos of Todd—often shirtless in an attempt to make ballet look sexy—were everywhere thanks to years of posing for magazines, fundraising calendars, even just regular publicity shots. They brought in larger audiences, and more women who draped themselves all over him. He had learned to accept it while gently removing himself from the situation.

Pauline wasn't like those women at all, which made working next to her that much harder. She respected his whole person.

"What are you thinking about?"

Pauline's question caught him entirely off guard and he almost missed the pot he was pouring water into.

"Other women."

"WELL, at least you're being honest." Pauline didn't even try to hide the sting in her voice, but she was fighting the desire to dump that pot of water over his head. It wasn't the lack of a costume holding her back, nor her mother's presence. Just its near-boiling temperature.

Todd's neck and shoulders stiffened. His voice stuttered. "That's...that's not what I meant. Not like that. We need to get desserts." He pulled her over to the display case and down to the floor. "What I meant was that I was thinking about how you're different from other women."

Pauline pulled her arm out of his grasp. "You're comparing me to other women? I'm supposed to consider this a good thing?"

But the look of worry in Todd's eyes told her she was wrong. He rubbed his forehead with his hand. "I'm not good with words all the time either. It's why I danced."

Pauline took a deep breath to calm down. She couldn't be angry at him for that. "I'm sorry."

She pushed open the display case door, and each of them, crammed in the tight space, began pulling out squares and tarts already pre-served on plates.

He lowered his voice, but whether it was to ensure no one could hear them or because he was scared, she couldn't tell.

"You're unlike anyone I've ever met, Pauline. I know a relationship makes no sense between us, because you're dedicated to a job you love in Toronto and I'm staying here." He stopped, perfectly balanced on the balls of his feet, but kept his gaze forward. "But I'm very attracted to you. In case that wasn't already clear." He turned to face her, as though hoping for a response.

Why did he have to open up his heart like that? His breath fell on the bit of skin over her breast bone exposed at the top of her sleeveless blouse, gently opening her own heart with every exhale.

He was right: a relationship wouldn't work, though for reasons he didn't know. But crouched here in front of her, his hands just as full with desserts as hers, was a man who understood her despite knowing so little about her. He even spoke in the silent language of movement.

Which meant...

They leaned into each other and his soft lips pressed against hers as she inhaled, the sweet scents of the desserts highlighting a spiciness in his mouth. She wanted to press her lips tighter against his without pushing him over. How would he feel about chocolate brownies smeared on his crisp, purple shirt? Then he'd have to take that shirt off to clean it...

Pauline didn't know how long they'd been kissing when her father interrupted them with a cough.

Pauline and Todd fell back, managing to save the desserts in their hands.

Richard chuckled as he slid a tray across the counter while they stood up. "The two of you are, um, quite nimble."

After they placed the food on the trays, Pauline topped up the tea pots with hot water, and Todd finished setting the tea on the tray so Richard could carry everything over.

Too embarrassed to face her parents and their friends, Pauline turned to the back counter, unable to look at Todd.

"What took so long?" Claire asked Richard.

Pauline dared turn around.

"Great," she muttered. "They're talking by exchanging looks."

"They've been married that long?"

"Almost fifty years."

Claire glanced in Pauline's direction, and Pauline's cheeks immediately flared up again. "Ahh…" Claire gave an approving nod, and everyone at the table turned their heads and smiled, too.

Pauline and Todd broke into giggles.

CHAPTER 17

The doorbell rang. Pauline bolted from her chair in the tearoom in her parents' house, almost running into Richard as he brought in the kettle. Sometimes her energy controlled her, and only after it had exited her body could she regain any control over herself. She threw open the door to a startled Todd.

"Hi!" Energy expended, she relaxed again, only to be enamoured by the wrinkles that formed at the corners of Todd's eyes as he smiled.

Todd was wearing khakis that hugged his legs the same way his slacks did at work. But instead of his usual button-down shirts with the sleeves rolled up to his elbows, he wore a deep blue golf shirt that showed his upper arms. As lovely as the bouquet of flowers in his hand was—it was likely for her mother—her eyes followed his arm up to the flexed bicep that kept the flowers upright. Pauline had obviously been around many fit men throughout her career, but there was something poetic about the way Todd held himself.

"They're for the hostess," he said of the flowers.

They stared at each other for a moment, and Pauline wanted nothing more than to drag him up to her bedroom for a little privacy. Her parents did it all the time. Why couldn't she? She was almost fifty.

Claire and Richard came out to greet Todd, and he passed Claire the bouquet. "Thank you for the invite."

She set one crutch against the wall and accepted the bouquet. "They're lovely, Todd, thank you, but to be honest, Pauline is the true hostess of this afternoon."

Pauline shot her mom a panicked look. That was so not true: Claire had prepared everything except the serviettes. This was supposed to be a welcome-to-the-business tea. Unless Claire had other intentions?

Claire passed the flowers to Pauline, and even Todd's cheeks turned red. He was clearly as embarrassed by this as Pauline was. Mmm. Bedroom would be nice right now.

She gratefully accepted the flowers and left to put them in a vase while Claire and Richard led Todd to the tearoom, which was through the kitchen, then the dining room.

"This is absolutely lovely," Todd said. "I feel a little out of place."

"Nonsense," Claire said. "Our home is your home. I'm so grateful that you're working for me. Had you not been there that morning, there's no telling how long I would have lain there in pain like that. Mondays are very quiet. In fact, I was almost considering closing on Mondays, too. But now with Pauline home to infuse a little of her energy back into the store, we'll see what happens after these renovations are complete."

Pauline joined them and Richard turned on the kettle.

"I haven't seen any ads in the newspaper for the reopening," Claire said.

Pauline explained. "Newspaper ads are expensive, Mom.

We can advertise on social media for a fraction of the price and reach thousands more. I already have a campaign running."

"But how do you support the community if you don't support your local newspapers?"

That would certainly fit her mother's goal: support the community. At the same time, with renovations beginning tomorrow, Claire's line of credit couldn't handle the extra expense. *I can pay for that*, Pauline thought. Plus, she didn't want to discuss her mother's dwindling accounts in front of Todd.

"I'll look into it tomorrow. I hadn't thought about it from that point of view."

"Thank you."

The kettle beeped, but first Claire passed the tea strainer containing the leaves around.

"I'll bet you won't guess what kind of tea this is, Pauline."

Todd's hands curled into fists on his lap, though the rest of him appeared at ease. Was he nervous? Pauline reached a hand over to his, and his immediately relaxed. Claire caught her daughter's comforting touch as she passed the tea strainer to him first.

Todd sniffed the tea. "Smells a bit like chocolate."

He passed it to Pauline.

The leaves were of medium length and dark in colour. She smelled chocolate and hints of hazelnut. She shrugged. "I don't recognize it. Not a scented tea, is it?"

A mischievous smile appeared on Claire's face. "No. I bought it in Todd's honour, but it's not one that would normally sell here. It's above our clientele's price point. Let me brew it."

Todd adjusted his grasp so his hand closed around Pauline's. *Why was this making him uncomfortable?*

"It's actually considered a rare tea," Claire said as Richard poured the water over the leaves. She turned the tea timer to five minutes, which made Pauline nervous. She usually preferred her black teas steeped for three minutes. Five minutes released too many tannins, making the tea too bitter, and she didn't add sugar.

Claire continued. "Your coming into our life, Todd, has been a blessing. I know the world of tea can be overwhelming for a beginner, but you have no idea how difficult it is to find someone who cares about my store almost as much as I do."

Todd tightened his grip, almost as though he were channelling his emotions into Pauline so he wouldn't show more than was socially appropriate on his face.

"But it's not just me who's benefited from your presence here. Jan told me that Austin has changed so much now that he's found a mentor in you, a man who loves ballet as much as he does."

Todd's grip tightened even more, and Pauline squeezed back.

"This is tea grown in Canada. On Vancouver Island, actually. Given your love of ballet and that you're from Vancouver, I thought it appropriate to celebrate your presence here with this."

Todd pressed his lips together and swallowed.

"That's very kind of you, Claire. Thank you. I must admit, I don't feel like I've contributed very much yet."

"Nonsense, Todd. You can't be expected to learn in two weeks what I've developed in a lifetime. It will come."

Claire's words should have comforted Todd, but his grip didn't relax.

The tea tasted unique—hints of hazelnut and cocoa, and no taste of tannins at all. The tea plant was greatly affected by where it grew—called its terroir—which was why Darjeeling, Ceylon, Assam, Keemun...all the black teas had different flavours despite being from one of two varieties, either *camelia sinensis* variant *sinensis* or *camelia sinensis* variant *assamica*. This

Canadian tea was no exception. Even a novice palate would discern the difference between it and a loose-leaf Darjeeling despite their both being the *camelia sinensis* variant *sinensis* plant.

Todd's voice was steady, but his hand quivered under the table. "You've been more than welcoming, Claire and Richard. Thank you so much for this."

"You'll bring your own stories to the tea shop, Todd," Claire said after her sip. "I learned about tea from my grandmother and mother. You'll learn from me, but you'll also find your own way of connecting with people."

"That sounds encouraging. I appreciate it."

Everyone savoured their Canadian tea.

"I do miss watching you connect with people," Claire said to Pauline. "I can't wait for the reopening. Todd, you should have seen her at her last job. She was a mountain lion. Literally."

Todd smiled. "Actually, Tracy caught me up on Pauline's career. Is that the one with the flip and then the slam dunk?"

Claire shuddered. "I still can't watch it."

"I'm surprised she's sitting here next to me," Todd said. His hand relaxed. "Off by an inch or two, and your chin would've been in that hoop."

"Or I would've been in the crowd."

He shook his head in amazement. "How much do those costumes weigh?"

"Twenty, twenty-five pounds. But the trampoline helps, of course."

Claire pressed her lips together and smoothed out the table-cloth in front of her. "I still can't believe the Peregrines didn't hire you for their mascot."

"No objections here," Todd said.

Claire drew in a breath and sat up straight, an immediate change in her mood.

"I didn't mean to offend," Todd said. "But Perry and I go

way back, and not in a good way. Obviously, whatever makes Pauline happy is what she should be doing. I apologize — I meant it as a bit of inside joke. Would only work if you knew my family, though."

Pauline wanted to ask more, but she couldn't risk divulging her actual job. She at least now had confirmation that his dislike of her team and role had something to do with his family. Hopefully, she'd learn more in time.

"So, you're not a Peregrines fan, eh?" Richard asked.

"Hockey was never my thing, though I attended the occasional game with my dad and brothers. Ballet was my calling."

"I see," Richard said. "I attend the local Kitchener Blizzard games if clients invite me, but can't say as I really follow hockey, though." He smiled. "Sorry, Pauline."

She reached for the savoury snacks on the second tier and waved her father's concern away. "I am actually fine discussing something else, believe it or not." That was true for many reasons.

"What does your family do, if you don't mind my asking?"

Now Pauline was all ears.

"Mom was a housewife." Todd smiled at Claire. "I'm certain she'd have been jealous of your life. She loved talking to people. She was always there for us. She died two years ago."

"I'm so sorry."

"Thank you. Dad and my brothers, Mark and Tim, run a hardware chain. You probably know DIY Home?"

Everyone froze. Of course they knew DIY Home. Who in the country didn't?

But, as a real estate agent, Richard was the most impressed. "*That* Parsons family? I know the CEO's name, of course. Who in real estate doesn't? I'm afraid I never paid much attention to the rest of his family."

"You didn't include that on your resumé," Claire said.

"I like to stand on my own two feet. I had no relevant experience from the family business to offer you, so it didn't belong on the resumé."

Claire nodded in acceptance. "Independence is important if you're going to stand behind the counter of Claire's Tea Shop."

"Actually, they're in Toronto right now for the playoffs and some business."

Pauline choked on her food. Richard rushed to get her a glass of water.

So that was why Todd's family was in the VIP section at the parade: DIY Home was the new sponsor for the Peregrines. She needed to talk to Ben. How was she going to have any hope of having honest relationships with the people at this table—the most important people in her life, and yes, Todd was becoming one of those—if she couldn't be fully open with them about her job? She wanted to share her happiness with them, but if Todd's family was sponsoring her team, and he was going to have a serious problem with all of it, she wanted to tell him. She knew it wasn't just the costume. Something deeper was lurking behind his dislike of her team, and if she couldn't be honest with him about what she really did for a living, then how could she have an honest relationship with him?

How could she have a relationship at all?

She needed to straighten this out with Ben. Immediately.

Her coughing spell over, she drank the glass of water Richard brought to her.

"Oh!" Claire said. "Well, you should certainly invite them over."

Claire and Richard knew even less about whatever was going on between Todd and his family, and Todd was nervous enough as it was.

Pauline pointed to the sweet desserts and asked, with as friendly a smile as she could muster, "Anyone want some?"

CHAPTER 18

"*N*o," Ben said.

"Not even my parents? They believe I'm in a job I hate, and my mother already suspects something. I'm lying to my family, Ben, and it's making for a very uncomfortable situation." Pauline's knuckles turned white, threatening to crack the case on her phone.

"You should've thought of that before you signed on the dotted line."

"Name one person in all the applicants you had with the almost thirty years' performance *and* community experience needed to build the community outreach program necessary to overcome what Nate did."

For once, Ben couldn't say anything. Pauline didn't know all the applicants, of course, but the mascot world was small. Most were young, usually in their twenties. She felt guilty for throwing Nate, the previous performer, under the bus, but he had been in way over his head. Pauline had worked in Toronto previously, and with her last gig being in LA, she had the experience needed to rebuild Perry's reputation. In fact, she was so certain of her abilities that she'd sent in her audition reel and application the moment she saw Nate's mistake go viral.

"You know I'm not going to get caught completely sloshed with Perry's head off in Belmont Village. Come on."

"Where?"

She rolled her eyes, since he couldn't see her. "Never mind. But this is my *family* we're talking about." *And Todd.* But who she kissed was none of Ben's business. "I just want to be honest with them."

"That sponsorship?"

"Yeah?"

"Your NDA prevents you from sharing this, too. You understand that, right?"

"Obviously, Ben, but that's not what I'm talking about. I just want to tell them that—"

"The answer's still no. I've already moved on to the next topic."

Pauline's hands were ready to crush her phone case—with her phone inside it.

"Because of the sponsorship with DIY Home, you have an additional twenty percent added to your budget. So, no, Pauline, you're not going to tell your parents anything. You know how this works: you tell someone to not tell anyone else, then they tell someone to not tell anyone else, and then they tell someone, and so on and so forth. Before you know it, you're out having a good time, you drink a little, and costume or no, you say something about the Peregrines, they say, 'Oh, wait! I heard that you're Perry, is that true?' Then someone else says, 'Really? It's you?' And you can deny all you want, but they'll put the pieces together. Then we have our second PR disaster in three years."

Pauline couldn't argue with Ben there. It was her greatest fear. She trusted her parents, but a tiny voice in her head gnawed at her: *Remember when your mother was a little loopy in the hospital? What if that happened again?*

"You do amazing work; the CEO thinks so, even the sponsor thinks so. He and his sons apparently appreciated that you got on a call with them to the rest of their family during the parade. Showed them you put family first."

Oh, crap. Crappity crap, crap, crap. If Todd found out, he'd probably assume she was on his family's side and not his. Not good. She was only getting into increasingly hotter water.

Thought the daughter of a tea shop owner.

And she couldn't even talk to him about any of it without risking a million-dollar lawsuit and losing her dream career.

Not to mention all the families she wouldn't be able to help anymore. If the Peregrines hadn't won the cup, she could've bided her time until another mascot role that required less secrecy opened up elsewhere. But with the cup win, hockey would grow in popularity in Toronto and surrounding cities. Heck, sports activities would experience a surge in registrations, and sports were healthy for kids. She could do so much with Perry to get more kids active because of all this.

"You're our employee, and Perry is our trademark. If you want out of this, I suppose you could quit. But I've just decided I'm going to increase your budget by thirty-five percent and your salary by ten percent. I don't need to tell you how many more families you can help with that kind of money."

No, he didn't.

"We'll meet after the fundraiser on Sunday. So don't plan to return to Belle Mountain right away Sunday night, or whatever your neck of the woods in Kitchener is called."

He hung up Ben-style: without saying goodbye.

Military personnel couldn't tell their families everything. Anyone in the health and legal professions had confidentiality duties, too. Maybe it wasn't that bad.

No, it was that bad. No one's life was at stake, nor was anyone's right to a fair trial compromised, nor was anyone's personal health information at risk of being shared. Ben Landry was scared of another PR nightmare, which Pauline knew would never happen.

She'd been working in this industry in some capacity for a long time. Besides, the stakes for her were much higher: being caught and publicly ousted would ensure no major league team would hire her again. Last she'd heard, Nate was selling running shoes.

Furious at Ben, she threw her phone across the room.

DUSK WAS FALLING, and Pauline was dripping buckets of sweat, but her feet wouldn't stop pounding the pavement. Infuriated by Ben's comments, she'd had to go for a run. After jogging for almost three-quarters of an hour along the Iron Horse Trail to Waterloo Park and around Silver Lake, she was nearing Belmont Village again.

She couldn't believe Ben was manipulating her with a deal her heart couldn't refuse. With that kind of money, she could also schedule more anti-bullying rallies at different summer camps throughout the cup tour.

Then there was her salary. The DIY Home sponsorship must have been huge, and Ben wanted to guarantee that she'd stay, but her salary wasn't as important as how much more she could now help others. The sponsorship would certainly make her last few years in her career out of this world.

But what would she do afterwards? It was a question she'd refused to even acknowledge until her mother raised the topic Thursday night. Working in her mother's tea shop, though nostalgic, was confining and agitating. Kids accompanying their parents didn't hug her, and although most customers were nice, when they couldn't get their favourite tea, some could become irate, almost like the opposing team's fans who dared show up at a home game. Sure, she dealt with her share of drunk and obnoxious fans, but as a mascot, she didn't have to smile and take it: she could either step out of the situation, or security would step in.

Besides, it was called Claire's Tea Shop, not Pauline's Tea Shop. Claire's voice shone out of every corner in that store, not Pauline's. If she could have explained how happy she truly was to her mother, everything would be so much easier right now.

"I could *kill* Ben," Pauline muttered through gritted teeth.

"Kill who?" said a male voice behind her.

She turned around to see Todd, just as sweaty as her, only now sexier than ever in workout shorts and a skin-tight Spandex T-shirt.

Her anger evaporated as quickly as the steam from a hot cup of tea outside in the dead of winter.

"Where are you headed?" Todd asked.

Home or keep going? The point was to burn energy from her phone call with Ben. As much as she loved staring at Todd, her blood pressure was still up from thinking about Ben.

"I think I'm going to run all the way to Victoria Park in Kitchener."

"Mind if I join you?"

She shook her head. Why did she have to fall for someone so kind and compassionate right now, when she couldn't be completely honest with him? Her role as Perry kept her so busy that dating wasn't even on the horizon. But Todd was special. She would've tried to make it work, and as a former performing artist himself, he would've understood her schedule. But whatever the bad blood between him and his father and brothers, she would need to find a way to be honest with Todd about her job for the relationship to really work. It was the right thing to do.

"Something on your mind?" Todd asked.

She had to give him some kind of answer. "Just thinking about Mom." It was half the truth. "She said if I ever wanted to quit my job with the Peregrines, I could take over the tea shop."

Pauline did not miss the hopeful expression that flashed across Todd's face. She couldn't mislead him. "But I love my job in Toronto, Todd. I said no."

She also didn't miss the look of disappointment that followed. "Must've been a tough conversation."

Made tougher by the fact that Pauline couldn't be honest with Claire either.

"Yeah."

How much did slime cost? She could dump that on Ben at the next game, claiming to confuse him for a fan from the visiting team.

"Sounds like she's hoping to pass the business down, like how dads hope to pass theirs down to their sons," Todd said.

"Maybe."

"Dad wanted to pass his down to all three of us. I proved to be a bit of a disappointment to him, I guess." He stopped and took a drink.

Pauline took a swig of her water, too. "How could your father be disappointed in you for teaching?" The more Pauline heard about Todd's father, the more she disliked him.

Todd didn't answer her question. "The Peregrines win has kind of dug up some old stuff. Sorry if I'm a bit of a downer in that area. I know you love your team and that the win is huge."

Pauline wiped away sweat dripping into her eyes. Another luxury of not being encased in a suit. "Seriously. Don't worry about that. I'm sorry to hear it's bringing up some old hurt. We work really hard to make the mascot experience great for everyone, but I guess it's easy to forget that not everyone likes Perry."

Todd smiled. "Nope, definitely not everyone."

He took her hand and she tried to lean her head on his shoulder, only it was too low.

Pauline laughed. "Sorry, that's too uncomfortable."

The corner of his eyes wrinkling, Todd leaned his head on her shoulder. "Ah, now I see what all the fuss has been about. The women I've been with have always been at least five or six inches shorter. And none have ever had shoulders like yours."

"Comparing me to other women again, are you?"

"I guess I am."

They stopped under an archway of trees and turned to face each other. A cyclist dinged his bell and Todd stepped out of the way, pulling Pauline closer to him.

"This is probably going to be the grossest kiss I'm about to have," she said.

"Hmm…you could name a new tea after it: Sweaty Kiss. Boil water, steep for three to five minutes, then add salt."

Pauline lifted her hands to his face. "I'm sure the customers will be all over it."

"Like I'd like to be all over you."

Todd slid his arms around her back and pulled her in.

CHAPTER 19

*P*auline and Todd returned to Claire's Tea Shop after having carried the last table to the empty neighbouring unit Monday afternoon. Todd couldn't wait to see how his and Pauline's ideas would come to life. His several decades in theatre included watching set designers transform empty stages into any world the choreographer desired, and he had to admit he'd picked up a few tips from his family over the years, too. Although his mother had remained a homemaker her whole life, she'd focused on creating a beautiful home and had also taught him a few things about that.

The store now closed for the week, and the flooring company starting tomorrow, they were clearing out what they could in preparation. Richard had rented a cargo van and driven the chairs and couch to the upholstery store. Next up: covering the entertainment equipment and the serving and prep area in old sheets.

Pauline gave Todd a kiss, sending chills all over his skin. "I prefer the less salty you, to be honest."

He brushed her ear with his lips. "I have to say the same

about you." Could non-Robinsons issue invitations to the back room?

You're an employee, Todd, he reminded himself. *Get back to work.* He pulled the first sheet off the pile, and with a little added flourish threw it over part of the back counter.

A knock on the front door surprised them.

"Hey," Austin said when he came in. At least he was talking, but compared to the animated teenager Todd had gotten to know last week, this sullen boy was practically a wooden set piece from a ballet.

She locked the door behind him. "How are things?"

He looked around. "A bit empty." Was he talking about himself or the shop?

"We've started renovations," Pauline said, "but nothing you can help with yet. Once the flooring's in, we'll be painting, and then we can talk. But if I'm not mistaken, you should be studying for exams, shouldn't you?"

Austin shrugged. "I'll probably fail." He looked at Todd with an expression that pierced Todd's heart; he was giving up hope again.

"I have to finalize a few things at the interior décor store," Pauline said, clearly making an excuse to leave the two alone. "And pick up some paint." It wasn't a lie, just something she hadn't planned on doing for another hour or so. "But we'll be sure to let you know when we start painting. I'm certain we can work in some time for you with your study schedule."

After she left, Austin leaned against the wall. "I just need someone who gets me." He slid down the wall and buried his head in his knees. Todd kept his distance at first, unsure if Austin wanted space or an arm around him. Space seemed like a safer place to start from.

A moment later, Austin looked up. "I stopped the caffeine, which is why I haven't been in touch. Made me a bit moody for a few days. But we've got an appointment tomorrow in Toronto, which is an hour of Mom drilling me about school, how I'm feeling, if I want to talk about anything. And then an hour back with her reviewing whatever the doc has said, asking again about school… And if we're stuck in traffic, it's even longer. It's the same questions every day, every week…all the time. Only I can't escape her in the car. It's like I'm a project. Nothing is about me anymore, just my messed-up brain."

"That must be hard." What else could Todd say? He'd never been in this kind of situation before and now felt stupid that with all the time he'd spent with Pauline he'd been more focused on his attraction to her and hadn't asked about how to talk to Austin.

"I wanted to dance all day, every day, not talk about therapy and…and…" He cut himself off. Did he want to mention what was going on at school?

Maybe talking about it was too much. Austin had said all he wanted to do was dance all day, and the shop was completely empty.

"I'll be right back."

Todd retrieved his phone from the back room.

"Do you know Kudelka's choreography for *The Nutcracker*?" He hooked his phone up to the entertainment system in the lounge area.

Austin swallowed. "I've been studying it since I was a kid. But I can't do it now. I haven't danced in a year."

Should Todd call his bluff? Or would that break the trust that was building between them? Todd drew on his teaching experience. Although he wasn't a teacher by training—he'd only ever been asked to teach because of his name—ballet had standards in teaching. Among them were directness and openness, though admittedly not all teachers used tact.

But if Austin had already stopped drinking caffeine—and

his lack of seizures in the few minutes they'd been talking appeared to show that—all because Todd had told him once to do so, that showed Todd the role he was playing in this teenage boy's life.

It was time to ask Austin to come clean.

"You've been dancing privately in your room all this time, Austin, haven't you?"

Austin stared at the floor. "It's not the same."

"No, it's not. But if you miss ballet so much, why won't you tell anyone?"

Austin stretched a leg forward along the floor, showing a beautifully pointed foot, even in his running shoes, lifted it forty-five degrees, and carried it to the side, all while seated. He clearly still had his strength.

He didn't want to talk, and Todd knew better than to force him. But Todd was going to encourage him to dance. "Being out of practice isn't the issue, Austin, it's that you need space. If you're worried you can't turn, do a *relevé*. If you can't jump, do a *grand battement* or walk like a prince. Heck, use the wall as a barre and do a *plié* with a *port de bras* if you're worried you're going to fall. At least you're halfway to the ground then."

Austin smiled at Todd's joke.

"But you need space to dance, today you have it, and based on your *ronde de jambe* you just did—seated, I might add—I suspect that despite only dancing in your bedroom, you've retained a lot of your strength. Let's see if I'm right."

Todd selected the piece. "Nutcracker Prince solo, opening of the Second Act, as performed at Claire's Tea Shop. Choreography by James Kudelka, with possible additional choreography by Austin Tschirhart."

Todd hit play.

∽

PAULINE RETURNED from the interior decorating store, several cans of paint in hand, and froze. Todd and Austin were dancing. Pauline immediately pulled out her phone, and recorded the pair for Tracy.

But where Todd's hands seemed to almost reach the ceiling when he jumped, Austin barely left the floor. Where Todd spun like a top, Austin executed perhaps two or three rotations. Todd's body moved in long, flowing lines and exploded with power. She remembered Austin as a six-year-old dancing with abandon, and although she didn't see that spirit here, she knew it was a miracle he was dancing at all.

A minute later, the dancers stopped, and Austin immediately hugged Todd. Pauline recognized the embrace of gratitude, one she often received. Why wasn't anyone telling her what was going on?

Like you have a right to know other people's secrets, she scolded herself.

She texted Tracy the video, but by the time she looked up, Austin had his back to Todd, his arms crossed, completely closing himself off again. Todd approached Austin and reached a hand to him.

Pauline had a feeling this wouldn't end well. She unlocked the door, propped it open, and carried in the paint.

"Leave—" Austin said before a seizure took over. After his seizure passed, he dropped to the floor and pulled his knees in. Had Austin wanted to escape, he could have run out the door, but he stayed in the shop. Pauline took this as a hopeful sign, but she and Todd had to tread very cautiously, otherwise Austin could dart. She left the door unlocked so he could bolt if he needed.

Todd stepped back and only now noticed Pauline. He raised his hands in confusion. Pauline suspected Austin had made himself too vulnerable too fast, and his seizure had embarrassed him. Whatever their relationship, Austin was trying to push Todd away to protect himself from whatever rejection he was expecting now from Todd.

She signalled to Todd to wait. Austin might let her in because their relationship meant less to him. He needed help, and based on what she had read about his form of epilepsy, calming his breathing and lowering his stress could reduce his seizures.

Her decades as a mascot kicked in and she mirrored his body language from a distance by sitting on the floor. She kept her gaze averted as she inched toward him, ignoring Todd for now. Austin tried to hold back sniffling: the dancing had probably released a lot of emotion.

No different than when I lift weights or go running, Pauline thought.

Only after a few minutes of nearing him without getting a reaction did she feel comfortable finally speaking. She kept her voice low and her gaze averted. "How can we help, Austin?"

He didn't answer for a minute, and Pauline didn't rush to fill the silence.

He pressed his face even tighter into his hands. "Make these seizures go away."

Pauline continued moving closer, still looking away.

"It's not fair!" he yelled into his hands. "My idol is here, and I can't dance the way I used to!"

His idol? Pauline glanced at Todd, who mouthed, "Later." She nodded, understanding his message: now was not the time for the full story.

She continued approaching Austin. If she moved too fast, she risked his shutting them out completely, and then she would need even more time to rebuild that trust.

"I hate it here," Austin continued through sobs. "I loved my ballet school. No one bullied me. I had a boyfriend who loved ballet, too, but my school's so far away it made no sense to keep seeing each other."

Pauline was now only a foot away from Austin, and he was talking freely. She beckoned for Todd to sit on the boy's other side.

"And here at school, I don't have anyone anymore, and the kids—" Pauline waited for his seizure to pass, but when Austin continued talking, she couldn't tell if he'd forgotten that he'd begun talking about the bullying or if he chose to stop talking about it. "And I can't get my driver's licence when everyone else is, and Mom's on me all the time about my seizures and everything…I just can't get away from any of it!"

Austin's naked pain pierced Pauline's heart, and the sadness in Todd's face told her he felt the same. But if they allowed their emotions to take over, they'd affect Austin's ability to clear his own. A mascot performer's job was to work with others' emotions and either build them up or help them dissipate. Austin's needed to dissipate, otherwise they would overwhelm him. Keeping them bottled up wouldn't help, but wallowing in them for too long would harm him, too.

She signalled to Todd with one hand to take a calming breath while she put her arm around Austin to distract him from her communication with Todd. She then indicated to Todd to also put an arm around Austin. The teenager continued sharing his pain with them, but he wouldn't mention a thing about the bullies at school. Within a few minutes, though, completely exhausted, he rested his head on Todd's shoulder.

Keeping her voice low, Pauline asked, "Would you like some tea and a snack? I know tea won't make your problems go away, but from what I've learned about epilepsy, stress is the one enemy you can try to control, and maybe a cup of tea will help you today."

Austin lifted his head, a weak smile on his face. "I guess I'm in the right place for that, aren't I?" He glanced at Todd. "Just, um, no caffeine."

Todd smiled back.

"Mom has some really nice herbal blends that are mild and soothing." She winked at him. "They even calm me down sometimes."

Pauline got up but pressed a hand into her hip. "Ouch. That's old age setting in." She asked Todd to help bring Austin to the back room, where he could sit at Claire's desk.

When Todd stood up, though, something cracked, and he groaned. She looked over, and he held his hand pressed into his back.

"My knee," he explained. "And now my back's spasmed again." But he still helped Austin up and supported him to the back room. Austin's face was pale, probably from all the emotion he had just released.

He wiped his eyes with his free hand and smiled at both of them.

"Looks like we're all a little broken."

CHAPTER 20

*A*fter Austin left, Todd shook his head in amazement. "What he's going through…"

"You did amazing," Pauline said. "He clearly looks up to you. As he opens up more, keep the empathy high and the pity non-existent. You're probably the first adult he's come to trust since his diagnosis. Make sure you keep listening like you have been. It's what he needs right now."

Todd shoved his hands into his pockets and leaned against the counter. "You've seen this before."

"It's changes like these that I live for. They don't happen often, but when they do…I don't have words for it. Don't get me wrong, he'll still get angry, but he's seen the light of trust. He'll find it again if he loses it, and it's in no small part thanks to you. Is it just because you're a man who loves ballet?" Then she remembered what Austin had said during his anger outburst. "Wait. He said before you were—"

Todd adjusted his sleeves. "His idol. Yeah. About that. Can I make you a Belmont Blizzard?"

Todd prepared the water and measured an appropriate

amount of tea into a disposable tea bag, concentrating as though he was performing a life-saving operation.

"Are you okay?" she asked.

He turned on the timer. "In about three minutes, I won't be."

The empty tea shop might as well have been an empty arena, the silence made it feel so gigantic. What was so terrible that Todd couldn't just come out with it?

"Nothing for you?" she asked.

"I'm not thirsty."

He watched the timer, remaining silent. No audience, noise, or outdoor space to absorb the energy collecting inside her, her leg began to bounce.

The timer finally beeped, and he removed the tea bag. When he turned to pass her the cup, she forced her leg to stop, but he wouldn't make eye contact with her.

"A relationship needs trust," he said finally. "We've kissed, and it shouldn't have happened without a full explanation of why I'm here. And that's related to Austin."

The energy in the room was full of electricity, and not the romantic kind. Pauline pressed her hands to the hot mug to keep them from shaking.

Todd glanced at the wall of photos. "Maybe I should take those down while we're talking." He brought a ladder over and climbed up.

Grateful at an idea that would let her move, Pauline set her tea on the counter to help Todd, but he insisted she stay where she was.

"I know you've got some busy days ahead, especially with your drive to Toronto tomorrow and such."

Why did that feel more like an excuse than a real reason?

He began to pull the photos off the wall and carry them to the counter, keeping his back turned to Pauline the entire time. "You really have never seen me on a poster in Toronto? Not even in LA four years ago? I guested with a ballet company there."

Until two weeks ago, ballet was far from Pauline's mind. "No."

"And Austin and Tracy really haven't said anything?"

"Said what? Seriously, Todd, I have no idea what you're talking about. I can see you're upset and scared about something, and I don't mean to be hurtful, but…"

Todd lifted more pictures off their hooks. "Pull out your phone and search up 'Todd Parsons' plus 'ballet.'"

KNOWING Pauline was scrolling through her search results right now was worse than watching from the wings while a group of critics took notes in the audience during the premier of *Gilgamesh*. Todd's heart was pounding in his chest. How would she react when she saw the scathing reviews about the first—and therefore last—ballet he choreographed, and the criticisms from his last years of dancing, where critics and supposed fans alike chewed him out for his diminishing performances? He'd poured his life into his art, but it all came crashing down like the metaphorical house of cards.

He peeked over his shoulder. Pauline was still scrolling and sipping her tea, a range of emotions jumping across her face. He continued taking down photos.

He'd planned to stay hidden longer than this, but that was obviously unrealistic. Austin hadn't meant to let slip that Todd was his idol. The comment had honoured Todd, and in fact, Austin had done a remarkable job keeping Todd's whereabouts a secret from fans. Tracy, too. Todd had worried this entire time that Pauline had been looking him up, but judging by how fixed her eyes were on her phone now, she'd really never heard of him before.

Maybe I shouldn't have said anything, he thought. *I could've just said that yes, I'd taught him, and that's how we know each other.* But something about her compelled him to open up completely.

He set the last photo on the counter.

"You're really amazing at ballet, aren't you?"

"Was," he corrected. He began pulling the picture hooks out of the wall.

"Are. I have my stunts, like slam dunk somersaults, but I don't have this…grace, I guess? I competed in gymnastics until I got too tall, and I played a lot of different sports — I don't have grace or elegance or this kind of attention to detail. I mean, I try not to set my costume on fire, but…"

Where was the disappointment he was expecting? Of course, she was a novice to all of this. It would come. She would figure it out.

Music emanated from her phone, and it took Todd four beats to recognize it before he grew cold.

"Like right there!" She pointed to her phone as though he could see what she'd just seen. But he knew the dance, anyway. "What your feet did there. That jumpy, switchy thing. Then…" Her eyes grew big. "Wow! What a turning thing! And I don't think I'd ever have that kind of stage presence without a costume." She looked up at him and blushed. "Sorry. I don't know what you call your steps." But her adorable smile turned immediately to alarm. "You're white as a ghost, Todd. Why? When I watch this, and compare it to that Russian dancer and the pig…actually, I think you're a lot better than him. But I'm embarrassed I haven't given ballet more of a chance." She watched a few more seconds. "This is absolutely incredible." She looked back at him. "Why didn't you show me this before?" She gasped.

"Was it my ballet comments? That it's boring? Oh my god, Todd, I'm so sorry. I really am." She watched more of the footage. "This is incredible. I'm so sorry that I hurt your feelings like that."

Todd hadn't even thought she would come to that conclusion. He had to set her straight right away.

"That's not it at all, Pauline. Those are some of my worst performances."

"What? These? Todd, you've got to be kidding me. They're amazing. Maybe you're getting the music mixed up. It kind of all sounds the same to me."

Todd allowed himself a little laugh. Another Pauline-ism.

She continued. "This one's from earlier this year. Don Quicksoat?"

Okay. That was worth more than a little laugh. He gave her the proper pronunciation of *Don Quixote*.

"But seriously," she said, "this is amazing. Makes you even sexier because I'm imagining you in bed." The corner of her mouth turned up. "I could seriously watch this all day."

No, you couldn't, not once you see what the young dancers today can do, Todd thought. It was touching that Pauline admired Todd's dancing, but she hadn't seen him at the height of his career.

"Oh…oh, no…Todd…"

His body filled with the burn of humiliation. *She's reading the comments.*

What happened to the Todd Parsons I grew up with? His legs don't even reach 180 on his jumps and he can't even clear those dancer's belly buttons with his own butt. It's like he's turned into my granddad overnight.

This isn't Parsons best work. He's doen better. Look him up like 5 yrs ago If u have never seen him before. He's missing turns. Only does 7 or 8 instead of ten. He's losing it, like hes loosing his hair.

Who is this guy? I can dance better and all I took was a kids class ten years ago.

MANY OF THE comments were written using language fit for the locker room. Many defended him, too, but even those comments contained hidden insults.

What do people expect? Dancers get old! He's still amazing, but let him age!

It doesn't matter if his abilities are getting worse, I'll always love him!

Just shut it! Dancers are allowed to get spare tires!!!!

What spare tire? Todd was super lean.

Pauline scrolled up to the view count, and her eyes almost popped out of her head like the lid off a kettle of boiling water: half a million! She returned to her search results and read similar numbers on many of the videos. Some reached well over a million!

He was some kind of world superstar!

But no sooner had his true career dawned on her that so had the next realization: he was a superstar whose career had come painfully crashing down on him because...

Because his body was failing him.

And because his art form required him to bare his soul in front of the world, whereas Pauline performed in disguise, these attacks cut deep. Pauline's flip that landed on another mascot was embarrassing to be sure and had landed—pun fully intended—on many top ten lists for most embarrassing mascot fails, but no one outside her professional circles and family knew it had been her. Pauline was truly impressed by the few minutes of Todd's dancing she'd seen on her tiny phone screen. When she watched Todd and Austin dance, she could see his passion for his art. She knew how much Austin had loved to dance as a kid. If Todd had that much passion—or even more—and had been able to make his dream career out of it...

She put it all together.

"You're here because you've been hounded out of a career you love and you're trying to move on without the whole world watching you."

He pulled out the last picture hook from the wall. "Yeah."

As a mascot, Pauline could sling insults back on social media. It was even expected and she enjoyed it. She was one of few people who got paid to be publicly—but playfully—vengeful and get away with it. But as a ballet dancer, Todd couldn't slip up even once without ruining his personal reputation and perhaps never getting hired again.

She set her phone down, went to him, and placed a hand on his shoulder. "I'm so sorry. I had no idea you were fighting this." She pulled him into her, and he leaned his head on her shoulder, his arms wrapping around her waist.

Through a costume, Pauline could only feel the intensity of an embrace and the size of a person's body. Now, without one, she could feel Todd's muscles ripple and twitch, as though they were fighting to accept that it was okay to let go of the pain and embarrassment he'd been carrying with him all this time.

She whispered, "It's okay. I'm here."

His body melted into hers. This was the first time in a long time Pauline had ever felt so deeply entwined with another man, where both lives blended together so perfectly. This had been missing her entire life.

But what would happen when she returned to Toronto? Any relationship, like Todd had said, required trust. She had to tell him about her job.

But what if this doesn't work out? Then I'll have lost my career and my relationship. No one would hire her if she jumped ship now: NAHA cup win, impending tour, contract breach.

His chest trembled: he was weeping. She stroked his back, desiring to comfort him. He stretched his arms around her, enveloping her in his loneliness.

But she was an actor playing a role that dangled financial disaster in her path if things blew up. Risk like this was impossible at such a crucial time in her career. She had to apologize and break things off. But why did every bone in her body tell her that ending this relationship was wrong?

Pauline needed to talk to someone. Dawn? No. She'd have to lie to their parents, too. Anyone in her professional circles was out. Rumours would spread like wildfire, and she couldn't lead Ben to believe she was having doubts about her career.

That left Tracy, an executive assistant who respected confidentiality for a living. *She even kept Todd's secret from me.*

Todd touched his cheek against hers, pressing his tears between them.

"I'm falling in love with you," he whispered in her ear.

His words infused with the emotions whirling inside her.

Tracy it was. Pauline couldn't handle this by herself anymore.

He pulled her in. She lifted her leg over his hip and planted her knee and a hand against the wall, pinning him. He hooked one hand under her raised leg and reached the other behind her head, drawing her in. Their lips touched, and they took tiny sips of one another, too scared for more, too shaken to admit what was happening. But the rising heat between them made a heady brew, and soon they gulped as though the pot could never be empty.

Pauline knew why splitting up with Todd would feel so wrong. When she could finally come up for air, she said, "I love you, too."

CHAPTER 21

*a*ustin sat in the back seat of Tracy's extremely clean Toyota Yaris, his monstrous headphones on, arms and legs moving to the music on his phone.

"If it weren't for his seatbelt," Pauline said from the driver's seat, "I swear we'd have to switch on the child locks on the back doors, otherwise he'd dance onto the highway."

Tracy's eyes glowed with happiness. "I haven't seen this side of him in a year."

Pauline was nervous about the upcoming appointment with the neurologist. Would it change Austin's mood again? Stealing this light from Tracy would be cruel.

"I'm so amazed by the career Todd has had and so sickened by how so many have turned their backs on him." She tried to keep only the facts in her mind about yesterday, but the hairs on her arms lifted as she remembered the feelings.

"I'm glad he's opened up to you. It was hard keeping his secret. I hope you're not angry with me."

How could Pauline be angry about anyone keeping a secret?

"Not at all. It shows how trustworthy you are. He's found very good friends in both of you."

Pauline stepped on the brakes as traffic came to a standstill for the umpteenth time. Why had she volunteered to drive on Canada's busiest highway instead of offering to pay the gas?

Oh, right. Because she needed her best friend's counsel. She wanted Todd and her career, but all she saw was oil and water. Hopefully, Tracy could be the emulsifier.

Pauline peeked in the rear-view mirror. Austin was completely absorbed in his world of ballet.

"While he's occupied back there, Tracy, there's something I need to talk to you about."

Tracy drew her eyebrows together. "Is everything okay?"

Pauline still wasn't sure. She could just tell Tracy she was under an NDA and leave it at that, right?

Traffic inched forward.

Tracy could be trusted. Not only was she used to maintaining confidentiality at work, but she'd already proven she could keep a big secret. Not that Pauline's secret was as big as Todd's—world-famous dancer!—but the consequences to her meant she'd be shelling out for the rest of her life. She could try out full disclosure with Tracy, see what happened, get Tracy's advice, and then decide if she wanted to tell Todd.

Of course, all without telling Ben.

"Okay," Pauline said, "I'm under a really stiff NDA for a job that's brought me more happiness than I ever dreamed, but it's beginning to cause me a lot of problems. I need you to promise that you won't tell a soul. If anyone finds out what I'm about to tell you, I could be sued for a million dollars. That's what my contract says. I'm not exaggerating."

Tracy's jaw dropped. "Seriously? Is this some federal secret? Is CSIS going to come after me? Because then I'd rather not know."

Pauline laughed at Tracy's overreaction. "No. You won't get in trouble, just me. The clause is meant to ward off any public relations disasters. I've already asked my boss if he can make an exception for my family, and he's said no. But I'm really conflicted about something and I need to talk to someone who knows me, not some random counsellor or psychologist or whatever." She glanced at Tracy and then back at the traffic. "Someone who really knows me. Can you promise not to say anything? Even to Austin? This is serious."

Tracy took a long look at Pauline. "You're really not joking, are you?"

Pauline shook her head as she kept an eye on the traffic.

"Of course, Pauline. Anything you need."

Pauline could still stop, but hearing Todd's whisper in her mind batted that idea out of the park. He had been honest with her; she wanted to reciprocate that trust.

"I've been keeping my distance from everyone since moving to Toronto in part because my job takes too much out of me: I can't get off the couch to visit. But also in part because I don't want to keep lying to everyone's face. I am in community engagement, but it's not a desk job." She took a deep breath... she could still back out...no, she needed this. "I'm the Peregrines' mascot."

Now the bird was out of the bag.

"Oh my freakin' lord, what?!"

"Shh!!!" Pauline was laughing at her friend. Well, in between panicked glances in the rear-view mirror. Thankfully, Austin was still lost in his world of ballet.

Tracy lowered her voice. "You mean you've reached your dream? Oh my god, Pauline, I'm so happy for you!" She gripped her seat as she realized something. "That means that was you with the prime minister? Although I guess he didn't know it was you. Oh my god, oh my god, oh my god! I could squeeze you so tight right now! You've reached your dream! All because some guy broke my heart!"

Pauline was grinning from ear to ear at Tracy's joy. This is what she missed. *Was this how Todd felt when he was cast as the Nutcracker Prince the first time?* Her family would've reacted like this for her had she been allowed to tell them she'd gotten the job.

Another moment of happiness Ben had stolen from her.

"Yup, all because of love and serendipity," Pauline agreed.

Pauline's phone rang. She'd hooked it up to Tracy's car via Bluetooth in case anyone called her for any reason: Claire or Todd with questions about the renovations, Ben to boss her around some more, Derek or the principal from Eby Heights to confirm plans for the anti-bullying rally or…well, that would've been about it.

But her skin tingled when Todd's name showed up on the dashboard.

"Speaking of serendipity." Tracy made smoochy kisses at Pauline as she touched the screen to answer.

"Mom?"

Pauline's gaze flew to the rear-view mirror. Had he actually heard? *The phone ringing probably distracted him*, she thought. But could she be sure? Her palms began to sweat.

"Why are you making kissing noises at Pauline?"

"Hello?" Todd said.

Tracy's face turned beet red.

"Ah, hey, Todd," Pauline said. "You're on speaker."

"Todd?" Austin said. "Wait…Pauline and Todd? Seriously? That is sick."

Todd chuckled. "Is someone going to tell me what I'm missing out on here?"

The women giggled.

"I see," Todd said. "I guess not. It's just as well. Giggling

women were never a good thing at any ballet company. Pauline,
Doris is here."

"And I'm out of my Dawn's Delight!"

Pauline could only imagine how un-delightfully Doris must
have marched into the tea shop.

"Do you mind if I sell her some? She knows she'll have to
pay cash. We have stock."

Even with a closed sign on the door, Claire's Tea Shop had
regulars who really gave meaning to that word. "Not at all.
Same for anyone else in a panic who has cash and doesn't mind
the noise and mess."

"Sounds good. Hey, Austin—good luck learning your new
choreography today, eh?"

"Yeah, for sure, Todd!"

"Thanks again," Todd said.

"Call if you need anything else," Pauline replied.

They hung up.

Tracy twisted around. "New choreography?"

Still smiling, Austin said, "That's how Todd told me to look
at all of this, like new choreography." He put his headphones
back on and immediately immersed himself in his music.

Tracy turned back to the front and sighed. "I thought I'd
said that once, too."

Pauline patted her best friend on the shoulder. "Hate to
break it to you, but if there's one thing I've learned in all my
years of silently working with kids, it's that parents are never
their kids' idols."

Tracy stared out the window as they passed transport
trucks. "Truer words have never been spoken. But back to you,
because I'm already tired of talking about me." She faced
Pauline. "You really like him. Like, like-like him."

"We're falling in love, Tracy, and I don't see how this is
going to work. He hates Perry and the Peregrines, and I'm not

exaggerating. How am I supposed to have a relationship with him if I can't be honest that I'm the Peregrines' mascot?"

Pauline slowed down to match the speed of traffic and checked the GPS to make sure she was in the right lane. She hated driving on the 401, which was why she'd never bought a car after moving to Toronto. Buses drove between Kitchener and Toronto every hour or two, and driving this highway was a nightmare.

"I think you need to tell him. He clearly trusts you if he told you everything last night. It only seems fair that you trust him, too."

"And if we break up?"

"He's a professional of the highest calibre," Tracy continued. "I've watched him since the day Austin started obsessing over him. I wanted to make sure my son was idolizing the right kind of man. He's impeccable. Believe me. You can trust him."

Pauline wanted to believe Tracy, but a million dollars and a destroyed career were a very high price to pay for love. And yet, Pauline had never felt this kind of love before.

Of course, she'd thought that with Gary, but they'd both been in their twenties. What did they know back then? Maybe with a little more time, she could figure this new, more mature love out. But she didn't have that much time left before she was headed back to Toronto for good.

Pauline and Todd? Seriously? That is sick. Those were Austin's words. Todd had to focus as much on staying present and friendly with Doris as he used to right before his big jump sequences. He closed the package of Dawn's Delight for her and reminded her about their grand reopening on Saturday.

Austin's words kept playing over in his mind against the backdrop of happy voices in the car.

"I'll be very surprised if you have this mess cleaned up by then!" She paid him in exact change.

Todd was all smiles when she left, his gaze floating to the spot along the wall where Pauline had pinned him yesterday afternoon. He inhaled deeply at the memory.

He had never expected to be turned on by the size of a woman's upper arm. It wasn't that professional ballerinas weren't strong—the strength in their backs alone could probably put any football player to shame—but Pauline's shoulders could function as shoulder padding.

> Your arms are as thick as my love for you,
> Your shoulders surround my heart like football
> protective equipment.

Good thing he had never attempted to break into the greeting card industry.

Nor did he ever expect to make out in a tea shop. Theatre catwalk, dressing room, stairwell...those locations were familiar to him, but a tea shop? As mundane as the location sounded, it was where he'd shared his public fall from grace with the most remarkable woman he'd ever met. The moment he trusted her with his deepest fear—rejection—his heart opened. Then to hear her say she was also falling in love, too...? It gave him the courage to hope that they might have a future together.

"I'll be right back to help," he told the floor installer, who nodded in acknowledgement.

Todd returned to the back room to put away the wholesale bag of tea he'd filled Doris's order from.

So...does that mean she'd have pictures of me now hanging in her locker? He smiled at the fantasy.

But they'd both agreed before that a relationship wouldn't work. When she shared her love for him, did she understand he still wouldn't travel to Toronto? Or had she changed her mind about taking over Claire's Tea Shop?

"Don Quicksoat." Even in the midst of all his sadness, Pauline had made him laugh with one of her cute mistakes.

But he couldn't travel to Toronto and expose himself to the public eye again. Not for his family, and, he had to admit, not for Pauline.

In truth, the Peregrines' win coupled with his family's team fanaticism and unexpected appearance in the area had caught Todd off guard. It wasn't that he disrespected the actor in the costume, but that bird had gotten more attention from Todd's family over the decades than he had.

"You're jealous of a costume, Todd," he said to himself. He shook the childish thoughts out of his head. He knew his dad and brothers loved him deep down. They just wished he'd chosen the same interests they had so they could do more things together. In and of itself, it wasn't such a bad desire, and Todd eventually had made the effort to join them for a few games.

But the win resurfaced all the excuses they used to give about why they wouldn't visit him backstage and take photos with him while he was in costume and makeup...

"We want to get to the car before everyone else gets to theirs."

"We have an early morning business meeting."

"Your brothers have to study for university exams."

Hmm... Maybe it wasn't that many excuses: they didn't come to that many shows, and where photos existed, their embarrassment standing next to him was obvious. Todd hadn't looked at those photos for years.

The workmen started hammering floorboards, pulling Todd back to reality.

"Pauline's not like that," he said to himself and immediately smiled. "Pauline and Todd. Sick."

He returned to the front of the café. When your dad was the CEO of one of the country's biggest hardware companies, you picked up a few skills.

And regardless of his feelings toward his family, Todd was going to put those skills to use to make sure that people like Doris were wrong and that this store was ready to go Saturday at nine o'clock, one hour before opening, precisely so that Claire could take pride in the legacy she'd built in the more than fifty years she'd been a part of this community.

He asked the workmen how he could help.

But the most important reason for ensuring the renovations finished on time was Pauline: Todd wanted her to know that, no matter his feelings for *her* employer, all he felt for her was love.

PAULINE AND AUSTIN sat in the car while Tracy pumped gas and bought some snacks.

"You and Todd, eh?" Austin had a mischievous twinkle in his eye. So this was the young man that dancing boy had grown into: charming, playfully sticking his nose where it didn't belong, and enjoying every minute of it.

Pauline's cheeks heated up and she made eye contact with Austin through the rear-view mirror. "I don't believe an adult relationship is any of your business." But any attempts at keeping a serious face were impossible and she broke out into a huge smile.

"I'm *so* jealous. If I were about twenty-five years older and, well, a woman..."

They smiled at each other, but a minute later, Austin turned serious. He undid his seatbelt and leaned forward.

A seizure preceded what he wanted to say. Pauline couldn't imagine her career with that kind of disability. In fact, it would be impossible.

"I know there's an assembly at school in two days with the Peregrines. I, uh, heard part of what you and Mom were talking about after Todd's call. There's something I wanted to ask you."

Pauline's stomach flew to her throat and she whipped her head around.

"Austin, you *can't* tell anyone." She blurted out the list of consequences faster than a peregrine falcon diving after its prey.

Austin slumped back against his seat, and Pauline immediately regretted her intense reaction. *So this is what happens when I tell one person*, she thought. *I'm completely on edge.*

Pauline turned around so she could comfortably face him. "I'm sorry, Austin. That was uncalled for." Guilt and regret multiplied inside her.

"I didn't know it was that serious," Austin said. "I promise I won't tell anyone. I've had my dreams taken from me. I don't ever want to do that to someone else. I don't have any friends to tell, anyway."

Pauline's fears were immediately buried by sadness at Austin's situation.

Austin bit his lower lip and leaned forward again. "There's something I was thinking about while you and Mom were talking, and knowing that you are actually Perry is making this easier for me." He paused, and Pauline could see the courage he was trying to muster to ask. "Being gay and loving ballet is hard enough already. I don't know why it's a hateful thing, but it is. Add this stupid epilepsy, and my life at school is a living hell. It also made my dad leave."

Pauline wanted to tell him that wasn't true—no parental relationship was that simple. But she also knew negating a child's feelings was the best way to shut them down. What

Austin was telling her was his reality. She had to accept it and tell Tracy about it later.

"And when I get stressed, my symptoms get worse. Like, you've probably noticed I have more seizures when I'm angry?"

Pauline nodded.

"It's embarrassing. But I can have more when I'm laughing really hard, too." He sighed and looked like he was lost in thought for a moment. But this differed from his seizures—his focus shifted from time to time. He eventually glanced in his mother's direction as though trying to gauge if he still had time to talk before she got back.

"I'm picking up my costume while you're at your appointment," Pauline said. "You can come to my condo afterwards and instead of listening to me talk, I can get dressed, and you can talk to a bird. I can't talk back in costume. It's habit now, but trust me, hearing a voice from behind the mask is also creepy."

That pulled Austin back to her and he laughed. "I guess it would be."

"Or did you want to still ask your question here?"

"Yeah. About the assembly." He took a deep breath, but another seizure followed before he spoke. "I'm tired of apologizing for who I am at school. Can I join you onstage? Just for a few minutes?"

Pauline blinked. That was the last thing she'd expected him to ask about. "Austin, I'd be honoured to have you onstage with me. What did you have in mind?"

Austin let out the rest of his breath. "You're kind of old, so you might know this. Have you ever heard of 'Swine Lake'?"

Pauline shot him a look. "Kind of old? Excuse me?"

As her answer, the twinkle of mischief returned to Austin's eye.

"Well," Pauline continued, "as a matter of fact, I have, but I'll have you know it's not because of my age; it's because of

Todd and your grandmother. They introduced me to it. It's with What's-His-Name and a dancing pig."

"What's-His-Name?" Austin broke out into the loudest laughter Pauline had ever heard from him, punctuated by a seizure. When Tracy returned with a few snacks in hand, she looked utterly bewildered at her son, who had resumed laughing.

Pauline could only shrug. "I keep forgetting the name of the Russian dancer in 'Swine Lake.'"

Tracy began laughing, too.

CHAPTER 22

$\mathcal{T}$odd was on his third cup of pu-erh, or fermented tea, which Claire recommended for moments in life requiring daring, and he learned today that the flavour of pu-erh was right up his alley.

He did a series of *entrechat six*, high, stationary jumps that involved switching the feet back and forth in the air.

Or what he would from now on lovingly refer to as "jumpy, switchy things," as Pauline had called them the previous afternoon.

The afternoon she'd admitted she loved him.

And now she was going to be here in ten minutes: the six-foot, all-muscle, forty-seven-year-old woman who used to somersault off trampolines dressed head to toe in twenty-pound costumes and slam-dunk a basketball, but who could also kiss so tenderly.

He had ten minutes to ensure a good first impression in his apartment.

He did a few more jumpy, switchy things. Talk about jitters! He remembered Pauline saying she used to get tea drunk on pu-erh. Todd had been drunk on alcohol before, but this didn't feel like that. This felt more like a new lease on life.

Nine minutes. He scanned his apartment and his eyes landed on his memorabilia box. Perfect. If he emptied it now, he couldn't lose himself in the memories of his career *and* he could toss one more box.

He opened the box, and right on top, wrapped in tissue paper was his Nutcracker Prince mask. He unwrapped it. Unlike many other productions, where the Nutcracker Prince mask was the full head, this one was just the upper half of the face, similar in style to what the National Ballet of Canada used for its production.

Ohh...it would be so much fun to put it on... But his watch now said five minutes. How had he lost four minutes? He set the costume piece on the bookshelf.

Next in the box were stacks of programs. He placed them on the bookshelf, too.

"See, Parsons? Easy peasy."

Now newspaper articles. Okay, those didn't look as nice on a bookshelf. He'd need time to think about those.

Underneath the newspaper articles were magazines...

"Nope, not touching those."

So much for emptying the box. He shoved it against the wall and closed the flaps just as his phone rang.

Pauline!

He answered, his heart racing. He let her in the building.

Wait a minute... She used to wear costumes for a living, so why not greet her in one of his? Getting dressed in ninety seconds was a skill he still possessed.

～

PAULINE SHRIEKED at the white half-mask with gigantic blue eyes staring at her, but had no objection to the mysterious masked man whisking her inside his apartment. He closed the door, and dipped her into a theatrical kiss.

The taste of pu-erh on his breath, coupled with his giddy mood, suggested he was tea drunk. But that didn't stop Pauline from giggling so hard her insides threatened to burst.

After they both stood up, Todd removed his mask.

"How was that for an entrance into my humble abode?"

"I've never kissed a Nutcracker Prince before, or any kind of prince for that matter." She pressed her lips to his then took another moment to drink him in. He wore a period red vest—from what period in history, she couldn't say—and a cream-coloured shirt with billowy sleeves. Instead of the usual tight-fitting slacks or khakis he wore, Todd had on white tights that showed *every* muscular curve of his calves and thighs. When her eyes reached his groin, though, she saw an interesting bulge.

"That looks like it would feel much more realistic than a jock strap."

Oops. Thinking about work again. Her real work.

Todd's shoulders slouched. "Why do women always get weirded out by a dance belt? My company even made me include it in an interview for a national newspaper once. It was like showing the country my underwear."

Another fit of giggles overcame Pauline.

"I mean, seriously," Todd continued. "Would people rather we men jiggle while we dance?"

Pauline prayed she wasn't hurting his feelings, but she couldn't stop laughing. "You're asking someone who's worn costumes designed to jiggle."

She was relieved to see Todd's rather bemused expression instead of one of hurt. He tucked that piece of her hair that habitually fell forward behind her ear, and shivers ran through her body.

"Had I known ballet dancers could be this sexy," she said, "I would've started attending ballets sooner." She ran a finger up the red, tight-fitting vest, then along his neck, and stopped at his chin.

"But then someone else might have found you first," he replied.

She nudged his face closer to hers with her finger, but before they could kiss, he let out a curse and arched his back in pain.

A hand on his back—a position Pauline was beginning to see all too often—he disappeared into this bedroom and three minutes later returned in jeans and a white T-shirt, holding a small, flat canister Pauline guessed was muscle rub.

"Don't want to ruin that costume. Too many good memories. But talk about killing the mood." He dropped onto the couch and opened the canister. "Do you mind, since you're here? I don't do it at your mom's shop because of the strong smell."

She kneeled beside the couch and dipped her fingers into the ointment. She had to admit, her mother would not appreciate the intense scent of eucalyptus in the shop. "Do you know what causes these spasms?" She massaged his lower back.

"Supporting women for over two decades," he said dryly.

Pauline chuckled. "I could read so much into that."

"You could, eh?" He pushed her hand off his back, pulled his T-shirt down and turned around.

"But I, for one," she said, "don't need support."

Pauline cleaned off her hands with a tissue and climbed onto Todd.

She smiled as she nibbled on his ear. They could order food later.

~

TODD THREW his shirt back on. Wow. Her smooth skin, the curves all along her body.

Her triceps when she was on top of him.

He laughed to himself. Parts of a woman's body he'd never noticed before.

While they waited for their pizza order, Todd prepared more pu-erh, and Pauline accepted a cup.

"You love old stories, don't you?" She perused his shelves. "That's why you did a ballet on *Gilgamesh*."

He sighed. She really understood him. Did she have to return to Toronto? The kettle shut off and he poured the boiling water over the tea leaves and set the timer.

Pauline flipped through some of his theatre programs. "Oh...I recognize some of these titles. *Cinderella, The Sleeping Beauty*... They made a ballet out of *The Handmaid's Tale*?"

"It's more recent, of course, but yes."

"And I always associated ballet with old things. I had no idea."

He wanted nothing more now than to swoop her into the air, but he'd never lifted a woman her weight. Then he panicked, wondering if he had insulted her by thinking about her weight. Could she read his thoughts? No, of course not. Humans weren't telepathic.

Her laughter pulled him out of his head.

"What?"

"I guess that's what I look like when I have a conversation with myself. Care to tell me what it was about?"

His cheeks turned hot. "Um...no."

He had less than two weeks left of enjoying her beautiful smile, when he'd love to enjoy it every day of his life.

~

THE WARM GLOW of the reddening sky reflected off Todd's face and highlighted his grey temples as they sat on the balcony. He looked relaxed and at peace with himself for the first time since she'd met him. They were still waiting for their pizza, and Todd was on his third cup of pu-erh that Pauline had witnessed. He also hadn't eaten anything. He had shared so much with her about his love for stories that she could only marvel at what else was in that head of his, waiting for her to discover.

But Pauline could sense he wanted to talk about something.

He gave a heavy sigh. "We've been working together for a few weeks now," he said. "And I still know so little about you. We've kissed, and now we've had sex, but you're still such a mystery to me. I'll be honest: I looked you up online, and aside from the amazing stuff Tracy pointed out to me, where I can't see your beautiful face, there's nothing." He looked longingly at her. "I was serious the other day when I said I was falling in love with you. I am in love, Pauline, but trust is a two-way street."

The evening had started on such a fun note. But at the same time, he was right, and since Ben wouldn't budge, and Pauline knew from her experience with Austin that she'd panic if she told Todd everything, she had to find middle ground.

She reached for his hand.

"I'm under a really strict NDA and can only say I work in community engagement for the Peregrines. I can't even disclose what I actually do to my parents." She explained the consequences to him.

Todd gasped. "Seriously?"

Pauline nodded.

Apology after apology tumbled out of Todd's mouth like pee-wee hockey players chasing after a puck.

Pauline squeezed his hand. "Todd, stop. It's not your fault. I should've said something earlier. I didn't realize..." She was having a hard time herself letting the words come out. "When I signed my contract, it was because I'd found my dream job. I didn't expect to fall in love outside my work. I don't know how to handle this."

He smiled. "And I never expected to fall in love with the enemy." He kissed her hand.

She raised an eyebrow. "Oh? So now I'm the enemy?"

He must have had a good amount of pu-erh before she'd arrived. His moods were on a roller coaster, and now they careened downwards as he shared story after story about how his father and brothers attended hockey games—especially Peregrines games—instead of his own shows.

"They even told me once that ballet was too boring for business," he said.

She was the enemy. But not just as Perry. She'd made those same comments herself.

"Todd, if anything I said when we met brought up those old memories, I'm so sorry."

"You didn't. I really did believe I'd forgiven them ages ago. But then the win, and when they cut me off for another picture with that stupid bird for their Peregrines' nest…it just became clear that I haven't forgiven them."

Pauline shifted in her chair.

"You okay?" he asked. "Crap. I really shouldn't be dumping all this on you, especially on our first official date." He rubbed his eyes. "Especially about your employer. I'm making an idiot of myself."

She gave her best fake smile. "It's the tea talking. You should eat something. It'll help."

Todd retrieved a bowl of pretzels from the kitchen.

"It's just that, when your dad and brothers have a Peregrines' nest for a man cave in your family house, and the only person who ever put up photos of you was your now-deceased mom, it gets to you."

So that's what a Peregrines' nest was. How many photos was she in? DIY Home had a Toronto office, so depending on how often Todd's family was in town, they likely had a lot of photos with her. Pauline sank further into her chair.

"I obviously don't expect them to have a Todd Parsons Hall of Fame, but they have exactly three photos of all five of us with me in costume and stage makeup. Three. And you know why?"

Pauline shook her head, afraid of the answer.

"Because Mom forced them to stand in them with me. Lots of the five of us with me in jeans and a T-shirt. Three in costume and stage makeup. Football tights and that black stuff under the eyes would've been fine."

Todd deserved to know who he was dating, because the anger he had toward his family involved her character.

Todd's eyes wrinkled as he smiled. His roller coaster was pulling back up. "I probably sound like a child the way I'm getting worked up over some guy in a costume." His eyes opened wide. "It is a guy right? I mean, it might be a woman."

"NDA. I can't tell you."

For once, she was telling the truth, but if she was being completely honest, now she was stalling. She hadn't expected her character to cause this much hurt. This was past finding mascots annoying or laughable or scary. In fact, she couldn't recall ever being aware of this kind of situation in her thirty years of work.

"Right. Of course not," Todd said.

Roller coaster going back down.

Pauline needed time to sort things out herself. If her character hurt him this much, would he tell the world who Perry was if he knew? She couldn't tell him, especially not in this state.

"Did I ever show you this? Look at how ridiculous they look. Leaders of a national company." He pulled out his phone and within ten seconds was showing Pauline the viral "Chicken Dance" video.

Pauline did her best to act like she'd never seen the video before, though it saddened her that Todd couldn't see the fun his family was having.

"I spent over a decade practising six hours a day," he said, the hurt in his voice unmistakable. "And they saw me perform three times before my career ended. But this took how long to plan? Two minutes?"

Actually, about thirty years of experience, followed by a stroke of luck running into them in the subway on the way to the arena, checking with security where they were sitting, engaging with them earlier to make sure they'd be game for the segment, coordinating with the technicians for sound and video, and having the right supplies on hand so this would all work, Pauline thought. But she knew he wasn't really comparing the perceived levels of skill. Instead, he was comparing the amount of fun his family was having with a disguised stranger compared to their son and brother.

That would be a stab in the heart.

He stroked her arm, his love for her shining from his eyes as his mood lifted again. "I bet you would've come up with some-thing way better." He sat back down and popped a few more pretzels into his mouth. "And get this: their life goal is to get me in a picture with that bird. Like that's ever going to happen." He leaned back in his chair. "It's all okay, really. Water under the bridge."

Pauline had to stop him right there. Things between him and his family were not okay. His father's intentions were clear to Pauline, even if they weren't to Todd. He'd chosen an awkward way to do it, but the intention was there.

"I think your dad's trying to reconcile with you. He just doesn't know how."

Todd waved her suggestion away. Whether that was him or the psychoactive compounds in the tea talking, though, she couldn't tell.

"If he wanted to reconcile, he could've just called and said, 'Todd, I'm sorry. I really messed up.'" He stared into the distance, suggesting the topic was over. "You're so easy to talk to, Pauline. I feel bad for dumping all my crap on you, especially tonight." He instantly put on a happy face and looked back at her. "So, what character was your most favourite to play?"

CHAPTER 23

Tracy welcomed Pauline in.

"Wow, that's a huge bag." Tracy pointed to Pauline's duffle bag on wheels.

"It's my life. Thanks for hiding us."

Austin tiptoed down the stairs. Instead of his usual jeans, T-shirt, and runners, he was wearing black leggings, socks, and ballet shoes, and a form-fitting white T-shirt. Pauline suspected it was a ballet uniform he hadn't worn in quite some time.

Tracy teared up, confirming Pauline's suspicions. "Austin, you haven't put that on —"

"Mother, I know."

Pauline touched her friend on her shoulder and smiled at Austin.

Tracy laid her hand on top of Pauline's. "It's amazing you're doing this." She looked at Austin. "Now, don't overdo it. If you stress yourself out too much —"

"Mother…"

Pauline understood Tracy's concerns: she'd heard similar worries many times over the years from parents who'd received life-changing diagnoses for their children. But she also under-stood Austin's need for independence. "Tracy, trust us. We'll be fine."

Austin let out a sigh of relief.

Tracy, though, wrung her hands.

Pauline's phone dinged. "Sorry—might be Ben. Just a second."

Everything set for rally tomorrow? Season ticket sales mostly Toronto. Need wider geo base for future profit.

Pauline rolled her eyes. "Excuse me. Just my manager being a jerk." She typed back: *Everything set to help kids be nicer to one another. Working on Peregrines stuff now. Will be in touch if any questions.*

"Am I getting you in trouble?" Austin asked.

"Heavens no. Ben won't know you're in the show until after-wards. I've already talked to Derek, my assistant, who hosts the show. And he's spoken with the stage manager, who has your music. We're all agreed your idea is fantastic." She pointed her thumb toward the basement door. "So, let's go." She looked her best friend directly in the eyes. "Put your feet up."

In the basement, Austin showed Pauline the space Tracy had cleared for them. Pauline pulled out Perry, happy to see the mascot face for the first time in over a week.

"Once he's on, my sight and hearing are limited and I'm six inches taller."

Austin studied the costume for a moment and looked past the top of her head. "Hmm…that reverses the traditional part-nering dynamics. I mean, you're already a little taller than me, anyway, which would make you the man in a traditional *pas de deux.*"

"A paw de what?"

"A *pas de deux*. A duet. Traditional ballet is cast with the woman shorter than the man."

"I've never danced a duet in my life, so you'll have to coach me."

Austin's chest puffed out in pride. A good sign. "I guess the first rule is that it's the man's job to watch out for the woman, or um, well..." He scratched the back of his neck, and blushed. "That sounds old-fashioned now that I say it out loud."

Pauline laughed. "Just be glad my mother isn't here."

"Or my grandmother." Austin took a moment to regroup. "It comes from all the lifts the man does, which we don't be doing. Even if I didn't have epilepsy, I wouldn't be lifting you. You're too heavy." He turned scarlet. "I guess that's another thing I shouldn't be saying."

Pauline held Perry's head in front of her face. "Why don't you say it to Perry instead. He doesn't talk back."

Austin relaxed. "Maybe I'll just play the music." But as he searched through the music on his phone, he bit his lip and cast several sidelong glances at Pauline.

Have I said something wrong? "You okay?"

Austin shrugged.

"You don't want to go through with this, do you?"

He slumped into an armchair. "It's not really that...I mean, it sort of is, but...I wish Todd could choreograph this. Then I'd know for sure this won't look stupid."

A tightness clamped around her heart. Todd couldn't be here because of her contract. "I'm sorry..." She had so many words for Ben right now. She needed to do something. Would Austin like it if Todd were at least backstage?

Austin's face lit up at the idea. "Really? You'd be okay with that?"

"The shop's closed for renovations, anyway. We just need to keep him out of the dressing room."

Pauline saw Austin's mood rise as the boy texted Todd. She pulled out her notes about the anti-bullying rally and reviewed where in the presentation they would be dancing. A minute later, Austin, all smiles, thrust his phone in Pauline's face, showing her Todd's acceptance.

"Great!" she said. "So, the best way to work with me is to start with the gloves and feet, because they'll affect how we hold on to each other and how I move around, but I'll be able to easily watch you and talk with you in a way I can't with the mask on."

She slipped her feet into the bags that formed the interior of the large skate boots and slid on Perry's hands, which reached up to her elbows and ended in elasticized cuffs. For the next half-hour, she and Austin experimented with a few ideas, but he soon fell into another slump.

"You can talk to me, right?" she asked.

He nodded but remained silent.

"Why don't I get fully dressed, and we can work on my part while you take a break." Maybe distracting him would help.

"Sure."

But no sooner had she completely disappeared into the costume than Austin said, "I can't do this."

Pauline shrugged, asking why not.

"I just can't."

Pauline's instinct told her to stay in costume.

Thirty seconds later, it all came out. "The kids at school will just keep bullying me, Pauline. They shove me into lockers, call me names. They even call me the…the…f-word. And once… one kid punched me while I was having a seizure…" His voice trailed off and he broke into tears. "I came out of it just as his fist hit my stomach." Pauline opened her arms and the angry teenaged boy who'd stormed into her mother's tea shop not three weeks before wrapped his arms around her in an embrace so tight she could hardly breathe.

Pauline had been hugged hundreds of thousands of times

over the years for joyous and sad reasons. She'd even been asked to stand by a child's bedside and hold their hand while they passed away. She had shed many tears of happiness and sadness in costume.

But none of those moments compared to this, where Austin, someone she knew, finally trusted an adult to tell them how others were humiliating him. Dancing with Todd had begun his healing. This moment was another step along the way. There was no telling when—or even if—his healing process would end. But he was finally reaching out to others.

But just as something had changed in him, it had also changed in her. She whispered through the mask, "It's okay, Austin. Your family and friends are here for you."

He squeezed even tighter, and sobbed. Pauline acknowledged his emotions by pulling him in more, too. Only after several minutes did his arms relax, and she mirrored his actions. Austin eventually stepped back and wiped his tears.

Pauline removed her gloves, undid the chin strap, and took off Perry's head.

A weak smile crossed Austin's lips. "Okay, a voice coming out of the costume was a bit creepy." He sniffled and Pauline handed him a tissue from an end table.

"Can I tell your mom what you told me?" Tracy needed to know, and this was one secret Pauline didn't want to keep. But telling Tracy without Austin's permission would destroy the trust she—and Todd—had worked so hard to build with Austin. "She wants to know so she can help. You can give me names, details, if that's easier for you."

He bit his bottom lip as he thought about it. "I can't live like this anymore. After that dance with Todd…I began to feel like my old self again." He glanced toward the door. "Can we dance first? I'll think about the rest. But right now, I just want to have fun."

"Sure thing. You call the shots."

Pauline put the mask and gloves back on, and for another half-hour, she and Austin rehearsed their dance. Tracy came down to check on them but Pauline chased Tracy back up the stairs wiggling her tail.

Not long afterwards, Pauline and Austin took a short break, and Pauline removed the mask.

"It must be hot in there," Austin said.

"It's a sauna, but you get used to it. There's a small fan in the head that circulates the air, but it doesn't cool anything down."

Austin stared at the costume, and Pauline saw the question in his eyes. "Do you want to try it on?"

His face lit up. "Can I?"

"No complaining about the smell."

Austin wrinkled his nose but agreed, and five minutes later, she was standing outside her costume with Austin in it.

"Oh god, it stinks!"

"Shh! You can't talk when the head's on. Remember how creepy that sounded?"

He gave a thumbs-up.

From behind the basement door they heard Tracy yell, "Wait just a sec! I'll get him for you!"

The basement door was torn open, and a grinning Todd stood at the top of the stairs. But as soon as he saw Pauline and Perry, his expression changed to one of embarrassment. In his hand he had the Nutcracker Prince mask from the previous night, probably to surprise Austin with, and instead found Perry.

The poor man.

Austin waved, and Todd waved back.

"Why is that bird here?" Then to Perry he said, "Sorry, no offence."

Austin waved Todd's concern away, and Pauline had to fight

with every ounce of strength she had to not crack a smile. She wasn't laughing at the pain Todd had shared with her the night before but at poor Austin stuck in her costume while his idol stood in the room. Tracy stood behind Todd, a hand over her mouth, suppressing her laugh.

"We're just rehearsing for tomorrow," Pauline said. "Austin's in the washroom. We're almost done. He'll be up soon."

Todd stared at Perry's feet. "The actor's a ballet dancer?"

Austin turned his feet parallel.

"He's just practising for tomorrow's routine." Pauline made a mental note to turn her feet out at the rally.

Behind Todd, Tracy's eyes were big with relief. "You can wait up in his bedroom. I'll send him up when he's done."

"Well, okay," Todd said. "Sounds good. Just don't tell him I have this." He looked at Perry. "Um, bye. Break a beak?"

Austin in Perry gave Todd a thumbs-up.

Pauline swallowed her laughter. "I'll be taking photos from the audience tomorrow, so I probably won't see you."

"I'm looking forward to it. It'll be nice to see what you do."

Her heart fluttered.

Tracy led him away and closed the door.

Austin took off the gloves and the mask, and then the rest of the costume.

"I had no idea he was coming!" She patted him on the shoulder. "But you did a great job."

"Poor Todd. That was the sports equivalent of the Mouse King."

"You forget I don't speak ballet."

"My idol saw me dressed as his arch enemy."

Pauline laughed as she began packing up the pieces of her costume. "Except he didn't know it was you, and he's not going to know, right?"

Austin nodded. "Promise. You're good for tomorrow?"

"You have nothing to worry about."

But the excitement in his eyes told Pauline his mind was already on the next event of the evening.

"Was that mask for me?"

"I'm not supposed to tell you—"

Austin bolted for the stairs.

CHAPTER 24

Of all the times to run into the Peregrines' mascot... It made sense that Pauline and the actor were here tonight, now that Todd thought about it.

Tomorrow's Austin's first show in at least a year. Maybe I should go so he can rest, Todd thought, standing up to leave. Suddenly, Austin ran in. Todd hid the mask behind his back.

"You're not going?" Austin asked before staring into space.

Todd waited until Austin's seizure passed. "I should've realized you'd be rehearsing tonight."

"I chose something pretty easy for the, um, the actor."

Austin stared again. When he came out of the seizure, he blushed. "Sorry."

"You don't need to apologize."

Austin shrugged. "Feel like I have to for some reason." He dropped onto his bed.

"You okay?"

"Just tired." Austin sounded sad. "Pauline does some amazing stuff. She's really nice."

Austin looked like he wanted to say more. Todd kept

Pauline's advice in the back of his mind: no pity, lots of listening.

"It was weird seeing that costume in pieces," Austin said. "Did you know it adds six inches to, um, the actor when he puts it on?"

Was Austin avoiding whatever he really wanted to talk about? Todd had to go with it. Pushing Austin to talk would likely just push him away.

He had wondered on his way over whether Pauline was the team's mascot. A job title of community engagement manager plus an NDA for what she described as her dream job would fit the bill. But her painful hip and shoulder would get in the way of that. And now he'd seen her with the actor. Evidently she wasn't the mascot.

"Explains why he's so tall," Todd replied. "You look pretty exhausted."

"I thought I had more energy than I guess I do. Not used to dancing without caffeine." Austin reached for a leg and pulled it toward his face, keeping it straight. "And I've lost easily four inches on this stretch. I'm worried about my extensions tomorrow."

Todd pulled the pillows off Austin's bed. "Relax your arms. Let me help you."

Soon Todd was helping him properly align his body to stretch his hamstring muscle. If the boy had lost four inches on this basic stretch, it only meant he could no longer touch his leg to his nose. He definitely had a dancer's body.

"Mom's taking Pauline and the Perry actor home. It's just the two of us for a bit." Austin switched legs.

"I actually came to bring you a little good luck gift." He handed his Nutcracker Prince mask to Austin. "I thought you might want it."

Austin shot up in his bed. "To keep?"

"If you want."

"Do I ever!" He held it to his face and looked around. "How do you see out of this?"

"With the stage lights on, you can actually see pretty well."

"This is the most amazing gift I've ever received. Thank you." He hugged Todd.

Was this what Pauline felt all those years in her work? If it was, why would she give it up?

"Can I get you something to eat or drink?" Todd asked. Despite his excitement, Austin still looked tired.

"Actually, that'd be nice."

Remembering from his last visit where Tracy kept dishes, Todd poured Austin some orange juice and placed some cheese, crackers, and grapes on a plate. He didn't know if Austin's condition required any special diet, but no one had said anything so far, so he assumed not. A balanced diet was best for dancers.

When Todd returned, Austin was turning the mask over in his hands, lost in thought. He eagerly accepted the snack and drink.

"Am I allowed to ask about the story behind tomorrow's dance?"

"I took inspiration from 'Swine Lake' but with a bit of a change—"

"Let me guess: 'Peregrine Lake'?"

"I hope you don't mind: I borrowed from *Gilgamesh*. Instead of an adult dancing pig looking for love in another adult, we're doing a teen boy looking for friendship with an adult peregrine falcon."

Todd's breath caught. Really? From his failed ballet? The artistic director at his company had said the youth of today didn't know who Todd Parsons was, and here was a teen boy who not only knew him but loved his work. If there was one, more were out there, right?

"Is that okay, Todd? It would mean a lot to me to kind of, I don't know, put a little inspiration from you into it. I hope it's okay? Maybe I should've asked your permission first."

Todd swallowed. He didn't mean for his delayed response to come across as an objection. He simply hadn't expected to be included at all. "I'm honoured."

Austin grinned from ear to ear, then popped some cheese into his mouth. But as he continued to eat, Todd could tell that something was on his mind. How could he encourage Austin to talk to him?

No pity, he reminded himself. He returned to that moment in the tea shop when Austin had felt so vulnerable that he'd pushed Todd away. What had Pauline done to turn that around? He reviewed every second in his mind. She hadn't forced anything out of Austin but had kept everyone calm and the energy moving.

Like an improvised dance.

Todd was used to communicating without words, but dance to him was a one-way street, not a silent conversation.

"You can talk to me about anything."

Austin studied him.

"I mean it." He didn't want to risk this boy shutting down again.

"What was it like?" Austin asked. "To live your dream?"

Was Austin avoiding his real question again? Or did he want to know about the future he might not have? Either way, honesty was the best way to build trust.

"Amazing, incredible, a privilege. A lot of fun." Todd smiled as a few memories came to him. "Things like—you know those boots men have to wear onstage sometimes?"

Austin nodded.

"Women always look fabulous in their pointe shoes. But when you point your foot in those boots, that line all the way down your body, the one you've spent six hours a day for over a decade to perfect can suddenly have this ugly bunching going on behind the heel. So, the guys and I would sometimes take the boots home and cut them open at the back and resew them ourselves."

Austin's eyes popped out of his head. "Seriously?"

"Yup. You know how it is: people pay to see gorgeous men jumping up and down. We didn't want to disappoint them."

Austin laughed, then picked up the mask and turned it again in his hands. So, that hadn't been the question.

"Why'd you really quit? It had to be more than just the criticism, because you've been criticized lots of times in your career."

That was the question, and it was time for Todd to be fully honest with Austin.

"I didn't quit. We got a new artistic director two years before everything went downhill with me. He saw my salary and my waning skill, saw my social media following, the growing complaints, and my lack of desire to appear on television. He said I couldn't draw in the younger crowds and he could no longer justify paying me what I thought I'd earned after two decades of professional work. So, he took me off the stage. Not as many people as I'd hoped protested at that move, sadly. He called me a choreographer. At first, I took it as an honour, but I later learned it was so he could simply raise more money. When that flopped, he fired me, calling me a has-been."

Austin's jaw dropped. "Please tell me you're joking. All the guys at my ballet school had you plastered in their lockers!"

Todd shrugged. "I somehow believed artistry was still important. But with guys not much older than you making a quarter of my salary, technically superior to me now, and practically able to rehearse all afternoon on a sandwich and cup of coffee…"

It took Austin a few moments to find his words. "But I lapped up every piece of advice you gave us about artistry! Open up your heart; expose yourself to the audience; connect with them; every performance is different because every audience is different; every time I play a character it's a different character, because I'm bringing whatever I've experienced in my life up to that point into the character, even though it might be the same character I played last year…I could go on and on. It's why your artistry was—and still is—the best!"

Todd had assumed his words forgotten after he'd taught that master class a few years before. So, young dancers—at least one —had listened to him?

"Um, well, thank you."

"I mean," Austin continued, "Patrick Swayze's knee injury kept him from dancing too much most of the rest of his life, but I always loved watching him dance when he did. Even the way Baryshnikov grooved in those clothing commercials a few years ago, and he was in his late sixties. And when Kudelka asked Evelyn Hart to come back onstage for a work, he convinced her by calling it 'heartfelt walking,' because she didn't dance anymore. Oh my god, Todd, how her emotions just flowed through her body… And I'd love to go out to Vancouver someday and catch Jeff Hyslop. Mom showed me all his kids' shows when I was young. They were fun. Involved this magic hat. But you a has-been? That's really stupid."

It was stupid, wasn't it? Todd had his injuries, and they prevented him from dancing in partnerships—a back spasm at the wrong time, like Austin's seizures, could seriously injure a woman. But that didn't mean he needed to stop dancing.

But was he ready to come out of his hiding spot? Or would the same negative reception greet him? The public cared that his hips couldn't clear six feet anymore. Would they let him evolve into another type of dancer, one who relied more on artistry than physical skill? Todd was enjoying his privacy and he wasn't ready yet to test those waters.

"All I can tell you, Todd, is that tomorrow, whatever happens, I'm aiming for 'heartfelt walking,' because that's what I need to share with my school: what my heart feels, even if all I have the courage to do is walk. If I can do more than that onstage, I'll be thankful."

"You'll be amazing, whether you groove like Baryshnikov or walk like Hart."

Austin's cheeks turned red. "Or dance like Parsons."

Todd had come here to pass on a gift as a token of good luck for tomorrow's performance, and instead Austin had given him a gift: reminding Todd that his teachings had helped others. Tomorrow, Todd would be backstage to support this young man as he showed his school what his heart felt.

"Or," Todd said, "dance like Tschirhart."

CHAPTER 25

Todd stood backstage at Eby Heights, wearing sunglasses and a baseball cap. With stage professionals from Toronto milling about, he wasn't taking any chances. Austin and Tracy stood beside him, watching the introduction of the anti-bullying rally from the wings.

Tracy rubbed Austin's back. "I'm so proud of you."

"Mom…"

"I know, I know, but I can't help it. I'm your mother. To see you ready to perform…"

"Mom!"

Todd knew Tracy's motherly love was annoying Austin — his mother had done the same to him when he was Austin's age — but it was heartwarming, too.

Plus, he felt the same way.

"Fine, fine," Tracy said. "I'll go into the audience now and leave you two alone." She kissed Austin on the temple.

"MO-THER!"

Todd summoned the Power of Jumpy, Switchy Things to not laugh, but the power failed him. Todd laughed, and after

Tracy left, Austin gave him the evil eye.

"Sorry. It was sweet."

The audience roared, and Todd suddenly felt what he could best describe as the nervousness of a father—if his father had been capable of such nervousness for him.

A student walked past, gave Austin the up and down, and snorted. Todd wanted to punch his lights out, but getting jailed for assault wasn't going to help anyone.

Austin stared at the ground.

Todd placed a comforting hand on his shoulder. "You're sharing your voice so that kind of thing stops."

Austin clenched his jaw, but he nodded.

"Good." Todd looked around. "Everyone seems ready to go. I see the hockey players."

As if on cue, Perry stepped out of the dressing room.

"And I see Perry. Figures. I come to Kitchener to sort out my life, and I have to share backstage during a really important show with that animal."

Austin laughed.

At least something good was coming of Todd's annoyance with that bird.

"I can't believe you still have a Perry thing."

"Well, believe it."

"Let me get this straight. You're forty-three and you've spent twenty-four years as a professional dancer. You've done eighty-three ballets, three major motion pictures...and you still have a Perry thing?"

Todd stared at him. "You know my entire resumé?"

Austin shrugged. "I'm a fan."

Todd could only laugh. He patted Austin on the back. "I guess I've never thought of my life in those numbers. Say, why is Perry pacing back and forth like that?"

"Um...stage fright?"

PAULINE COULDN'T STOP PACING. She'd performed in this rally hundreds of times since creating it in her first year as Perry. Why had she given Todd the morning off from the tea shop and allowed him to stand backstage?

Because you have a heart, she told herself. After seeing Austin's fear last night, Pauline knew that having Todd in his corner would give Austin the courage to follow through, especially when she couldn't be two places at once. Austin would never forgive himself if he backed out, and she couldn't step out of character to help him. Not only did her NDA play a role here, but in that sea of fifteen hundred students in the gymnasium were other kids like Austin. She had to help them, too.

I hope I don't forget the choreography, she thought. Her days of memorizing gymnastics routines were long behind her. It was one thing to learn stunts and gags, but the intricacies of ballet choreography, even the simple routine Austin had created for her, required a lot of Belmont Blizzard this morning while she practised in her parents' basement.

She looked in Todd's direction and shook out her nervousness. Remembering Austin's turned-out feet from yesterday evening, she turned out her own.

"IS that a different actor from the one at your house?" Todd asked Austin.

"Why?"

"The one at your house turned out from the hips. This one's turning out at the ankles like an amateur."

Perry attempted a *plié*, knees bending forward like a novice instead of over the toes like a trained dancer.

Like Pauline had when Todd had showed her the basics.

Before Austin could answer, though, Todd's phone vibrated. He pulled it out of his back pocket to make sure it wasn't the floor installer.

"You must be joking," he muttered under his breath. Of course his father was trying to call him at the moment the Peregrines' mascot was staring him down with a terribly executed ballet step.

Todd tapped, *Will call back*.

"My phone's in my locker. Can you take a picture of me and Perry? You might have a Perry thing, but I don't."

Todd pasted his best stage smile on his face. "You're trying to get me back, aren't you?"

"You have to say yes, because you're my idol and you don't want me to think bad things about you." Austin beckoned to Perry to come over. "Photo?"

Perry nodded.

Todd worried the mascot would invite him to join them. He could stand eight feet from the bird and take a photo, but he wouldn't stand in it.

He still had his pride.

He hoped.

The bird didn't gesture to him, but just as Todd was about to snap the photo, Austin asked Todd to join them, anyway.

With that mischievous twinkle in his eye.

"You wouldn't want to ruin my big day, would you?" Then Austin turned earnest. "I promise it won't go public. It would just mean a lot to me."

Todd couldn't deny Austin that kind of request.

~

"FINE," Todd said, "but I'm not standing next to Perry." To Perry, he said, "Sorry, no offence, long story."

Pauline waved it off, suggesting it was all right, and motioned to a stagehand to take a photo with Todd's phone.

"So," Austin said to Todd once he got his phone back. "How are things going with Pauline?"

He is so going to get it! Pauline thought.

"You're about to go onstage, and you're asking me about my love life?"

Love life. Butterflies flew all around Pauline's stomach. *Get your head in the game, Perry,* she thought. *You've got a show to do.*

"Well?" Austin asked.

"I think things—"

"Perry?"

Ugh!

The stage manager interrupted the conversation. "You're up."

Pauline gave Austin a high-five and then followed the stage manager to her wing. She would ask Tracy and Jan to share baby stories about Austin with her and Todd in front of Austin. But she couldn't help but enjoy his sense of fun. And given what they were about to show his entire school, she was glad to see his lighter mood.

THE LIGHTING AND MUSIC, along with the host, had raised the energy in the gym to a level Todd had never seen when he danced. The host announced the names of the five hockey players who'd joined in for this show—Todd had learned they didn't always participate. A pang of jealousy reminded him again of the lack of popularity of his art form. Yes, his name used to easily fill a four-thousand-seat theatre several weeks in a row, but not a twenty-thousand-seat arena for months.

At the same time, that was why he couldn't disappear in Toronto but could drive an hour away and hide in Kitchener. But even he knew who Evanoff was when the Peregrines' centre entered the spotlight.

Austin gripped Todd's arms. "I can't do this. The students aren't going to cheer for me." He faced Todd. "I'm going to be a disappointment when I get onstage."

Todd placed his hand over Austin's. "I've never had that kind of reaction either. We're ballet dancers, not hockey players. It's simply a different crowd."

"Which means we don't share a crowd." Austin pulled back from Todd. "I can't do it."

Perry was strutting across the stage while the host was saying something about teamwork and accepting people as they were. The atmosphere they were building was the right one for Austin to share his message. As an adult Todd could see that, but he now had to help Austin, whose teenage world had turned upside down in the past year, see it.

Todd took off his sunglasses. "Listen to me. Whatever you and Pauline choreographed, she wouldn't have let you choose something that would make a fool out of you. She knows what she's doing, and so does that actor. I'm sure they've done this hundreds of times."

Austin watched for a few seconds, his eyes still wide with fear.

"You've also got professional hockey players out there who understand how a team functions, and the professional actor in that costume is an expert in improvising. Trust your performers and trust yourself."

Todd didn't like to think of himself as anyone's idol; it seemed selfish. But Austin did look up to him, and the teenager needed all the strength he could get from those who cared about him to complete his goal of sharing his heart with everyone. Todd knew not everyone in that audience hated Austin. In fact, he suspected most didn't even know Austin existed. Once Austin shared his story in his own beautiful way, he would certainly find new friends.

"Listen to me again. What you do up there is up to you because you're surrounded by professionals who will help you. You can groove like Baryshnikov, walk like Hart…"

"Or dance like Tschirhart."

"You've got it."

When a Peregrines assistant came over to ask if Austin was ready, the teen bravely said, "Yes, I am."

CHAPTER 26

The stage lights dimmed and the gym grew dead silent. Todd's heart pounded so hard he was ready to throw up.

"And now," the host's voice boomed, "give it up for Eby Heights' very own Austin Tschirhart!"

To Todd's surprise, the gym broke out in the same cacophonous cheer he'd heard only moments before.

The lights came on, the cheering died down, and Austin sat on a chair downstage left. A few snickers from the audience pierced the silence and Todd's heart. Had Tracy heard them?

Had Austin?

No. 14 from Tchaikovsky's *Swan Lake*, "The Swan Theme," played over the loudspeakers, and Austin sat at attention. A smile crept over his face as he pulled from behind his chair the Nutcracker Prince mask Todd had given him the night before. He secured it to his face and his head tilted back, his body relaxed, as though the music were pulling him into his imagination. He stood up and, holding on to the back of the chair, executed a few *rondes de jambes*, his leg perfectly straight through his foot to his toes as it circled around the floor.

When the trumpets added their threatening tone to the piece, Austin pretended to fight to keep the mask on.

The mask is the dream world where he's accepted, Todd thought. *He's trying to stay in it.*

The music crescendoed again and diminuendoed. Austin burst into a jump and landed on the floor. The taunting—the bullying—had broken his dream world.

But upstage, the lights had now lifted onto Perry and the hockey players, who had seen the bullying. Austin placed the mask on the chair and mimed weeping.

The voices were gone, but the music was quiet, too.

Perry signalled to the others that he'd talk with him. The sensitivity of Perry's reaction surprised Todd, because it stood in stark contrast to the high-energy, motivational character he'd seen in the previous segment.

Perry offered Austin his hand, and Austin accepted. What followed honoured Todd in a way he'd never experienced.

Austin hadn't only used Todd's idea from his ballet: he'd used an actual piece of choreography. Todd had taken traditional partnering intended for a man and woman and re-created it for two men, something he was criticized for. Todd's chest expanded as he saw his work in a new light.

Perry held onto Austin's hips as Austin pirouetted and then extended his leg to the side in a high *developpé*. The mascot actor also properly supported Austin on jumps, which must have been no easy feat with those gloves on and the beak in the way.

Except that the actor's lower back stuck out.

"Hopefully he doesn't strain it."

Lower back sticking out. Wait a minute…

Todd shoved the suspicion out of his mind and continued watching. Many people stuck out their lower back.

The hockey players, in jeans and team jerseys, formed the *corps de ballet* and provided a fun background with simple arm movements.

The music became softer again. Austin gripped Perry's hands tight, and Perry nodded. Was the actor really encouraging Austin for this last segment? Or was that choreographed? Todd couldn't tell. But he knew what was coming up, and Austin certainly wasn't aiming for just heartfelt walking.

Todd hadn't noticed a single seizure during the last two minutes. Hopefully, Austin wouldn't have one in this last part.

Austin now stood upstage right and glanced in Todd's direction. Todd gave him a thumbs-up, and the music picked up. Todd held his breath: one false move and Austin could twist or break an ankle. With only dancing in his bedroom this past year, injury was a real possibility.

Austin performed a series of turns to get his momentum going and then broke into a sequence of *grand jetés*, each one followed by one *chaîné* turn in fast succession.

One…two…three…four…five…six…seven…eight!

The students cheered.

The stage was so small that Austin was back where he started instead of in the opposite corner. He adjusted the following choreography accordingly and finished the dance in an embrace with Perry and the hockey team: Austin's character, once alone and bullied, now had friends.

Todd shot his arms into a "V" over his head. The hockey players hit the floor with their sticks, and the audience followed suit with thunderous applause while Perry thrust Austin's hand high in the air. Austin's chest heaved as he caught his breath, and his face glowed with pride.

The dance now complete, Perry signalled to a player to move the chair downstage centre and a stagehand brought out a bottle of water and a microphone for Austin. Perry led Austin to the chair, kneeled beside him, and placed his gloved hand over the mic. The actor appeared to be talking, too, because Austin talked, paused to listen, and talked again.

Pauline said she never spoke in costume. That nixed Todd's suspicion.

Perry rubbed Austin on the shoulder before standing up. Certainly not the kind of behaviour Todd expected from a character whose purpose was to brag about winning. He had to admit, he was impressed. Whatever unhappy memories Todd had of the character, this actor had just created a very pleasant one for him.

Perry stepped back, and a spotlight fell on Austin.

"Uh, hi. I'm, um, I'm Austin. I...I...I—" When Austin came out of his seizure, he looked for Todd.

Todd stepped closer to the stage and pressed himself against the downstage side of the wing to remain hidden from the audience. He took off his sunglasses and placed his hand over his heart to signal his gratitude for the performance he'd just seen.

Austin faced the audience again, the words just tumbling out of him now. "I was born to love ballet and, well, to love guys. For some reason, though, that's a thing. There's this dancer, Todd Parsons, I've always looked up to. Some of that choreography was his, actually. He was also teased for being gay because he loved ballet, even though he's straight. So, I know it's not just me. But I don't know why I'm still getting bullied here at school about it. And I've got this disease. It's called epilepsy. I think I just had a seizure a minute ago. I stare, and I don't always know I'm doing it. It's become another reason why some kids bully me. This disease isn't contagious. It's just something else I was born with and it really sucks. But I wanted to show all of you who I am, and I want to tell the kids who for some reason think bullying me is fun to stop. I'm not just telling school administration about you: I'm telling the entire school that it's happening. If you think you're that tough, I dare you come up onstage right now and try that jump sequence. I'll bet you lunch tomorrow you can't do it." He waited a moment. No one came onto the stage. "I thought so. That took years of practising to execute like that. Punching me in the middle of a seizure takes five seconds of cowardice."

Todd's stomach tightened. Who would punch someone in the middle of a seizure?

Some kid yelled out a curse in support of Austin's confession.

"Yeah, I know," Austin replied. "That's how brave these kids are. They find me when I'm alone, like when the washroom's empty or something, then they punch me when I'm basically unconscious but standing. Because of how I was born, of how I identify, of who I am. I'm done with it."

No one snickered, coughed, laughed, sneezed, unwrapped a candy, or sent a text. Having said what he'd wanted to, Austin stood up, and a gentle knocking began. It took Todd a moment to realize what it was, but when he did, his tears started to flow: the players were hitting the stage with their sticks in unison, increasing the volume to match the lights now coming up. Perry made his way downstage, clapping overhead to the beat the hockey players had begun, and the audience joined in. Todd couldn't help but clap, too. Once Perry was standing next to Austin, he began stomping, raising the volume of the more than fifteen hundred people to a thunderous storm of acceptance.

Even if Pauline wasn't the actor in the costume, that she had orchestrated all of this so one young man could touch over a thousand young adults added to the rush of emotions pirouetting through Todd. He couldn't let her get away—he had never met anyone so remarkable in his life.

Austin hugged Perry for a full minute. Stagehands began preparing for the next segment, and Todd put his sunglasses back on and removed himself from the wings just as Tracy entered the backstage area, tears streaming down her face, too.

Perry led Austin offstage, and Austin ran directly into his mother's arms. Todd had planned to thank Perry for the touching performance, but the mascot immediately returned to the stage.

Austin then pulled away from his mother and rushed over to Todd. "I did it!"

Todd's heart couldn't have filled with more joy. "You did."

"Thank you!"

Tracy touched him on the shoulder. "Austin said you helped give him the courage to go through with it. That was so beautiful."

"He had the courage inside him the whole time. I just pulled back the curtain."

A woman holding out a phone approached them, flanked by someone holding a camera. Todd recognized the appearance of a reporter and accompanying photographer and immediately backed away, like a vampire seeing a cross. So much for courage.

Tracy and Austin ushered the media pair into the school hallway, and Todd thanked the powers that be for Kitchener's lack of ballet love: the reporter hadn't recognized him at all.

He suddenly remembered his father and pulled out his phone. Michael had left a message.

"Todd, it's me. Listen, I know you don't want us visiting, but if you're close by, I want to see you. I've actually watched a few of your ballets online and it's made me regret not seeing you live more often. I'm really sorry. Please call me."

Pauline was right: Michael was trying to reconcile with Todd. But was Todd ready for that conversation?

He stuffed his phone back in his pants pocket. The rally continued onstage, but any time Todd lost himself in memories of his relationship with his family, clapping, stomping, or cheering pulled him back to reality.

If he ignored his father's request, Todd risked losing him for the rest of his life. Did he want that? This Peregrines win had made Todd realize he had never fully forgiven his father for ignoring his passion for ballet all those years. But believing that he had forgiven his father these past few years had been nice, even if it had been a façade.

This time, it could be real.

Perry had brought a few student volunteers onstage and was having some good, clean fun with them. Everyone was laughing.

Now there was an idea: Todd in costume in a photo with his family...and Perry. The more Todd thought about it, the more the idea made him happy.

But the more Todd watched Perry, the more he realized that the performer did move like Pauline...with self-assured, big movements. The height matched, but many people were Pauline's height.

Perry did an aerial on Pauline's preferred side.

Wait...did Perry just limp for a second there on his left leg?

Was it Pauline after all?

He laughed again. *Figures I'd fall for the actor who plays Perry.* They had only known each other for a few weeks: it was understandable she wouldn't tell him, especially if she was contractually obligated not to. She had said that not even her parents knew about her real job.

But wait a minute. If that really was Pauline... The worst thing about being tea drunk was that you remembered everything you said.

Every. Single. Word.

~

PAULINE NEEDED a few minutes to decompress before she changed. She couldn't remember an anti-bullying rally as intense as this one. She'd cried throughout almost all of Austin's performance and hoped it hadn't shown through her body language. Speaking to Austin onstage to make sure he was okay was a first for her. He trusted her, but she couldn't remove the mask in front of everyone, and she needed to know he was comfortable continuing with his plans.

Someone knocked on the dressing room door, so Pauline stayed dressed. She and Derek had agreed that if she was still in costume and therefore unable to answer, he could enter after three seconds. One, two, three…

Derek opened the door, and Tracy burst inside and beelined straight for Pauline, clutching her in an embrace before Pauline could even fully open her arms.

"Um, Tracy's here," Derek announced. "I'll leave you two alone." He closed the door behind him.

"You've brought me back my son. He's talking to an LGBTQ group right now," Tracy said.

Pauline sobbed and only then did Tracy let go.

"Oh my god, Pauline, I'm so sorry. You can't exactly blow your nose in there."

Pauline shook her head as she took off the gloves and mask.

Tracy gasped. "You look horrible!"

The high school best friends broke into fits of crying laughter while Pauline set Perry's head on a fan to begin drying out the interior.

"All these years of working as an EA have left me more than prepared. Here." She gave Pauline wipes and tissues. "Derek's a good assistant."

"The best I've had, though I'm certain he's not better than you."

As Pauline cleaned her face, one thing became clear to her: this was still her calling, not selling tea.

CHAPTER 27

*B*ack at the tea shop that afternoon, Pauline's heart was so full, it threatened to overflow. The flooring had been installed, and she and Todd could paint walls. She couldn't jump all over the place, but at least she could move.

Todd, on the other hand, looked glum. He continued sneaking glances at his phone, which was unlike him. Had someone begun posting about him online? Pauline wanted to ask, but she also wanted to respect his privacy. She had reached for his hand several times, and he'd responded with a smile, but his sadness had remained and he said not a word.

Or had it been the show this morning? Todd had said nothing about it to her either, even though she'd asked a couple of times. Had it hurt him too much to watch?

Pauline had to lift Todd's mood somehow. Whatever was bringing him down wasn't doing him any good. She couldn't offer him tea: the floor installation had left too much dust to safely uncover the equipment. They had already mopped the floor once, but not behind the counter.

A little acting it was.

She dramatically pushed the back of her hand against her forehead and collapsed. "So, so tired. Too much energy taking photos at a high school."

She glanced up at Todd to see if she'd gotten a reaction. He stared at her, but it wasn't enough. She heaved another dramatic sigh. "Too many photos. *Far* too many photos. Ohh, my poor thumbs. I *long* for the days of film when you could only take thirty-six pictures." She peeked at him, and he lifted an eyebrow. "Twenty-four photos? Twenty-four photos would have been *too* much less work."

Todd snorted. "You really are too much sometimes. You're tired because of *photos*? I installed half this flooring after the rally. That's what those extra years you have on me do to you. See? I can keep going." He jumped in the air, his legs splitting to the side.

Pauline snapped back to her feet. "I only complained about my thumbs." She flipped upside down into a handstand but soon found herself somersaulting out of it in response to her shoulder. Maybe not taking time to recuperate after the rally was a mistake. "I'm going to add my shoulder to that list of poor body parts."

Todd stuck his chin in the air. "See? How about this?" He kicked off a shoe and completed ten rotations on one foot with his other knee pulled up and turned to the side.

Pauline would not be beaten by a spinning letter "p." She jumped and tucked her knees in, completing a backflip, only to crunch her bad hip on her landing. "Dang it. And my hip again."

Todd did a few turns moving forward, then jumped in the air, his legs tight together, and rotated three times.

Pauline threw her hands in the air. "Ugh! You win! The Patrick Swayze Jump. Doesn't work in a twenty-pound costume."

Todd laughed. "That's what you call a *tour en l'air*? A Patrick Swayze Jump?"

"It's what he does after he jumps off the stage in *Dirty Dancing*."

"I see. So, the Patrick Swayze Jump doesn't work in a twenty-pound costume, but a backflip does?"

"Easier to get power off the ground that way. Depends on the costume, too, though. Not sure I could do it as a hippopotamus anymore, for example. You know, extra padding, snout." The pain in her hip stung, and she pressed into it to quell it. "Ouch." As fun as this challenge was, it was too much on top of the rally today. Three years ago, this wouldn't have been an issue. Maybe seeing a sports medicine specialist would help her find new ways to heal faster.

"That looks bad."

"Just needs some ice. How come my body breaks apart in ten seconds and your back stays put for once?"

Todd jogged to the freezer in the back room to get Pauline a pack of ice. "Luck of the draw, to be honest," he called back. "You haven't talked to a doctor about that yet, have you?"

"A little ice, and it's fine again."

He returned with the ice pack, and Pauline pressed it to her hip. Deep down, she knew she wouldn't be able to keep this up, but she just needed to get through this year. Then she'd have next summer off and could see someone about it.

"You know," Todd said, "that was the first time in ages that I've done ten pirouettes."

"It's nice to see your spirits up again."

Todd ran his fingers through her hair. "You are quite good at that."

Pauline stroked his arm. "You seemed down. I just wanted to make you happy."

He wrapped his arms around her waist and tilted his head.

"Well, it worked." He pulled her in for a kiss.

The bells over the front door jingled. "There's a back room for that, you two," Claire teased as she entered on crutches.

Todd pulled away immediately and ran his fingers through his own hair.

Pauline groaned. "Mom, not in front of the employee."

"Shall we start our meeting in the other unit?" Claire asked.

Pauline's face burned with embarrassment. She'd been floating on cloud nine and then been preoccupied with lifting Todd's mood. She'd forgotten about the meeting to discuss the reopening.

"Just let us cover up the paints, and we'll be right there."

Claire gave her daughter and employee a mock-suspicious look up and down, but then she broke out into the warm smile she was known for. "Come over as soon as you're ready."

Richard held open the door for Claire and winked at Pauline, who rolled her eyes at him.

Pauline and Todd covered up the paint cans, trays, and rollers.

"Does your mom play matchmaker all the time?"

Pauline took hold of Todd's hand and pulled him in close. "I guess only when she's trying to keep me home."

Todd cupped his hand behind her head. "But I thought she supported your dreams…"

"I think now she's trying reverse psychology on me, and I'm quite okay with that."

But instead of landing a kiss on his lips, Pauline dabbed straw-coloured paint on Todd's nose and dashed for the door.

TODD TRIED to rub the paint off his nose before he entered the other unit.

Maybe she's not Perry, he thought with a grin. *She's the devil.* He wanted to ask her about Perry, but if that role was the reason for her NDA, then forcing her to choose between her dream career and a man she'd only known for three weeks wouldn't be fair. He'd never tell a soul, no matter what, but he did hope she would trust him enough someday to tell him everything. He would love to hear her stories, and he imagined she needed someone to share the heartaches with, too.

Claire and Richard were laughing when they entered, and Richard discreetly pointed to a spot on his own nose where Todd had missed some paint.

Claire was already seated at a table with a box of desserts in the centre next to a pitcher of what Todd guessed was iced tea. She passed out disposable plates, cups, and cutlery. He could see where Pauline got the energy to perform as a mascot: Claire had to greet every customer with positive, high energy every day. If that was Pauline this morning at the school in front of fifteen hundred people, then Todd had seen only a fraction of her capabilities.

They all sat down on some folding chairs the building owner had lent them. Richard explained to Todd that he'd been the owner's real estate agent since before he and Claire had met, hence the owner's willingness to provide a few favours.

Claire thanked them for coming. As much as she loved her home, living there all day, every day for these past three weeks was becoming an absolute bore. She loved her first few days off, watching reruns of *The Monkees*, and Todd caught that familiar exchange of knowing expressions between the long-married couple.

Richard filled him in: he was a Stones fan and Claire a Monkees fan, but back in the sixties, he had to admit defeat over an argument in authenticity between the groups.

"You only admitted defeat to go on a date with me," Claire said.

Richard smiled and kissed her. "True." He began serving everyone iced tea.

"I actually did also read Mike Nesmith's memoir while I was in bed. It'd just come out. Sadly, I've lost a piece of my pride. Turns out The Monkees *did not* outsell The Beatles and Rolling Stones combined."

Richard slapped the table. "I knew it! There was no way a bubble gum band like them could've sold so many records!"

Claire playfully shook a finger at Richard. "That doesn't mean they're a bubble gum band, my Keemun."

While the two lovingly debated further, Todd leaned over to Pauline. "I have no idea what they're talking about."

"They're just carrying on with an argument that's older than their marriage. Why don't we get the photos while they're trying to settle it for the umpteenth time?"

As soon as Pauline stood up, she cried out in pain and pushed the table when she clamped her hands on its edge, her knuckles turning white.

"It's just a cramp," she said through clenched teeth.

But Todd knew it was much more than that.

"Have you called the doctor about this, honey?" Claire asked.

"Not yet."

Claire's face became stern, the way a mother's did when a child didn't do as she was told. Claire pulled her phone out of her purse. "Then I'm doing it right now."

"Do you want me to get some ice again?" Todd asked.

Pauline took some deep breaths. "It's just a cramp. I'll be fine." She tried to lift her leg to shake it out, but the painful expression in her face said she couldn't.

Richard looked concerned. "Honey, what's going on? What

aren't you telling us?"

"Nothing, Dad. It's just a cramp. Happens when you're active."

Todd helped her lie down on her side, and he dug into her hip muscles with his elbow.

He recognized her behaviour right away: denying something serious was wrong, in the hopes it would go away, because it signalled your body was aging. He was guilty of it himself, but because it reminded him of the career he'd lost.

And it's reminding Pauline of the career she's about to lose.

She had to be the Peregrines' mascot. Nothing else made sense. It was clear she wasn't taking any painkillers, probably to avoid side effects that could affect her performances. But if that kind of pain shot through her while she was in the air, she could seriously injure herself. And what if Perry reacted like that? It would frighten the kids, not to mention harm the brand.

So...she couldn't be the Peregrines' mascot. But then why all this denial that something was seriously wrong? Did she simply believe she was too young to have these problems?

He usually saw this kind of pain in ballerinas and suspected its cause was arthritis. Arthritic pain came from both friction in the joint and increasingly tightening muscles pulling on it. But Claire was making a phone call to their doctor, so he'd let the doctor diagnosis it. After all, maybe Todd was wrong, and the last thing he wanted to do was frighten Pauline: she was already avoiding eye contact with him.

The muscles in her hip began to relax. He shifted to her front and slowly lifted her knee onto the floor. Then he gently pressed against her shoulder to stretch the hip. She closed her eyes in relief and placed a hand on his, squeezing it in gratitude.

"Our doctor will see you tomorrow morning," Claire announced, and Pauline let out a meek thank you.

Richard brought the photos and then the new frames to the

table. Pauline told Todd she could take over stretching from here.

As Richard sorted the photos and new frames on the table, Todd leaned over to Pauline.

"Let me support you."

She nodded but continued to avoided his gaze.

By the end of the meeting, Pauline was walking again, Claire had been caught up to speed on the renovations and reopening, and the historic photos had been reframed. Todd marvelled at how the Robinsons could mesh family and business so harmoniously. In his family, work came first. End of story.

"So," he said to Pauline. "Ready to—" But she was already walking away from him. "Pauline?"

"I need time alone. I'm sorry. I'll be back in half an hour."

She limped slightly as she stormed off, the electricity just buzzing to explode from her, and Pauline striving to contain it.

If she would only open up to me, he thought. *She's spent so much of her life listening to everyone else, but she needs someone to listen to her.*

Back inside Claire's Tea Shop, he stared at the half-painted walls, the equipment covered in drop cloths, and the empty room that still needed all the furniture moved back in. He glanced back in the direction Pauline had walked off.

"She's completely overwhelmed by everything, and who knows what else is going on inside her. I have to make this easier on her." He also worried if the shop would be done in time for the reopening. "Not without my working sixteen hours a day the next few days." He had to admit, he didn't know if his body could handle it. After decades of dancing six hours a day, his body was also slowly calling it quits.

He took a deep breath, pulled his phone out of his pocket, and dialled.

"Hey, Dad, it's Todd. Any chance you brought work clothes with you?"

CHAPTER 28

auline felt guilty for leaving Todd alone for thirty minutes, but she needed air, and ideally a large crowd and noise to drown out everything rushing through her mind right now. Music on her phone would work if she had earbuds with her. Would a band be playing in Uptown Waterloo on a Thursday afternoon? Doubtful. But she headed down the Iron Horse Trail in that direction just in case. Maybe a bar had an afternoon concert going on?

Also doubtful. This was Waterloo Region. Kitchener, Waterloo, and Cambridge all had arts and culture scenes, but nothing compared to downtown Toronto where you'd find music somewhere at any time of day.

But Pauline was desperate: she felt like she'd drunk ten litres of tea and could swing from the trees that lined the trail. She certainly couldn't do a series of back handsprings and aerials—she'd injure herself more.

And Claire scheduling that appointment for tomorrow morning was finally forcing Pauline to face the truth: what if the doctor told her to stop performing?

She was so angry she wanted to scream. *Had you looked into this earlier*, she berated herself, *you could've probably done physio and found meds that wouldn't affect your performance before things got too serious*.

She jogged a few steps and stopped, thinking the better of it. She couldn't risk another episode like that with her hip.

Was it time to retire? She leaned against a tree and closed her eyes. What she wouldn't give to be in her costume right now, where nothing mattered but the people around her.

Like her family. Like Todd.

As they'd reframed those photos, Claire and Richard reminisced about all the customers who'd come through the doors of Claire's Tea Shop over the years, and Todd had listened intently.

All of them cast glances in Pauline's direction.

Glances that suggested Claire and Richard hoped Pauline would take over the store, and that Todd hoped she'd stay because he loved her.

Enough was enough. She was going to tell her parents the full story. Then she'd tell Todd. She knew all of them only wanted the best for her. The only reason they believed her staying in town was a possibility was because they didn't know she was living her dream.

She didn't have to tell Ben anything. Why was she lying to her family and not her manager? To the people who cared about and loved her rather than the one who treated her like she was expendable?

Claire's first husband had silenced her, and although Pauline didn't know the details about that marriage, Pauline had options with Ben. It was time she exercised them.

She hoped for another few years as Perry, and she'd find out tomorrow if that was feasible. But she wasn't going to lie to the people she loved any longer.

She turned around to head back to the shop. She'd tell her parents tonight.

The phone rang. It was Ben.

"I'm a genius! Have you seen the news? Noticed the number of views on the video of that boy's dance today?"

The rally had exhausted her so much, without a game to re-energize her, she'd focused on Claire's shop to try and regroup. "No."

"Having that boy as part of the rally was the best idea I've ever had. The CEO loved it."

Pauline's jaw dropped. This was the most audacious selfishness she'd ever heard from him. "Ben! That was Austin's idea one hundred percent. And if I recall, I didn't even tell you about it."

"I noticed. That we'll talk about later. We've already sold over two hundred seasons' tickets from your area and it's only been seven hours! So, I want you to find me a kid like that at every rally from now on."

After the emotional morning, the fear that her career could be over because she'd been avoiding her body's warning signals, and then listening to nostalgic tea shop stories while receiving signals from her parents that she should move home, Pauline had nothing left in her. She sat on a bench and rested her head on her other hand. "'A kid like that?' Do you have *any* idea what Austin went through to drum up the courage to speak on that stage in front of his tormentors? Any at all? In fact, he didn't fully open up to me about it until I was in costume."

"He knows you're Perry?"

"Yes. And so does his mom. We were best friends in high school."

"So, you've breached your contract."

"And I'm about to do it again with my parents." So much for lying to him.

"Are you asking to be sued?"

"You're not going to sue me, because I'll turn that trial public—"

"And you'll never work again, you know that. No franchise will pick up an actor with that kind of track record."

Pauline sighed. He was right. At the same time, her career was almost over, anyway. "I've been experiencing really strong pain in my hip for a while. I probably don't have much time left in my career. So, I have nothing to lose at this point, but you could lose at least thirty years of your career if this trial goes public, because it would go against the family image I've built up for you. Plus, you'll lose the biggest sponsorship of your career. I'm the best mascot you've ever had, and if I hadn't told Austin, that video would not have happened, and you wouldn't be gloating on the phone with me about an idea that was never yours in the first place. Tell me, Ben, what were those viewership numbers?"

Pauline had never enjoyed silence this much before.

"Looks like you win this time. But all I need is for that kid to get on social media and tell his friends—"

"He has no friends to tell, Ben! He was being bullied at school so badly he couldn't even tell his mother... He couldn't look a human being in the eye to talk about it. It took the costume for him to open up."

Ben didn't speak for a full minute, and Pauline checked her phone's display to see if he'd maybe hung up. Was he livid with her now? About to fire her, anyway? Why couldn't this conversation have waited until she'd returned to Toronto? Heck, even a video call would've been better. *This* silence was uncomfortable.

"Ben? Are you even there? I've had enough of your crap. I'm working really hard—"

"Just stop, Pauline. For once, stop talking."

"Sweet words coming from you."

"You're right."

"Wait...what?"

"I didn't know he couldn't tell his parents—"

"His mom. About the time he got his diagnosis, his father walked out on them."

"Really? Okay. Listen, let's put it this way. If you ever meet kids who want to share their story, then you have my permission to include them in the show. They'll need to sign a waiver, so I'll have Legal draw something up that their parents—or parent—can sign. They'll need to sign an NDA, too."

Pauline glanced around to see if anyone was listening to her. "Ben! Stop it with the NDAs! It's already destroying my relationships. Do you know what Austin's mom said after the show? I wasn't out of costume yet, and she said I gave her back her son. Even Evanoff cried, and he didn't cry at his grandfather's funeral last year. Your best chances for preventing another PR disaster are by hiring the right person in the first place. Nate was known for getting drunk. You just had to ask around. But look at that one Indiana football team: he unmasks as part of their high school presentation all the time, and he's hugely successful."

"You're sure they won't—"

"Austin's mom, Tracy, is a senior EA in the tech industry, so confidentiality is practically her middle name. And Austin believes he's had his dreams taken away by epilepsy, so he doesn't want to be responsible for taking away someone else's dreams. And he knows how important this career is to me."

"Fine. But this is where it stops. No parents, no family, no boyfriends. Ever. Everyone works through Derek in the future. Understood?"

She sighed. "Yes, Ben."

"I should get going." He wasn't even just hanging up on her.

"I'll have Legal draw up a waiver for future shows. And, um, nice job on the rally. Crappy job on your NDA, but I'll give you one pass. Don't waste it. I still need your feedback on Sunday's fundraiser for the children's hospital. Everything has to look perfect: we announce our sponsor. Lots of opportunities for photo ops, that sort of thing. Then enjoy your final week at your mom's. We're all looking forward to having you back in Toronto."

Ben hung up, leaving Pauline frozen. What was happening? Ben Landry *played* nice. Nice wasn't in his nature. But what exactly was he planning? Pauline noticed the time on her phone.

"I can't believe I left Todd at the shop alone for even this long."

She limped back to Belmont Village. Come hell or high water, she was going to get her mom's shop ready for Saturday morning, no matter what it took.

"I'LL LEAVE the cutting for Mark," Todd said to himself as he evaluated the reno to-do list. "That was always his thing." Todd would rather spend hours rehearsing the most difficult, intricate footwork combination known to humankind for the next ten years than cut along the wall-ceiling crease with a paintbrush.

His family had done some sleuthing on their own, had found that horrible review from that woman in Todd's first week, noticed that the background from that photo and what they'd seen in their video chats with him had matched, and were on their way.

Or maybe they were here. A car had just pulled up.

Pauline had been right about his father wanting to reconcile.

How could Todd have missed that? The efforts his father was making went far beyond anything he'd done in all of Todd's life.

Todd's heart beat fast as his negative memories began to surface, but he took a lesson from Claire and Pauline and offered his own positive energy when his family walked in. He had, after all, asked them for help.

Tim, who'd turn fifty soon, had inherited their father's hair-loss pattern, but with his Peregrines baseball cap on, you couldn't tell that half his head was bald at the back. "What? No hug?" Tim asked, his arms open. "Because of the hat? Or is it because I'm twice your size now and your arms won't reach around me?"

Todd laughed. "Neither. It's just that I'm covered in paint, and you're wearing designer jeans and a T-shirt."

"I'll just buy them again." Tim hugged Todd, though their embrace felt stiff.

Mark, now forty-seven, didn't look much thinner than Tim, but like Todd, he had most of his hair. "Nice to see you again," Mark said.

"I left the cutting for you." Their hug, too, felt more polite than warm.

But what was Todd expecting? They'd been pushing each other away again for months, and both sides...perhaps he needed to stop thinking of sides. They were a family. *Each member* had contributed his part to this moment.

"I was happy to get your call," Michael said, offering his hand.

Todd shook it. "I'm glad you were already on your way."

"You're reopening in two days?" Tim asked.

Todd couldn't tell if he'd heard judgment in his brother's voice or if he was reading decades of sibling rivalry into a simple question. He opted for the latter, only because he was trying for reconciliation.

He sighed. "Yeah. That's when the curtain goes up, and I'm going to get it done." And on cue, Todd's muscles spasmed. He pressed his hand into his back.

"You okay?" Tim asked.

"Yup."

"What's wrong?" Michael asked.

Todd pulled his knee to his chest. "I've been getting back spasms. And my usual knee pain. It'll work itself out. I need to find a physiotherapist here. And get back to barre exercises. I just haven't had time since my boss dislocated her knee on my first day."

Which was a lie. He was as much in denial about his situation as Pauline was about hers. Two peas in a pod, the pair of them.

Maybe it was time he pulled out his barre. But the moment that thought occurred to him, his gut wrenched. Pulling out his barre reminded him of company class he'd attended almost every morning for over twenty years.

"Okay, boys," Michael said, taking charge. "Enough chit-chat. There's a lot to do if opening day is two days away and we're returning to Toronto tomorrow morning again."

"You have no idea what my boss and her family and friends have done for me. I need to get this finished. Pauline, their daughter, is a ball of energy. She'll be a big help, too. She just stepped out."

Tim and Mark got to work, leaving Michael and Todd alone for a moment. Todd stared out the storefront window, wondering if Pauline was okay. Michael followed Todd's gaze, unable to make direct eye contact with his son.

"I should prop open the door to air out the paint smell," Todd said.

While Todd searched for something to place between the door and doorway, Michael began. "Your brothers showed me a lot of what people have been saying about you online. I can't believe they'd say those things about my son."

Well, you've said and done some pretty thoughtless things to me, too. Todd wanted to let all the hurt that had reappeared these past few weeks have its moment in the spotlight. Maybe now was that time, but then he remembered Pauline's advice: listen lots, say little. What would happen if he applied it to his relationship with his father? Todd would keep his thoughts to himself, at least for now.

Michael continued. "I'm seventy-five. I don't know when my time on this Earth is done: it could be tomorrow, it could be in ten years. I've been an idiot with all those shows I've missed, and now your career is over. I love my Peregrines, but never more than my sons. There was just a part of me that...I don't know...I was hoping all three of my sons would love my team, like my father and grandfather did with me. We'd be like a team together, and I'd pass down my business to all three of you."

Was that enough of a reason to forgive his father for treating him like an outcast all those years? As a father, shouldn't he have known that love was not a feeling one of his sons was receiving?

No. Todd needed to hear everything.

"You were too embarrassed to even stand in a photo with me if I had my costume and stage makeup on, Dad."

Michael's face turned bright red, and he stared at the floor. "I'm so sorry. I...I held old-fashioned ideas of..."

Todd waited. He wanted to hear all of it.

To his father's credit, Michael finished his confession. "I held old-fashioned ideas of what it was to be a man."

Todd's skin burned.

Michael added right away. "But that was long ago, Todd. I did change. In recent years, we never came because, well..."

Todd waited some more.

Michael sighed, regret clear on his face. "Ballet's boring. Which I know isn't much better. When you wouldn't tell us where you'd moved to or how long you'd be gone, I just realized that the last thing I wanted was to be lying on my deathbed regretting that I didn't take your passion...your *life*...seriously."

Michael was right: no one knew how much longer they would be on this planet. How much longer was Todd going to hold on to his anger? His father was making an effort to close the rift between them.

Michael now looked Todd in the eyes. "I'm sorry if our videos and phone calls with all this Peregrines stuff have been overbearing. It's unfortunately the only way I know how to reach out to you. I just want to say to you—in person—that I'm sorry."

Todd knew from all his years in the spotlight that many boys who loved ballet had fathers like this. That Michael had come around, even though it was too late to see Todd perform live, was something Todd was grateful for.

"That means a lot, Dad."

This time, they embraced.

Michael squeezed Todd's biceps. "Wow, you have kept in shape. Not like your brothers."

Todd smiled.

They both picked up rollers and got to work.

A gust of wind blew through the shop as the back door opened and slammed shut.

"Sorry about that," Pauline said as she entered. "Front door open?" She startled when she saw Todd's family. "Oh, hello."

"Pauline Robinson," Todd said, "meet my family: Tim, Mark, and my dad, Michael." Why did she suddenly look like a deer in headlights? "Family, meet Pauline Robinson. She's..." Was it okay to say? "We're dating. She knows everything about me. She's the community engagement manager for the Peregrines."

"Seriously?" Tim asked, his eyes wide.

"You're joking, right?" Mark said, regressing in age by about thirty years. "*You* are dating someone who works for the *Peregrines*?"

Here we go, Todd thought.

"Oh, perfect!" Michael said. "An insider! Do you have time for a coffee—or, um, I guess tea—tomorrow morning before we leave for Toronto? I need help with this Ben guy. Wow, is he a piece of work when it comes to money."

Todd's jaw clenched. After all his father's attempts at reconciling with him, he had withheld yet another secret.

"Dad..." Tim warned.

"What?"

"That's why you're still in Toronto?" Todd asked, trying to keep his tone friendly. "You're sponsoring the Peregrines? Sounds perfect for DIY Home. Are you also sponsoring a ballet company then? Or you're going to try one in Vancouver? Or the ballet school where I studied? You probably have a few dollars left over, right? I mean, if you can afford to sponsor the Peregrines now?"

Michael looked like he'd been caught with his hand in the cookie jar.

CHAPTER 29

*P*auline could've used a straight-up ginger tisane, the nausea in her stomach was so strong. What was Todd's family doing in the shop? And what argument had she walked in on?

"Um, tea tomorrow morning? Sure." She wasn't going to say no to the man who'd increased her budget by thirty-five percent.

"What do you need to discuss?" Todd asked.

"It's covered under an NDA," Michael said.

"Gotta love those NDAs. Convenient when you don't want to tell your outcast son everything."

Her heart ached for him. He must have felt so alone all those years if it was him against these three.

"You want to reconcile, Dad, and that's great, it really is. But it's really hard when you don't trust me."

"Whoa," Tim said. "You didn't trust us with your hiding-place secret either. You knew we were in Toronto. *One hour away.*"

"It's never been about keeping secrets from you. It's been

about helping you not lie to the press so your reputation remained intact. There's a huge difference."

"And it's the same with us," Tim countered.

"If that were the case," Todd said, "then where's the sponsorship for a ballet company? You've supported charities all these years. Lots of ballet companies are non-profits, so the tax benefits are there. Why not support them? No. You didn't tell me because you knew this announcement would make me mad, and you were right."

Tim opened his mouth, but Michael signalled to him to close it. It had become clear in the few minutes since Pauline had met the family—out of costume—that Michael was still very much in charge.

"Todd, ballet just doesn't fit the image of a do-it-yourself home improvement business."

Pauline's breath caught. How could a father say something like that to his son?

"Right, because far be it from me to fit the family image."

"That's not what I mean."

"But that's what you're saying." Todd blinked and looked away.

One thing Pauline could do as herself and not as Perry was speak, and Todd needed the support. No wonder he had "a Perry thing." The character symbolized exclusion from his family, not inclusion as Pauline had tried so ardently to build into the character these past three years.

She had to stand up for Todd. He would do the same for her in a heartbeat.

Or in a jumpy, switchy thing.

The sponsorship was already out in the open. She just had to make sure she didn't give out any further details, including her own role in all of it.

"Actually," she said, "ballet is the perfect image for a

company like DIY Home, just as any sport would be. Ballet is all about self-improvement and dedication." She looked at Todd. "Didn't you study ballet for over ten years?" Todd nodded. "No different than most major league athletes. And I'm sure you know how hard it is to perform at Todd's level. It needs the support of a family to get there, and DIY Home is all about family. Did you see the anti-bullying rally we did today at my old school?"

Michael shook his head. "We were in meetings all morning and then drove here."

Pauline plugged her phone into the television and played the YouTube video. The animosity in the shop disappeared as Todd's family watched Austin's dance. The eyes of the man behind her budget increase were moist. On the screen, Austin held her hand and leaned forward as one arm reached for the sky while his back leg curved up behind him. The expression of victory on his face was unmistakable.

What am I doing? This relationship with Todd could never work. Pauline knew how to find opportunities for people like Austin so they could be themselves again. She didn't find her purpose in finding "kids like that," as Ben had so callously put it. She simply knew how to create warm, welcoming, exciting spaces for hundreds, even thousands of people at once. Sometimes those spaces attracted people who were at a place in their lives where they needed help to move forward, like Austin did. Other times, people just wanted those spaces to celebrate, like they would at Saturday's reopening. To expel her own boundless energy, Pauline got fans amped up at games. She loved the attention, too.

She could have all of that.

Or she could sell tea to maybe two or three thousand people in a year.

Her mother was a rock in the community, but Pauline could

never be that rock. She was restless, more like water destined to overflow if it was dammed up for too long. Todd wasn't ready to enter the public eye again, and she wouldn't have time for frequent returns to Kitchener, especially with more money at her disposal and therefore an even busier schedule.

Michael pulled Pauline out of her thoughts. "Who arranged all of that?"

"I plan that presentation along with Derek, the host, and the actor who plays Perry. But the routine and the boy's speech? That was Austin's work with, of course, some of your son's choreography. When Austin heard we'd be doing this presentation, he asked me if he could participate." She looked back at Todd. "He wanted to tell his story."

Mark picked up a paintbrush and climbed a ladder to continue cutting along the ceiling, but slowly, as though he wanted to listen. Tim and Michael, however, gazed intently at Pauline, as though business decisions hinged on this conversation.

"So," Michael said, "did the bullying stop?"

"This was only this morning, so I honestly don't know. There were definitely some positive outcomes, but they're too private to share."

"Of course. I don't mean to pry. But all of that because of this routine?"

Pauline nodded.

"Incredible," Michael said.

Michael surprised Pauline. Aside from his puzzling exclusion of Todd's passion for ballet, he was remarkably respectful and polite.

"All I wanted to show you with that clip was how ballet and sports combined to help that family. It would absolutely fit DIY Home's image."

"I was backstage," Todd added, "and I think I can share that the embrace between Austin and his mom was one made for the movies. I've only known the family a few weeks, and when I first met Austin, he was so angry, and both his mom and grandmother told me that he barely spoke to anyone. He was even angry at me."

"You?" Tim asked. "You didn't know him."

"*I* didn't know him but Austin could rhyme off every ballet I've ever performed in and in what year. But he was angry at me for disappearing. He was looking to me to lift him up, and I wasn't there for him."

"Like I wasn't there for you," Michael said to Todd.

He took Pauline's hand in both of his. "Never in a million years did I expect to have an epiphany about family in a tea shop." He gave her hand a squeeze and let go. "Now, let's get back to work. I've also never in a million years left a job unfinished."

CHAPTER 30

*P*auline lay on Todd's couch, her head in his lap. It was Friday night. She and Michael had tag-teamed Ben—Pauline on a call mid-morning, and Michael and his sons that afternoon in a face-to-face meeting to address any final concerns with Sunday's fundraiser. Something had changed in Ben, but she still had a feeling he was *playing* nice.

Whatever. She was fully prepared for Sunday—Perry was clean, though it had involved a white lie to her parents about why he was in their washing machine and hanging in her bedroom after Thursday's rally—and she and Todd, along with a little help from Austin after his exam, had finished the shop renovations.

Todd stroked her hair. "What you did yesterday with my dad…I spent decades fighting with him about that, and you explained everything to him in, oh, I don't know, five minutes? And you didn't even serve tea."

Pauline smiled. "But I didn't get you a sponsorship for a ballet company."

"Still. At least he understands me better."

Pauline sat up. Seeing the conflict between Todd and his family play out before her had made clear she needed to discuss her work with Todd—without breaking her contract.

She held his hand in her lap. "But can you really be with someone who works for a symbol that reminds you of being an outcast in your family all those years?"

Todd kissed her hand. "After seeing that dance with Austin, whoever's in that costume, I have to say, has started to change my opinion."

That answer came too fast for her liking: Pauline found it hard to believe that he'd forgiven Perry so quickly after everything Todd had told her about his father, and after witnessing his hurt yesterday.

"This is important to us, Todd. It's just that I feel like everything I love causes you nothing but pain, and now that you know your dad's sponsoring my employer... It's just that I love my work, and if what I do really bothers you, I guess I need to know or..."

Or what? Had she really left that question dangling? *I guess I have*, she thought. But Michael's sponsorship would help her reach so many more kids. What happened yesterday with Austin was just the beginning. She loved Todd, but she didn't want to find out whenever she was allowed to tell him that he couldn't fathom the thought of dating the team mascot. She wasn't giving up her work for him.

What she needed to know was: did he support her dream? Only, she couldn't really tell him what her dream was.

Todd stood up from the couch and walked over to his kitchen. "I need a cup of tea. You?" He gestured to his basket of the tea samples he'd collected over his first few weeks at Claire's Tea Shop.

"Sure."

"What kind?"

But even Pauline didn't know what to recommend, because there was also the result of her doctor's appointment from that morning.

"If you look after your hip properly, including regular physiotherapy, I'm sure you have at least a year, maybe even two, before you need hip replacement surgery. But a specialist will need to make that call. Do you want to be referred to a rheumatologist in Toronto or Kitchener?"

He had said those words as if he were offering her dessert options at a restaurant. Pauline knew she was supposed to take comfort in having "at least a year," but that year was supposed to be the best year of her career.

"Pauline? What kind?"

"What? Sorry. I don't know."

Todd came back around the breakfast bar and cupped her face in his hands. "The appointment didn't go well today, did it? You haven't mentioned a thing about it."

Because it had ruined her day and threatened to ruin the rest of her career. But Pauline forced a smile and wrapped her arms around his waist. "It wasn't too bad. Diagnosis: I'm getting old." She kissed him quickly and stepped out of his embrace. She needed to change the subject. "I was so thankful your dad brought in the cleaning company he uses for the stores. That was really nice of him. It was so hard to keep Mom away today —she's not used to trusting her shop to someone else. But I want it to be absolutely perfect when she sees it for the first time tomorrow."

Todd filled his kettle with filtered water. "He felt guilty for the argument yesterday. So did I. But Claire's Tea Shop is ready to go. And thank you for relegating me to the back room for the day. Not only can I avoid any media, but I'm still having a hard time memorizing all these teas. Your mother's going to fire me after she sees how little I've learned."

Pauline studied the samples he had and glanced at Todd's notebook, which lay next to them.

"You've got these organized by name."

"So I can easily look them up in your mom's bible. But I can't look after a lineup of customers this way."

Pauline agreed with him.

"Plus," he continued, "how can I look up someone's emotion, problem, or celebration? It's like looking up a word in a dictionary based on its meaning."

Pauline sighed. "I guess Mom's drunk so much tea in her life, she knows how it feels in her mouth and body. Then, when she hears her customers' stories..." It clicked. "Todd, your stories! Do any of these connect with all those stories you love?"

Todd froze for a full minute, and then the most magical thing happened. His eyes darted to a tea, he stopped, then his body made small movements as though in a private dance. He mumbled something like, "Yes, that's it," and wrote it down. Over and over again, in fast succession. Some movements were quick and choppy, others slow and fluid, his face making a vast array of expressions to match. Pauline sensed that different characters from different ballets were travelling through Todd's body as though taking momentary possession of him.

She slowly backed away, leaving him to his discovery. She perused his bookshelf of ballet programs and books when her eyes travelled down to the box of memorabilia still left open on the floor. However, the newspapers had been cleared out, leaving only a stack of magazines inside. The magazine lying on top drew her hand in right away and she picked it up.

The cover title read, "Todd Parsons: 15 Years of Stardom."

She peeked over her shoulder. He was immersed in inspiration. She didn't want to disturb him. She opened up to the main article, hoping to enjoy an exposé on the kindest and most talented man she'd ever met, but instead was greeted by page after page filled with photos of Todd and his partners.

Todd lifted them over his head in the most beautiful positions; he supported them as they leaned on him, their long, thin legs extended in the air; he held them while they stood on their tiptoes, their smiling faces bright and cheerful.

All of them small, elegant, graceful, fairy-like dancers.

And behind, beside, and under each woman was a man who did indeed support them, one deeply in love with his art form, who'd been cruelly ousted from his professional world.

Pauline still had her career, still had at least a year left. *Maybe two, if I really take care of myself*, she thought. There would never be a magazine with her face on it, announcing her thirty years of work. But that wasn't why she did what she did. She performed to make others happy, and as a mascot she could make thousands happy in one performance instead of maybe a few dozen in a day selling tea.

No one would be jumping over the counter to give her a tight embrace of gratitude.

"Have you decided yet?" Todd asked, a huge grin on his face. "I could offer you something that would make you feel like Cinderella at the ball, or the Cheshire Cat in a tree, or—dare I say it—Gilgamesh and Enkidu about to slay Humbaba?" He didn't stop to let her answer, he was so excited by the ideas this new system had sparked. "I'm afraid I don't have Belmont Blizzard. It fits into the magical scene where the nutcracker becomes the Nutcracker Prince, so it's about transformation, including falling in love." Then he frowned. "But if I drink your tea, am I falling in love with myself, since I've danced that role so often? Okay, now I've thoroughly confused myself."

Pauline laughed and held up the magazine at a two-page spread. "Or how about a role in here?"

~

SEEING old pictures of himself surprised him, though he didn't know if it was a good surprise or a bad one. It was one thing to talk about his former life with Austin—that boy had nothing but pure light in his eyes for Todd. To see the younger generation excited in ballet ignited Todd's desire to pass on his knowledge.

But with someone as attractive, trustworthy, intelligent, strong, and compassionate as Pauline, everything about his former life wanted to be heard. He could be completely open with her, which, for reasons he didn't fully understand, made it hard to just remember the good times.

"Todd?" Pauline lowered the magazine. "Sorry. I didn't think again. You probably still miss this."

Of course he missed it. Morning class with the company. Rehearsal in the afternoon. A show at night. Travelling the world. It was why he couldn't bring himself to assemble his barre to do his exercises and reduce those increasingly painful back spasms. They hurt less than the realization of what he'd lost.

"Do I miss being myself every day of my life? Yeah, I do."

She stared at the magazine. "You won't visit me in Toronto, will you?"

A knot turned in his stomach. This discussion was inevitable, but he'd hoped they could delay it until she had to leave for the tour. Something about flying away on a plane made the end of this beautiful relationship final.

But the question also meant she wanted a future with him. This was no longer just love but love plus a future. She wanted to know if he was committed to her. He was! He so was! Just not publicly.

"I guess that means you're not taking over your mom's tea shop?"

She shook her head. "I will be in Kitchener more often, but I don't know if it'll be often enough to make us work. If you're not able to find a way to feel comfortable in Toronto..."

She didn't finish the sentence, but he predicted its ending.

There was no way she worked in community relations when she had a hard time saying the right thing, worked extreme hours that prevented her from visiting family, had a strict non-disclosure agreement...it was all adding up to the truth that she worked as Perry.

But where did her weakening body fit into this? And if this was a career she loved with all her heart, and she was considering a long-term relationship with him, why was she still withholding her true career? Hadn't he shown her enough trust? Or was she so terrified of this Ben that she couldn't fully open up to Todd?

"It's the kind of job you just don't cut back your hours on," she added. "Especially when you know you're making a difference for thousands of people."

She *was* Perry. Was this her way of telling him without telling him? Based on the photos and articles Todd had seen of the character, he knew the mascot visited all over Toronto, including the children's hospital. That work had to take an emotional toll on the actor.

"I need someone who supports my work, Todd, because it is my life."

But if they were going to have a relationship, hints were no longer enough for Todd.

"How can I do that when you won't be honest with me about what it is?"

"I work in community engagement. That's all I can say. You know that."

Her voice was so cold, as though the last three weeks hadn't happened. Pauline wasn't going to tell Todd her job because work came first.

Todd knew how that story would end.

~

PAULINE AND TODD showed up at nine on the dot the following morning.

"Morning," Pauline said to Todd.

"Morning," Todd said to Pauline.

Good, she thought. *We'll be like the professionals we are. The show must go on.*

They were back in their professional clothes: Todd in his slacks and button-down shirt with sleeves rolled up to below the elbow, and Pauline in her dress pants and sleeveless blouse.

Pauline unlocked the back door, and they entered. Tracy would join them in an hour, Austin mid-afternoon during a study break. Richard would be bringing Claire by any moment, so Todd turned on all the lights while Pauline called her sister on Skype.

Dawn looked chipper in her sports bra and ponytail.

"You're already awake?" Pauline asked.

"Getting ready for my morning run. Can't wait to see what you've done with the place!"

The front bells jingled and Pauline held up the phone so Dawn could see as Richard and Claire walked in. Richard waved to their younger daughter, but Claire was immediately in awe with the new interior.

She clapped her hands together in front of her heart. "Oh, my goodness! This rich straw colour is sunny! The perfect colour for a daytime café! I love the pastels of traditional tea rooms, but this is Belmont Village. People have places to go, things to do, and yet they also need a place to rejuvenate. This colour is perfect. The dark brown metal of the chairs with the rich brown wood of the floor anchors the furniture." She ran her hand along the new light blue upholstery. "This feels wonderful."

Claire walked behind the counter and inspected every nook and cranny. "Oh my, oh my, oh my. You've really outdone your-selves with the cleaning."

Pauline smiled and explained she had now contracted the same cleaning company as the local DIY Home stores, and that the first cleaning was a gift from Todd's family.

"Then all you and Todd have to do is vacuum and do the dishes at the end of each day. And check this out." She handed the phone to Todd and instructed him to keep it pointed at Claire while she dashed—without jumping over the counter—to the back room and returned with a duster on a telescopic arm. "You can still do your weekly thank-you ritual with your photos, but without getting on the chair."

Claire immediately tried it out, leaning on her cane with one hand and dusting the photos with the other, a grin on her face.

"If we weren't opening in an hour, I'd say this calls for another serving of Canadian tea!"

If Claire was willing to serve them the most expensive tea she had, Pauline knew they'd done an amazing job. She and Todd smiled at each other.

"Hey, wait a minute!" Dawn said on the phone. "I see Dad and Mom, and Pauline told someone else to hold the phone. Who's there? Mom said Todd. Is Todd holding the phone? I haven't met him yet. Turn the phone around."

Pauline laughed. For the 'quiet sister,' Dawn could certainly be demanding when she wanted something. But that only happened when she felt comfortable, which she appeared to be with Todd in the room, even though she'd never met him...

Todd turned the phone around, and the easygoing, talkative

man she'd come to know was replaced by the shy one she'd met on her first day.

Pauline didn't want to answer any questions about her and Todd. She pointed out the drafting chair she'd purchased that would allow her mom to sit at standing height behind the counter.

Claire touched her hand to her heart. "You've truly thought of everything, Pauline."

"Well, not without your input. This is, after all, *Claire's* Tea Shop."

Claire opened her free arm wide and pulled her daughter into an embrace. "What you have given me in these three weeks, I will never forget."

Dawn joined in. "Wish I were there with you guys."

Pauline and Claire looked up. Richard was standing next to Todd, smiling at the women in his family, and Todd held the phone so Dawn could see her sister and mother hug. Todd offered to take a family photo with Richard's phone. After good-byes, everyone got down to business.

A half-hour later, rapid knocking at the door caught every-one's attention. A smiling Tracy with a beaming Austin performing jumpy, switchy things beside her was outside.

Pauline let them in. Tracy opened her mouth to speak, but Austin wouldn't let her utter a word. He wrapped his arms around Pauline just as tightly as he had onstage.

"They got expelled, the bullies! They got expelled!"

CHAPTER 31

*P*auline dropped onto the couch in the lounge area, absolutely exhausted. The nice thing about rental costumes was that the company cleaned them. She wrinkled her nose: certainly a job she would not want after retirement.

Sales had been through the roof—Todd would have to order fresh stock on Monday. And Austin had shared even more good news with Pauline and Todd: he'd try medication again after exams—he just didn't want to risk dealing with side effects during such a crucial period in his schooling.

"Ready to vacuum and mop?" Todd called out from the back room.

It was about eight o'clock. Most of the shop was clean, thanks to everyone's help, but this was the longest Claire had stayed out of the home since her accident, and Austin still had two exams, so he needed his sleep.

Todd had remained in the back room most of the day and Pauline had been in costume, so they hadn't interacted much with one another.

You just have to finish cleaning up. Then you can head home and you won't see him until Monday, she thought. They needed the break from each other.

"I guess we should get this over with, eh?"

Pauline lifted the couch cushion. Yup, crumbs.

Todd emerged from the back room, looking withdrawn and quiet, like the first day they'd met. He set the vacuum cleaner down by the lounge area.

"I also put a tin of Belmont Blizzard and some disposable tea bags in your bag." He shrugged. "I know you'll be rushed when you get back to your condo tomorrow. One less thing for you to worry about."

Pauline swallowed. Her heart raced.

Todd stared at the floor. "I...I don't know where we are anymore, Pauline, but that doesn't change the way I feel about you. I still love you, and if I said anything last night to hurt you, I'm sorry."

Why was life forcing her to choose between a man she had grown to love and a career she had loved most of her life?

"I got to see you perform again today but on a different stage, so to speak. It was so much fun." He smiled. "The kids really loved you."

"I love what I do." She continued toward the back room and paused as she passed him. "I can't talk about what I do because I was stupid enough to sign a contract that forbids it. I'm so sorry, Todd."

She loved him, but this wasn't going to work. They had each found the right person but at the wrong time in their lives.

Todd reached for her hand, but before he could grasp it, she continued on her way and returned with the hand vac.

"Shall we keep going?"

An hour later, she collapsed again on the couch. She didn't know how much energy she had left in her. They still needed to mop the floors and move the tables and chairs back, plus she hadn't packed her overnight bag yet. She should've done that last night, because she was taking a morning bus to give herself time for some emotional prep work before her day began, something she couldn't do at home. Just thinking about the children she'd meet weighed on her heart.

Todd joined her.

"May I?" he asked, lifting his arm over her.

She nodded, her heart winning in this moment: she wanted to enjoy what might be their last time together. She nuzzled into him as his arm wrapped around her shoulders.

"It's still hard for me to think about what I loved so much, because then I have to remember how it was snatched away from me and that I can never have it again," he said.

He lived the future she feared. Returning to the Peregrines was the right decision for her.

"But coming to Toronto?" she asked, hoping.

"You really can't get enough time off to come here, can you?"

"I need three days in a row off to make that work. It won't happen often enough with the win."

It would be so nice to have a real shoulder to cry on tomorrow as she let out the sadness and happiness—some children were terminally ill, but she almost always celebrated with at least one child who was being released from hospital with a clean bill of health.

She sniffled and Todd sat up to look at her.

"You okay?"

Pauline wiped away her tears. "It was always really hard to see kids fighting for their lives in a hospital when the only thing they should be fighting for is the TV remote at home."

Todd sighed. "That must be tough. Visiting fans in the hospital isn't something I've really ever done."

The anticipation of tomorrow, coupled with her exhaustion,

brought more tears. "You have to exude all this energy—you're still a character, not a human, as far as everyone around you is concerned. But you have to get the energy from somewhere. You can't collect it from thousands of fans, but you need it to fight the sadness that can overcome you if you're not careful. You're there, because everyone's expecting you—the character, not the human being underneath—to relieve them of that sadness for a time. But then you find this...I don't know how to describe it. There's this...this other energy you're sharing in the room with everyone. It's a different energy..." She drew big circles with her hands. "I really can't describe it."

Todd jumped up from the couch as he scrolled through his phone and walked over to the tea shop's sound system. He plugged it in, and a beautiful song played over the speakers.

"This is 'Four Dimensions' by Luduvico Einaudi. I feel like it has a little bit of all emotions. This is what I love about dance. It lets me express myself without finding words."

"This is your cup of tea."

A corner of Todd's mouth curled up. "Exactly."

He held out his hand, inviting her to join him.

Pauline shook her head. "Aside from the fact that I'm completely wiped, I can only dance in costume." *And my hundred and sixty pounds would break your back if you tried to lift me*, she thought. "Besides, I can't do ballet."

Todd took her hand and pulled her off the couch, leading her to the middle of the floor. "No one's watching, this isn't a performance, and I'm not talking about Patrick Swayze Jumps or jumpy, switchy things."

Pauline's terminology sounded cute coming from Todd's lips.

"Ballet is more than tricks. It's above all emotion and move-ment, which isn't much different from your work, if I'm not mistaken. Just let the music and your feelings reflect one another, and let my body support you as yours will support mine, even though we're more drained than a pair of flat tires. Follow along as though you were in costume and improvising. Just be yourself. Be the woman I've fallen in love with."

Before Pauline could object, Todd raised their grasped hands to shoulder height. He released his fingers, so she followed, and he pressed his hand against hers. She followed again.

The pressure between their hands moved outwards and down. At first, Pauline simply copied Todd, turning her back when he turned his, leaning her head back onto his shoulder when he did so with his head to her shoulder. But once their cheeks touched and she closed her eyes, something changed: the energy she imagined feeling in a room of people now surged through them, the music leading it. She found herself stepping away from Todd as they each dropped into a deep lunge, held together only by their hands, feeling alone and barely able to hold on but by a metaphorical thread, a feeling she experienced sometimes when visiting terminally ill children. She couldn't talk about it to anyone outside her line of work because it upset them too much. The closest she could get was others in her profession, usually big, strong, young men who turned to puddles at the mere mention of sick children and changed the topic.

Pauline and Todd pulled themselves together as the music got louder. She lowered herself halfway to the ground as the invisible sadness of a hospital cancer ward pulled her down. She flattened her back like a tray, as though she were preparing herself to carry as much sadness as she could, and pressed her elbows into her thighs for support as she felt Todd roll over her. This all happened through instinct. Nothing hurt.

When he landed on her other side, he hooked his arm into hers, and she twisted around to him.

Like someone coming to help me, she thought.

Holding on tightly to her forearm, Todd kicked both legs into the air in an arc behind himself, his chest staying in line with her shoulders. When he landed, she spun under his arm and they finished back-to-back again.

Her years of working in her mother's tea shop had taught Pauline how tea could help her when she was alone and couldn't reach anyone. But these past three years in Toronto had begun pulling her away from those she loved. She'd been able to hold out on her own, perhaps lean on Derek and her colleagues a little, but it wasn't enough. She needed her family and Tracy back in her life. And she wanted a man she could make love to, who she could share her triumphs and embarrassments with when she got home each day, who she could be herself around all the time.

Todd was that man.

He stretched his arm out and she followed, but this time, she tugged him in. Amused, Todd twirled into her like she had into him that night in Uptown Waterloo.

Pauline realized this dance was like the afternoon when Todd bared everything to her about his reason for being here.

Only it was now about her.

HIS BACK TO HER, Todd stepped his right foot to the side into second position, bending forward and pulling Pauline on top of him.

"Lift your legs," he whispered in her ear. Pauline needed to know what it was like to fully trust someone, to let him support her for once. Whatever she was going through, she was carrying the weight of the world on her shoulders.

She reached her arms around his chest, and her weight transferred to his hips as she lifted her legs. Her head was next to his, her hips over his. She felt heavier than he would have expected for a woman of her size. True, he'd danced exclusively with women who were considerably smaller and lighter than her —such was his world of professional ballet—but this wasn't about physics. He was feeling more than a number on a scale: Pauline carried a heavy emotional burden in her, he was certain of it. He breathed in deeply and let out his breath, hoping she would mimic him. She did, relaxing even more into him.

"Now let go," he whispered. The gift of trust she had given him that afternoon when he had shared his story was something he'd always be thankful for, no matter what happened between them. He wanted to give her that gift now.

"I can't."

He reached behind her back. "I have you. You can trust me."

It took Pauline a few tries, but she eventually released his torso from her tight grip. Once he sensed her balance centre, he let go, too, and gently swayed back and forth to the music.

WHAT PAULINE WOULDN'T GIVE to have Todd by her side in Toronto. Yes, he would comfort her at the end of her difficult days, but Pauline would happily listen to anything he wanted to share with her, too. And they would laugh so much together! But so long as her calling was in Toronto, and his healing was in Kitchener, this wouldn't work. What good was Pauline in Kitchener? She could only accomplish what she'd done for Austin with the platform she had through the Peregrines.

Todd slowly rose, and Pauline slid off his back. No crashing at all. Staying behind him, she grasped each of his hands in hers. The music sounded like the waves of the ocean. Staying pressed against his body, she lunged to the side, and he followed her movement. He turned to face her, and their eyes met as they came to standing, their knotted hands pressed between them, Todd's heart beating as fast as hers.

Pauline had never opened herself to anyone like this before. She had barely said a word this entire time, and yet she felt like she'd shared her entire life with him.

Todd cupped her face in his hands. "You can't let go because you feel like all the attention's on you. Is that it? Like everyone's relying on you to always be there for them. You'll be in costume tomorrow, won't you?"

His expression was one of hope, not anger. He simply hoped Pauline would finally be honest with him.

"I…" Her emotions were so raw, she couldn't close them off and lie to him. Pauline loved Todd Parsons with her soul.

Tears welled up in her eyes as she remembered many of the children she'd met over the years. Todd gently wiped them away as they fell down her cheeks.

"You've helped so many people, Pauline. I imagine you stopped counting how many eons ago."

The memories—happy and sad—now made their rounds in her head, and the tears streamed down her face, refusing to stop. Todd gathered her in his arms, and she nuzzled her face into his neck. He stroked her hair, and finally, she could let out everything she had been holding onto since she'd moved to Toronto.

Todd whispered in her ear. "You can tell me whatever you need to, whenever you want to. I'm here for you, Pauline. I always will be."

The only wall standing between them was this one truth, the one that would break her contract. She could return after the fundraiser and take over Claire's Tea Shop, never finishing the best—and probably last—year of her career that awaited her.

But that would force Ben to hire the next person who

showed up with the biggest and best stunts for more publicity. Who would find more "kids like that." To Ben, kids like Austin were money-makers, not people who wanted to fight to be heard.

She wouldn't be able to help kids the way they needed to be helped: by someone with an open heart who would help them speak up on their terms when they were ready.

Pauline had to finish her last year and ensure that the next actor was the right person. Lying to Ben wasn't an option: she couldn't keep her love for Todd a secret, and her million-dollar NDA was going to come crashing down on her.

She let go of Todd. "I've told you, I'm not Perry." She stepped back. "I don't do that anymore. I wish people would stop asking me that." Her energy had come back, but it wasn't the energy she wanted—bliss, joy—it was the energy she needed—panic, the need to escape. She wiped her face dry on the back of her hands. "I have to go. I'm really tired. I have to leave. Too much to do tomorrow."

"Pauline…"

"Meeting with Ben Monday. Maybe community event Tuesday. Have to check the team calendar." Now she was making things up, but she didn't care. "Don't know when I'll be back."

She rushed to the back room, grabbed her things, and ran out the back door before Todd could catch up with her.

Even as the pain seared through her hip, as though her body was screaming she was making the wrong choice, she ran. Down the alley, turning right, heading to her parents' home. She had to pack her bags, she had to pack everything.

Because she wasn't coming back.

CHAPTER 32

"*I*'m at least driving you to the station," Tracy said from Pauline's speakerphone. "You're not taking a taxi."

"Fine, but please order that ticket in case I can catch the next one. When is it?" Pauline shoved clothes into her tiny suitcase.

"In two hours. You just missed the last one."

"Fine. Book it. Please." It was hard to remain polite when trying to process your crumbling world at the same time.

"Pauline, talk to me. What's going on?"

Pauline stubbed her toe on the corner of her bed and silently cursed.

"What's all this panic for?"

She certainly wasn't going to tell Tracy the real reason. "The doctor thinks I've got arthritis in my hip and will eventually need it replaced. I probably have a year, maybe two, but he's not sure. And that's with meds and regular physio. And if Ben even allows me to keep performing."

She shoved papers from her desk into her laptop bag.

"You're not going to tell Ben, are you?"

"I've told him it hurts a lot. That's all he needs to know."

"Pauline, this is nuts. You could seriously injure yourself."

"I'm not the only mascot performer to ever face something like this."

"No, you're not. But don't they all take a break? If I recall, didn't Toronto's basketball team mascot bring in someone—his 'cousin' or something—while the usual one took some time off?"

"They hadn't won their league cup yet. Do you have my ticket?"

"It's more than your hip, isn't it? You wouldn't be leaving in a panic like this because of your hip."

Pauline just wanted to leave. "My ticket."

"I'll print out your ticket and bring it with you when I pick you up. I can tell you're in no mood for talking right now, but you're telling me everything in the car or I'll hit the brakes. I'll pick you up in an hour. We can grab something to drink at the station."

"That sounds nice. I'll see you soon."

They hung up.

Pauline surveyed her bedroom. The only thing left to pack was Perry. She picked up his head. The motivational, "Go, get'em!" expression moulded into his face made her smile.

"I knew you'd be trouble, but I had no idea just how much."

She loved him in a way. She really did.

Standing in front of the full-length mirror hanging on her closet, she slipped on Perry's grey fleece leggings with the Pere-grines' red hockey shorts attached. His red hockey boots had silver platforms underneath that were meant to give the impres-sion of skate blades. The boots were made of a soft foam and fit snugly around her own shoes, so she could easily walk in Perry's feet for hours if she wanted. If real hockey skates were on the agenda, Pauline used other boots that functioned more like spats so she could skate. A third pair of boots didn't have the silver platforms and were used for days—like the parade—when she expected to do acrobatics.

She zipped up the back of Perry's boots, pulled his outer body and hockey jersey over her head and zipped that up, too. From her sleeves hung Perry's wings, and on her back, his falcon tail. Because Perry always appeared with the Peregrines jersey on, the torso and upper arms of his outer body were made of a mesh fabric instead of fleece. This made it slightly cooler and lighter.

She set Perry's head over her own and tucked her hand up behind her head to adjust the ratchet system inside the helmet so it was snug. She fastened the chin strap. Last, she pulled on the three-fingered gloves.

Feeling as though she was wrapped in a warm blanket, her heart rate slowed down. Pauline had rappelled from stadium ceilings in costumes like this, used T-shirt canons to shoot T-shirts high into spectators' seats, collected teddy bears tossed onto the ice during charity events, let herself be pummelled by the opposing team's mascot, played hockey with kids' community teams, enjoyed all-star mascot games...

How could she have courage to do all those stunts and engage with strangers but not find it to stay in a relationship with Todd?

Because that was what this was really about, wasn't it?

She remembered Todd's embrace right before he whispered he was falling in love with her. These costumes had never allowed her to connect with someone on such an intimate level.

Then there was Claire's embrace after she'd seen the renovations to her tea shop. Another level of intimacy—from mother to daughter—that Pauline hadn't experienced in a long time, and that she wouldn't have had with the costume on.

But what about Austin? He'd feared sharing his humiliation

so much that he couldn't talk to a human whose eyes he could see. He knew Pauline was in the costume, so it had very little to do with who he was talking to.

It wasn't just Perry. During her years working in Florida, parents hugged her almost as much as their kids did. The notes of appreciation she had from some families told her she had a talent and she was using it the right way.

She was going to Toronto tonight and not returning, at least not to help with the store. She'd tell her mom after she'd packed away Perry. Todd had figured out a system for recommending teas now, and because of the renovation, he knew every detail of the store. Pauline would continue to manage the store's social media accounts for now, so she wasn't leaving her mother completely in the lurch.

But she was finishing her year with the Peregrines. What-ever came afterwards would depend on her prognosis. This was the life she was meant to live. Her mother would want Pauline to reach her dream and see it through. Claire's Tea Shop, Pauline's Mascots. She just needed five minutes to pack up Perry, and then she'd talk to them.

Someone knocked at the door.

Pauline's heartbeat raced as she scrambled to pull off her gloves. Not accustomed to changing quickly, she couldn't grasp Perry's fingers fast enough.

"Pauline?"

"Just a sec."

One glove off. She reached for the chin strap, hoping to undo it with one hand.

"Pauline? Are you okay?"

Maybe she hadn't spoken loudly enough under the mask? But it was too late. Her parents opened the door just as Pauline undid the chin strap.

She lifted Perry's head off and immediately diverted her

gaze to the floor. What she had seen on their faces already sent her stomach to her throat.

"Why the lies?" Richard asked. That he'd found his voice before Claire had found hers cut Pauline's heart even more.

Unable to speak, she removed her other glove, pulled a printout of her contract from her laptop bag and pointed to the relevant clause. Richard took the contract in his hands. She opened her phone to show them the budget and salary increases and passed that to her mom.

Pauline stepped out of Perry and packed him away while her parents absorbed everything. Finally standing as herself, she found an ounce of strength to speak, though her voice was weak. "I could reach my dream and help more people if I stayed quiet."

Claire's voice was stern. "And not lose a million dollars. What a horrible, selfish man to silence a woman. Does he not know what it means to have a family? How could he manipulate you like this?"

Pauline shrugged. "I wanted the job so badly...I didn't know it would come to this."

"He took what was most important to you—your love for others—and turned it into your price, all because the performer before you couldn't hold his liquor."

The story with Nate was more complicated than that, but Pauline didn't have the strength to explain everything to her parents.

Richard looked around her room. "You're packing everything? You're not coming back, are you?"

"Todd doesn't need me anymore. He has a way to learn Mom's system of teas, and I can manage the shop's social media accounts from Toronto." She wiped tears from her face. This was it.

Richard passed Pauline tissues from her desk. "We wouldn't

have told anyone. Your mother's the furthest thing from the town gossip, and you don't know a single celebrity I've sold a house to, and trust me, there've been many."

Pauline dried her face. "After I told Tracy, and then Austin found out, I was already on pins and needles—"

Claire interrupted, her voice a whisper. "You told a friend you've barely been in contact with for years over your parents, who've supported your dreams all this time?"

Pauline couldn't remember ever seeing her mother so hurt. She had told Tracy first because she wanted to avoid this very moment, but she realized now this moment was inevitable.

Claire continued, her voice still low. "Your father and I have done everything to support your career, and when you hit your pinnacle, you lie to us and tell someone else instead." She tossed Pauline's phone onto her bed. "Understanding tea is more than just memorizing my system. It's about knowing who you are, understanding what tea means to you, and helping others understand what it could mean to them." She straightened herself up on her cane. "I hope Todd's up to the task, as you say he is, because clearly my own daughter never was."

Pauline stared at the floor. "He is, Mom. He's found his voice."

"And where's yours? The one that included your family in your life? You can save yourself any guilt you might be feeling about not wanting to run the store, because I don't want you running it." Claire hobbled out of the room. "You need to know who you are, Pauline."

"Claire," Richard called out to her. He tugged at his collar. "I'll go talk to her."

He called after her as he followed her. Pauline appreciated her father's help, but she didn't want to come between them either.

Pauline had always felt like the odd one out: her parents and

Dawn were always polite and refined and led professional lives. Whenever Pauline told people what she did for a living, she'd get looks and questions that, even if they were intended to be polite, were rude.

Todd fit right in at the tea shop. He was refined and professional, and now that he had a way of categorizing Claire's teas, he was set to go. She didn't fit with him any more than she fit with her own family. At least with the Peregrines, where everyone knew what she did, she could be herself. She didn't have to dress in professional clothes or refrain from jumping over furniture, or lie about her job.

She lifted Perry's head out of the bag.

"I see courage in you. Through you, I know who I am." She held his head beside hers and looked at both of them in the mirror. "But who am I without you?"

She packed him away, unsure of the answer.

CHAPTER 33

"*Y*ou're supposed to be my idol, not an idiot!"

Todd groaned. It was mid-morning on Sunday. After Pauline's escape, he'd spent an hour dancing in anger with a mop in a broken-heart-inspired rendition of a Gene Kelly routine. Why had he asked Pauline to go against her contract?

Incidentally, Gene Kelly also danced ballet. And actually infused hockey he'd learned from his Canadian father into his dance style, now that Todd thought about it.

But he probably hadn't spent mornings on a couch of ice packs under the glare of a teenager who was being honest with him about his love life.

The teen's mother was staring down at him, too. "Austin! That's no way to speak to anyone."

At least she was on Todd's side.

"But seriously, Mom, how can he not see how perfect they are for each other? They're both performing artists—"

"She *is* a performing artist." Todd groaned as he adjusted an ice pack. "I *was* one. Can someone get me some ointment from the bathroom counter?"

When Austin returned, Todd rubbed some of the ointment onto his lower back.

"So, what happened?" Tracy asked.

"I must have said something to scare her off when I was telling her I missed my old life."

Tracy shook her head. "Something's not adding up. She's miserable, Todd. And so are you. Has she told you about the suspected arthritis in her hip?"

He closed the ointment and cleaned his hands on a tissue. "No, but I figured it out. She's hardly told me anything. It's like she doesn't trust me."

Tracy sat down in an armchair. "She wouldn't tell me anything when I took her to the bus station either. I threatened to pull over until she talked, and *she* threatened to walk. It's Kitchener: she would've been there in thirty minutes on foot. In the interests of saving her hip, I kept driving."

Austin had found Todd's theatre programs. "Are these all the ballets you were in?"

Todd smiled. "Yes, but I'm keeping those."

"Can I put them in chronological order?"

"Go for it," Todd said.

Evidently, adult relationship talk was no longer on Austin's radar. Good thing.

Tracy snapped her fingers. "Chronology. Time. The doctor thinks she has one, at most two years left before hip replacement surgery. She's trying to finish this year."

"What I wouldn't have given to have that chance. But then why didn't she tell...?" Todd clapped his hand over his eyes.

"What?" Tracy asked.

He sighed as he lowered himself to the floor and split his

legs open into straddle to stretch. He reached over his head to his left leg. "Did she tell you what happened when I got tea drunk?"

Tracy laughed but stopped after noticing he wasn't laughing with her. She shook her head, and he filled her in.

"I was just so angry with my dad and brothers at the time," he finished, "but also feeling so giddy from that pu-erh, and in love with this amazing woman, I lost the ability to control what I was saying. I mean, I knew what I was saying, and I at least knew she worked for the team... Anyway, I can only imagine what she felt."

Tracy crossed her arms. "Maybe that's why she wasn't inclined to risk breaking her contract. You were insulting the job she's loved the most in her entire career."

Todd switched sides in his stretch, grabbing his right foot. "With the Peregrines' win and my family nearby...I guess all my issues with the team kind of put up a wall there."

"Plus you're still in hiding. How was she going to have a relationship with you if her job's in Toronto?"

"I was hoping she'd find a way to work less and come here more often."

"Do you know everything Perry does?"

Todd nodded. "I'm related to his biggest adult fans."

They hadn't noticed that Austin had disappeared from the living room until he'd cried out in excitement from Todd's bedroom.

"Oh! My! God! Is this your—" A few seconds later, Austin started his question over. He seemed to be forgetting what he was saying less often. Todd took this as a good sign. "Is this your Nutcracker Prince costume?! The one you wore every Christmas with your last company?"

"Austin! What are you doing in Todd's bedroom!" Tracy's face turned red. "I'm so sorry!"

"It's all right," Todd said, chuckling. "Glad someone's appreciating it."

Austin came running out with the costume on a hanger. "Is this it? Like, *the one*?" He stared again. Emotional excitement clearly triggered seizures.

To hear someone call it "the one" was cute. "Yes, it is."

It was also the costume he'd surprised Pauline with. Although some embarrassment accompanied those memories, so did her laughter when he'd greeted her at the door in mask and costume: she accepted him as he was.

"Mom, can Todd dance this evening with me?"

Todd raised an eyebrow. "What do you mean?"

Tracy parked her hands on her hips. "Austin, *I* was supposed to bring that up."

Austin's voice became small. "Sorry."

"What's going on?" Todd asked.

Tracy sat back down in the armchair and leaned forward, appearing to bide her time as she thought about what to say. "After seeing the wreck Pauline was last night, I assumed...you would be in the same state, too. Austin's right, Todd. You two love each other."

Of course he still loved Pauline, but if she didn't want him, what could he do about it?

"Anyway, Pauline asked me..." She sighed. "Your father was so moved by Austin's performance with Perry that he's asked Austin to do it again at the fundraiser this evening. Pauline asked me to tell you."

"My dad couldn't tell me?" Were Todd and his father back at square one?

"According to Pauline, he didn't know how you'd feel about it—he was worried you were still angry with him, and he wanted to give you some space. He wanted to give Austin a chance to dance in front of an important crowd and help raise some money. Plus, your father wanted to show you that ballet's important to him."

Todd brought his legs together and lowered himself to the floor. He pulled one knee to his chest. "He could've told me himself, but I appreciate his efforts."

"Why is your barre still in its box?" Austin asked.

What was it with this family today and their knack at uncovering every buried truth in Todd's life? But he might as well open up about this, too.

"I guess because returning to a regular ballet routine would remind me of what I've lost."

Disappointment replaced Austin's excitement. "Wait a minute. You're the one telling me about dealing with the new choreography in my life and you can't deal with yours?" The look he shot Todd stung. Why did this teenager have to be so observant and...so right?

Austin removed the lid from the box.

"Austin!" Tracy said. "Put that lid back on and apologize. That doesn't belong to you."

Todd stood up, one hand pressing on his back. "He's right, and actually, I'll help him. It's because I've been avoiding this that my back's in the shape it's in. If I'd kept up a daily ballet routine, I wouldn't have had to spend my morning on the couch."

"Does that mean I get to have a private ballet class with you?" Austin's eyes grew brighter. "And will you join me onstage tonight?"

"I'm not sure I'm ready to appear in public yet, but I'm happy to do a private class with you."

Austin ran his hand along the barre. "Oh. I guess that's okay."

Tracy pulled her son aside, but Todd's apartment was small enough that he could hear their conversation.

"Austin, it's amazing that you have courage to dance in front of an audience again but think of how long that's taken you. You need to have some understanding."

Todd remembered watching videos of Pauline's failed stunts. Of course, no one knew who was under the costume, but she knew. She also had courage every time she visited hospitals to hang out with kids, no matter their health. She attended all manner of events, not knowing who she'd meet. Not to mention the abuse she took from rambunctious fans. The woman he was in love with had the courage of a lion.

"Do you think Pauline will want to see me tonight?" He couldn't help but smile at Austin's glowing face. "I'm not saying yes yet—I need to take her feelings into consideration. She has to perform tonight."

Tracy smiled. "She's as much in love with you as you are with her, Todd, and I know tonight will be easier for her if she sees you first."

Austin darted into Todd's bedroom and reappeared with his costume. "Where's your stage makeup?"

Part of Todd was terrified at seeing Pauline so soon after last night, but part of him wanted to do a jumpy, switchy thing out of excitement precisely at the thought of seeing her so soon.

Tracy arranged to drop off Austin's things so he could have his private lesson with Todd, then study for a little. "I'll have almost three hours to myself." She smiled. "Maybe I'll get a manicure."

Austin wasn't the only one who'd changed in the last three weeks. This was the most relaxed Todd had seen Tracy, too.

But Todd couldn't help but wonder if Pauline really wanted to see him. If he reminded her of everything she was scared of, and he had insulted what she held dear, why would she want to see him anymore?

I guess that's part of your new choreography, Todd Parsons. You have to have hope your audience will love it.

DEREK BROUGHT PAULINE A WARMING PACK. The doctor had suggested it, believing that her ice baths, though beneficial for her muscles, were contributing to the pain in her hip. She could at least make this change to her pre-show routine right away.

"You okay?" he asked her in the hotel room she was using for a change room. The fundraiser was taking place in the hotel's ballroom. "You look rougher than usual. Two hospital gigs in one day too much?"

Pauline held the warming pack to her hip and shook her head. "Just wondering why Tracy and Austin aren't here. Any messages from them?"

Derek checked her phone. "'Traffic's bad. Will be there ASAP.'" He handed her phone to her.

Pauline texted back that they'd put in Austin's dance whenever it worked out then dropped onto the bed.

Derek tilted his head as he stared at her. "Is that all? You seem more down than a peregrine that's crashed into a bay window."

Pauline attempted to smile at the joke. "Just life crashing down on me."

"Life or love?"

"Maybe both." She sat up and sighed. "How can I play a character who's nothing but courageous yet I feel like a complete coward?"

Derek placed a hand on her shoulder. "You spent hours with sick children this afternoon. You even held the hand of a boy who passed away. Why do you feel you're a coward?"

The boy was fourteen and had been fighting leukemia for three years. His parents had welcomed Perry into the room as though he were family.

"I can only do it dressed as someone—or something—else."

Derek sat next to her and put his arm around her. "What's happened to you? I know these visits have always been hard, but I've never seen you like this. Are you sure you can go onstage tonight?"

What else could she do? Cancel her appearance at a fundraiser she'd helped plan? A fundraiser that would hopefully raise several million dollars for the hospital foundation? Absolutely not. She had to pull herself together.

She nodded.

"Then what's going on?" He dug into her duffle bag. "Here's your Belmont Blizzard." He held up the tin Todd had packed. "I can brew this up for you. We've still got half an hour."

Her eyes moistened. "I really screwed up, and I don't know what to do."

The door lock clicked, and Ben barged in. "I want to do some publicity shots with the Parsons before we—oh, cripes, what now?"

Pauline wiped her eyes. "I'm fine. This afternoon was a bit much."

"Just don't start drinking."

Derek stepped in. "A boy died today while she was holding his hand. Have a heart, Ben."

"We're trying to raise millions tonight so that doesn't happen again." He handed Pauline some tissues. "Pour your heart out to Derek if you have to, and then meet us onstage in ten. Tonight has to be picture-perfect: it's DIY Home's first sponsorship of this magnitude." He turned on his heel and left.

"Forget him. How can I help?" Derek asked.

Pauline shrugged and glanced at the bedside clock. "I should get going before Ben gets ticked off again." She walked over to the desk, where Perry's head and gloves lay and set the heating pack down.

"You asked me the day of the winning game how I manage this job with my family," Derek said.

"You said you just make it work."

He nodded. "But I take time off. You're so dedicated to your work that you don't take off time for anything else except a week each summer to visit your family. You've put so much energy into bringing Perry back since you took over from Nate that you have no energy for yourself or those you love. You're burning out."

Pauline pulled out the tin of Belmont Blizzard. "Todd packed this for me because he thought I'd forget to pack my own today. He was right. Only three weeks working for my mom's store, and he knows me that well."

"And he knows teas that well, too."

Pauline smiled. "Actually, my mom's system of teas was so complex that he couldn't figure out a way to learn it. The other night, we figured it out: he needed to use his love of stories to categorize Mom's system. He said Belmont Blizzard fits into this scene where the nutcracker becomes the Nutcracker Prince. He said it's about transformation…" Pauline gasped. "Oh my god, Derek. That's it!" She jumped into the air. "I've got it!" She hugged him hard. "I *am* burning out! And I know why! But I know how to fix everything! Oh my god! How could I not have seen this before!"

She grabbed Perry's head and gloves.

"This is the most interesting type of burnout I've ever seen," Derek said, "but I'll take it."

"I'm going to go back to Kitchener tomorrow, but first we have to raise a few million dollars."

She put on Perry's head, fastened the chin strap, and slipped on the gloves. She flexed her arms. But this time, when she looked through Perry's eyes into the mirror, instead of seeing Perry, she knew exactly who she saw.

And that person was Pauline.

CHAPTER 34

*T*odd and Austin had put their makeup on in the car during stalled traffic. Both now wore sunglasses: Todd, to hide his identity, and Austin, because he didn't like wearing makeup in public. All they needed to do was get inside to get changed and let someone from the Peregrines production team know they were there.

"We're sorry, ma'am, but you need a ticket."

"But I'm Tracy Tschirhart. Michael Parsons of DIY Home wanted my son to perform with Perry…"

The two women at the desk outside the ballroom door shook their heads. "Sorry," one of them said. "We have no one on our guest list by that name."

"No, we're part of the fundraiser. We're not guests."

Todd removed his sunglasses. "I'm part of the performance, too, but it's confidential, which is why you weren't told about it."

Both attendants' eyes almost fell out of their sockets.

Toronto ballet fans.

They nodded vigorously and allowed them in.

Tracy pushed open the door to the hotel ballroom, and Todd and Austin followed. A few heads turned to see who was disturbing the event, but no one said anything; it must've been too dark.

The room was lusciously decorated, and several hundred people were in attendance. Judging by the plates on a nearby table, the main course had been served. Todd recognized some of Toronto's elite who also held season tickets for his former company.

His heart leaped when he saw the tall peregrine falcon next to the speaker onstage.

"So, Perry, what do you think?" the man asked. "Should we talk more about the work our incredible healthcare teams do?"

As important as the topic was, Todd wanted Pauline to shake her head and mime that she needed a break so he could wrap her in his arms and tell her he loved her and that he was sorry.

Instead, Pauline nodded exuberantly and clapped her hands together a few times. The speaker rhymed off a few names, and everyone clapped, including Pauline.

Tracy, Austin, and Todd slid across the back wall, hoping to find a way backstage.

Suddenly, someone jumped out of their chair and aimed a camera at Todd's face. His years of living in the public eye took over and he smiled as the flash went off. The reporter gave her name and news outlet and held a recording device in front of him. "What are you doing here? And where have you been?"

"Let the speaker finish. He's congratulating healthcare workers who've done an amazing job helping the kids in this hospital's care. We can talk later, I promise."

But the damage had been done. The entire table was staring at him, and within thirty seconds, people were whispering:

"Is that Todd Parsons?"

"Todd Parsons is here?"

"I thought Todd Parsons died?"

The speaker appeared to notice something, too. Todd felt guilty for the disruption.

"Wait here," Tracy said. "Let me straighten things out."

She walked down the side of the room, the murmurs seeming to follow in her wake. She signalled to the speaker as she got closer.

"My apologies, ladies and gentleman. Just a moment here," the speaker said.

THE CHAIRMAN of the board stopped talking. Pauline scratched Perry's head but she had to be careful: she didn't want to appear like she was making fun of a potential emergency. They were about to announce the DIY Home donation as part of their Peregrines sponsorship, so the interruption had to be important. They'd worked everything out with Ben, had settled on a format that highlighted the children and their families, and Pauline had even persuaded Michael to offer a matching donation that would secure the full development of a private communication platform that connected families across the country with their healthcare teams and each other.

Wait. It's Tracy. Yes! And not an emergency. She mimed listening in on the conversation.

Finally the chairman took the microphone once more. "I'm quite all right with a minor change in plans, especially if it raises more money. Are you, Perry?"

Pauline gave him a thumbs-up.

"Ladies and gentlemen, you may have seen a viral video of a school performance that happened last week with a young gentleman, Austin Tschirhart."

Yes!

"It was called 'Peregrine Lake,' co-starring, of course, Perry.'"

Pauline bowed humbly. Austin deserved all the praise, but he was probably getting ready.

"I've just learned that Perry managed to find none other than ballet great Todd Parsons, who's agreed to perform with Austin tonight! He'll be joining us shortly."

What the...?!

The audience erupted into applause.

"Perry, how could you keep such a secret from us?"

Pauline had to follow his lead, whatever was happening. She held a hand up to her beak and bounced up and down, mimicking a snicker reminiscent of old cartoon characters.

But this means Todd's here, and I'm trapped in this costume!

"I understand he and Mr. Tschirhart are getting changed. As you may know, Todd is the youngest of Michael Parsons's sons. Michael, Tim, and Mark, would you please join me? And Ben Landry, the director of marketing for the Toronto Peregrines?"

They came onstage to polite applause, but now that the audience knew Todd was here, construction guys and a newly promoted Ben weren't as exciting. They announced the new communications platform, and Pauline could hear the excitement in the chairman's voice. Even Michael's eagerness to support the project seemed genuine.

"This, ladies and gentlemen," said the chairman, "is what your donations are going toward, in addition to the amazing research we conduct here." He paused. "Yes, it appears they're ready now. Ladies and gentlemen, may I have the pleasure of presenting to you...Todd Parsons!"

The audience stood on its feet, startling Pauline, but she bowed deeply as though Todd were royalty when he entered. When she stood up, her breath caught: Todd was indeed dressed in the Nutcracker Prince costume he'd worn the evening of their first date, but without the mask. He was wearing stage makeup, ready to perform, to show himself to the world again.

Todd swept his arm out to his left, and Austin entered, dressed in a ballet uniform.

"And Austin Tschirhart, one of our patients in neurology," the chairman said. "Austin has made it his mission to show other youth with epilepsy they don't need to be embarrassed by their seizures. A strong message indeed, Austin."

Pauline walked in front of Ben and the four Parsons men, sticking her beak in the air and eliciting a good laugh from the audience. Once she reached Austin, she mimed asking for someone to take a picture of the two of them.

"Should I take it?" Michael asked, laughing.

Pauline nodded and posed with Austin.

"So, Perry?" the chairman asked, smiling. "Are we ready for 'Peregrine Lake'?"

Thinking of Austin's seizures, she faced Austin and pretended to hold a camera to her face and take photos again. Austin understood her message and walked over to the mic.

"I need to ask people to not take any flash photography," he said. "It might cause seizures. I hope that's okay?"

The chairman leaned to the mic. "Austin, never ask if it's okay. Your safety is more than just 'okay.' Right, everyone?"

The audience clapped, and Pauline joined in.

But as Austin crossed the stage to his beginning position for "Peregrine Lake," he spoke quietly to her. "Can I do this just with Todd?"

Pauline didn't need to be asked twice. She pushed Austin toward his mentor.

Austin explained to the audience it had always been his

dream to dance with Todd Parsons and that in Kitchener it hadn't been possible.

Pauline stepped into the wing where Derek was watching, and removed her mask. Derek passed her a water bottle he always carried in case she could take a break.

"Did you want me to get paper towels for your face?" he asked.

She shook her head. "It's not important. For once I get to watch this with my own eyes, and I'm not missing a single second of it. I need you to stay to make sure no one sees me. Tracy and Austin are the only ones who know. Todd's family doesn't, of course, and neither does Todd. I promised Ben I wouldn't tell him so he wouldn't sue me for telling Tracy and Austin."

Derek swore under his breath.

TODD TOOK his position upstage right while Austin placed his chair downstage left. Todd couldn't see Pauline from where he stood, but he was certain she was watching.

When the music began, though, instead of Tchaikovsky, Todd heard a piece from *Gilgamesh.* He held his breath. Austin hadn't mentioned a word about this change.

Austin turned around, worried, but Todd smiled: it was really okay. That Todd's work was giving strength to a young man experiencing turmoil had already turned his failure into success.

Austin didn't have the Nutcracker Prince mask with him, nor did he have the voices of children taunting him play over the music. Instead, Austin used mime to show the audience that he wanted to play with others but was rejected time and again.

Austin ran to centre and sat on the floor, pulled his knees in, and mimed crying. That was Todd's cue. Improvising, he threw an imaginary baseball into the air and caught it, as though he was on his way to a neighbourhood game. Austin turned around, pretending to have heard him, and Todd threw him the imaginary ball. Austin caught it.

WHEN THE MUSIC HAD STARTED, Pauline needed a moment to recognize it. But was Todd comfortable dancing to a piece from his failed ballet? When she saw his smile, though, she knew he'd be fine. She still dreamed of someday being the dancing pig—or peregrine falcon—with Todd, but letting Austin have his dream of sharing the stage with his idol was far more important.

Besides, Pauline could witness the magic that had begun that afternoon at the tea shop as teacher and student now danced together in their glory, their joy shining through and filling the ballroom.

WHEN THE CYMBALS in the music crashed, Todd and Austin turned and jumped into the air, their front legs extended straight ahead, their back legs curved in a jump named for Baryshnikov. When they landed, they followed with another turn and jump and continued the sequence for a total of eight Baryshnikovs, crossing downstage, and coming full circle upstage again. They followed the jump sequence with ten *chaîné* turns down the centre of the stage, then a Patrick Swayze Jump, before lowering themselves quickly onto a knee, each dancer lifting one curved arm over his head into fifth position as the music ended.

As one, the audience jumped to its feet and erupted into

applause, and before Todd could even lower his arm, Austin wrapped his arms around him in the tightest embrace of gratitude Todd had ever received.

~

PAULINE PUT her mask and gloves back on and came onstage, clapping her hands over her head. She raised both dancers' hands in victory.

"Guess my dad gets his photo of me with you," Todd said as he smiled for the cameras.

Does that mean Todd knows? If he believed someone else was in this costume, he wouldn't have said that, right?

But she had to stay focused on the show. Pauline patted him on the back and beckoned Todd's family to join them. She was going to make sure Todd got his photo in costume with them, too.

Michael walked onstage, his arms open, and he embraced Todd proudly.

"That was beautiful, son, absolutely beautiful."

"Thanks, Dad."

Pauline's tears flowed as father and son clapped each other on the back. Michael then embraced Austin, too.

Ben took over the microphone. "Tonight is for every child and teen—like Austin—who'll be helped by *your* donation. DIY Home is starting the night off with donating one million dollars to the hospital and will match *your* donations, dollar for dollar!"

The audience applauded even louder, and so many flashes went off that Pauline was glad for her mask lest she go blind from all the light.

But wait—the flashes. Austin. She looked over, and he seemed fine. She gave him a thumbs-up to inquire.

"I'm not lifting anyone," he said to her. "And they don't hurt, so it's o—" After he came out of the seizure, he said, "It's really okay, Perry. If anyone caught that on camera, then people can see what my seizures look like."

Michael stepped up to the microphone. "We're so proud to help an organization like the children's hospital of Toronto. Family is important to us, and we want all kids to grow up and achieve their dreams."

"Dad!" Todd yelled across the stage. He stood right up to Pauline, his hands parked on his hips, and he stared at her through her mask. "I know how important this cause is to, um, Perry, which is why I came back in the public eye sooner than I thought I would. I know that...I know that Perry likes a challenge, that it makes him happy, that a good challenge shows Perry how much he's loved."

Pauline's heart started to race. He knew it was her in the costume.

And he just said he loved me.

"If I can beat the bird in a challenge of physical skill, I'll donate the first fifty thousand."

The audience oohed.

Fifty thousand?!

"So, bird?" Todd said. "What do you say?"

CHAPTER 35

Pauline stuck her hands out as if to stop him.

"Ohh…" Ben said, playing along. "Perry doesn't like being called 'bird,' do you, Perry?"

Pauline had to keep playing her role. She shook her head, turned her back to Todd, and flipped her tail feathers at him, getting a laugh from the audience.

"Because I'm new to this," Todd said, "I need a coach, and I choose Austin."

Pauline knocked her knees together in mock fear as Austin crossed his arms like an important Olympic coach. He really was quite the performer. Todd and Austin pretended to confer on a strategy.

Todd walked to the middle of the stage, placed one foot forward and one behind, and spun like the letter "p." Pauline counted one rotation…two…three…ten…eleven! He'd spun *eleven* times in public! She wanted to jump for joy while the audience clapped, but she couldn't. After all, this was a challenge.

She flexed her arms and marched to one side of the stage.

She did a round-off followed by a back handspring and backflip and thrust her arms into a "V" for victory to more applause. She turned up her beak at Todd, much to everyone's amusement.

Todd and Austin conferred again, and Pauline shuffled up to Michael and stuck her face in his suit jacket, getting another good laugh from the audience. Did someone take a shot so he could add it to his family's Peregrines' nest?

Todd did a few turns to build up momentum, and...yes!!! *The Patrick Swayze Jump!!!*

Perfect.

The audience cheered even louder for him.

Pauline marched up to him and began clapping overhead and stomping, getting the audience to join in. She flexed her arms, squeezing each bicep for extra emphasis, then grabbed him by the hips, and in her best slapstick manner, attempted to lift him overhead. Todd played along perfectly by staying firmly planted on the ground. He even faked a yawn, which the audience loved.

Pauline hung her head and drooped her shoulders in defeat. A moment later, she thrust Todd's hand high in victory to thunderous applause. She dropped it and hugged him. She remained in character but said through her mask, "I love you, too."

Todd squeezed back even tighter.

Their embrace must have lasted a while, because Ben said, "Perry? That's a little long to be hugging the visiting team."

The audience laughed, and the two broke apart.

Todd mimed signing a cheque, and Ben nodded.

"Fifty thousand dollars is our first donation, folks," he said. "And it's actually a hundred thousand, because DIY Home will be matching it!"

Todd waved to the crowd to more applause and, joined by Austin, exited the stage.

Pauline joined his family and Ben by the microphone, eager

to finish the evening. Just a few more stories, then collecting pledges, and then closing remarks.

"I've got a special treat for everyone tonight," Ben said. "But you have to promise to donate more than you'd originally planned when you came. Perry, why don't you head to the centre of the stage again."

Pauline gave a thumbs-up, but something felt wrong.

"So, Toronto, here's the deal. I'm going to trust you. You see, tonight couldn't have happened without the help of a very special person, and if you promise to donate more, we're going to show you who that is."

Oh, crap.

"You met the planning committee on your way in, you've heard from the chairman of the board, and you know me."

Yes, Ben, we all know you.

"But there's one person no one has met in the past three years and who's been responsible for the incredible community work you've seen with the Peregrines. That person is standing right there."

Pauline pretended to look for someone in case Ben really wasn't talking about her.

"If we show you tonight the mastermind behind our community engagement—the person in that costume—will you increase your donations by ten percent?"

What is he thinking? I'm not some celebrity who'd be worth the reveal. She loathed the thought of publicly taking credit for her work.

But cheers and applause answered Ben's question.

"Can we get cameras up here?"

Then she realized what this photo would look like. She had given so much of herself these last three years, had sacrificed the most important relationships of her life because of Ben's insistence. Yes, she had chosen to sign on the dotted line, but she also wanted to help as many people as she could, not fore-seeing the true sacrifice she would make.

She would continue to give of herself in whatever capacity she could, but for ten seconds of her life, she was going to enjoy Ben's expression when the mask came off, because after all he had put her through, he would finally see what that looked like.

It would not be picture-perfect.

"How long has Pauline been in that costume, Derek?" Tracy asked, standing backstage with Austin and Todd.

"Easily two hours, though she took Perry's head off while she watched Todd and your son dance."

"You're taking photos?" Tracy asked.

Derek held up a camera hanging around his neck. "You bet I am. Ben thinks he's going to get a Kodak Moment that will make him look magnificent, when what he's really going to expose is the heartache and compassion she feels in that costume. And I'm passing those photos around to staff tomor-row. You want some?"

"Please," Tracy said. "I'll share them with her family."

They high-fived each other as Derek left.

"And you two met, how?" Todd asked.

"At the rally," Tracy replied.

Of course. Tracy hadn't been hiding that day, just Todd.

"We're getting Pauline out of that stupid clause," she explained.

"What's a Kodak Moment?" Austin asked.

"Instagram shot," his mother translated. "Minus the filters."

Ben, his chest puffed out, strutted over to Pauline. He placed both hands on either side of Perry's head and lifted...

Austin snorted when Perry's head didn't come off. "He doesn't even know there's a chin strap in there."

Todd furrowed his brow. "And how would you know that?"

Austin's face turned red and he averted his gaze. "Remember when you—" Austin stared, and Todd waited. "Remember when you came down to bring me your mask?"

Todd's mouth dropped open. "That was you inside?"

Austin nodded, and Todd ruffled his hair.

Now Ben lifted the mask off and immediately stepped to the side, grinning at the cameras as they flashed. "Pauline Robinson," he announced proudly.

Then as Ben faced Pauline, disgust bodychecked his pride off the stage. Pauline's hair was matted to her head from sweat, her eyes were bloodshot, snot had dried above her lips, and salt was caked around her eyes and down her cheeks where tears had flowed.

But to Todd, she was beautiful: he saw the emotions she had so often hidden from him.

Pauline was smiling for the cameras as though she didn't know what she looked like. But after thirty years in costume, she must. He smiled, realizing her moment of happiness came both from no longer having to hide and because she knew this wasn't what Ben was expecting. Todd's smile soon turned to laughter as he watched Ben struggle to find his composure.

Tracy was enjoying this far more.

"That was your idea?" Todd asked.

"Derek's and mine. We knew how much she was suffering. But I convinced Ben to unmask her, and Derek was more than happy to record the moment. I said it would be good publicity to show a woman inside the costume."

Austin was alternating between seizures and laughing.

"I have to save her now." Tracy grabbed Todd by the hand. "And you're coming, too."

"But I'm not kissing her like that."

Tracy laughed and pulled wipes out of her purse. "For a ballet dancer, you really know how to kill the romance."

Once onstage, she practically threw Todd at Pauline, who playfully shielded her face from him while she gratefully accepted Tracy's wipes with her other hand. As soon as Pauline had cleaned herself, she wrapped her arms around Todd.

"I'm so sorry I left," she said. "I love you."

He couldn't believe he'd ever doubted her love for him. "I love you, too."

Camera flashes and questions interrupted them.

"Where were you, Todd?"

"In Kitchener."

The reporters fell silent, as though Todd had just announced he'd grown twenty heads.

Finally, someone said, "But no one likes ballet in Kitchener."

Austin piped up from the side of the stage. "That's not true! I love ballet and I'm from Kitchener! And there are over twenty dance studios in Waterloo Region! Lots of people there love ballet!"

Todd laughed. That kid had so much passion. Maybe one day he'd become an artistic director and open his own ballet company in the city.

"I needed some time to myself," he said.

"How did you meet your girlfriend?"

Todd smiled at Pauline. "She rescued me from a horde of tea lovers."

"What's the full story?"

Pauline blushed. The contradiction between the extreme self-confidence he'd just witnessed onstage and the shyness he was seeing now made him fall even more in love with her.

"If you don't mind," she said, "it's a bit of a disservice to the character if I stand here half-dressed. There are still stories to share about what the money is being raised for, and that's a lot more important than me and Todd. Let me get changed, please focus your attention back on this evening's purpose, and we'll answer all your questions afterwards."

She's always thinking about those she can help, Todd thought. His heart just did its own jumpy, switchy thing, followed by a back-flip, an aerial, and a Patrick Swayze Jump. He was never going to let her go again.

AFTER SAYING goodbye to his family, who were flying home to Vancouver in the morning, Todd rode back to Kitchener with Tracy, Pauline, and Austin, first stopping by Pauline's condo so he could pack her some clothing for the week—Pauline had fallen asleep by the time they'd arrived.

All her Peregrines paraphernalia had made his family's Pere-grines' nest look like a candidate for a minimalist reality show. But in truth, he couldn't wait until after her tour when he'd stay over and soak it all in: tons of photos, many of them with community groups and families, hung everywhere. So many stories were displayed in those rooms, and he wanted to hear every single one of them.

Todd spent the ride back to town in the front seat, keeping Tracy awake and enjoying stories about her family and the Robinsons, while Austin and Pauline slept in the back.

In Kitchener, they pulled up to his building, and Todd reached around the passenger seat.

"She looks so peaceful," he said to Tracy.

"You won't see that side of her often. She tries so hard to help everyone else, she rarely takes time to help herself."

"I guess that's what tea's for."

"And someone who loves her."

He nudged her knee, and Pauline opened her eyes. "Time to go inside," he said.

Once upstairs, Pauline collapsed onto Todd's bed. "Can you at least open the duffle bag to air him out?" she mumbled.

She meant Perry. "I can wash him right away if you want."

Pauline groaned and shook her head. "Tomorrow." She rolled over and fell back asleep.

Todd unzipped the bag and a wretched stench emanated from it. "This is the side of Perry my dad and brothers don't see," he said to himself with a laugh.

Two shoeboxes sat on top of the costume pieces, though, so he removed them. As he did, the contents of one of them spilled out: piles of notes and letters addressed to Perry.

He opened one. The handwriting was clearly that of an older adult.

Dear Perry,

Thank you for finding time in your very busy schedule to come onto the field with us for what became our last family photo with my brother. He succumbed to his cancer that night. We're all convinced he was holding out for a last happy memory. You made that possible. After 64 years with him, this was my happiest memory.

Sybille Grayson

He opened another.

Dear actor who plays Perry,

My son was always scared to get on the ice, especially because he's 11 and never learned to skate when he was young. But the way you made him feel comfortable—he LOVED how you slipped on the ice, too. I'll admit, I don't know how you do it in that costume, especially with that beak. When we signed him up for skating lessons, we were scared he wouldn't go, but he did! Now, when he falls, he laughs and gets right back up the way you showed him.

    Matt Guildner

And another.

To Perry,

    My name is Sam. Kids at school are meen to me. Granma takes me to peregrins games. Wen I see yu, I feel stron. Thank you.

    From,

    Sam

These letters were from people who had taken the time to find a way to reach Pauline. There were thousands more out there she'd helped.

"Could I do the same?" he asked himself. He had fans around the world, after all, and Pauline could certainly teach him how to help them.

Todd would find a way to keep her in his life despite her schedule. He glanced over at Pauline. What was she dreaming about? Helping children in hospitals? Skating with families she could barely see through Perry's eyes? Wild sports fans in bizarre makeup? All of the above?

He smiled. "It's probably something really random, like teacups dancing around doughnuts being baked in the ocean."

But in the meantime, Todd could at least offer his fans an update. He pulled out his phone, took a selfie, and posted, *Sorry I've been gone so long. I needed some time to regroup. You may have heard: I met the most amazing woman at a tea shop. Her name is Pauline, and aside from having helped thousands through her work as a mascot, she can do a backflip in a 20-lb costume like nobody's business. Do you have someone in your life who loves to help others? Tell me something nice they've done.*

He couldn't wait to see the responses.

But even more important: he couldn't wait to work side by side with Pauline again at Claire's Tea Shop. He only had one week left with her before she went on tour with the NAHA cup. He was going to make every moment count.

CHAPTER 36

*P*auline woke up the next morning, still in her clothes from last night, to the sound of gentle music playing outside the bedroom. Last night raced through her mind in a blur: the fundraiser, her *schadenfreude* at Ben's botched photo op, and the most glorious part of the evening: Todd and Austin's dance. They may not have been father and son, but their connection felt like that in a deeply spiritual sense, and only through dance could she fully appreciate it.

She groaned as she sat up, surrounded by the contemporary but minimalist white walls of Todd's room.

"If I move in here, I'll need my cluttered sports corner," she said to herself, a smile forming on her lips. But they had a couple of months to talk things over. The tour came first.

She combed her fingers through her hair and walked into the living room. Todd was lost in ballet exercises at a short metal bar set up in the middle of the room.

As she watched, he held on to the bar with one hand. His other arm was extended to the side, slightly curved, away from her. The leg closest to the bar stood straight as a post while

Todd's other leg swished back and forth, his foot reaching as high as his shoulder up front and forcing his body to tilt forward when it swished to the back, creating a beautiful arch, almost like the Nike logo. The movement reminded Pauline of a bell swaying back and forth. After doing a certain number of repetitions, he brought his legs together, rose to the balls of his feet, turned to face the other side, and repeated the kicks on the other leg. Pauline was more than content to lean against the doorframe and watch. Only after he finished did he notice her, and the smile on his face warmed her more than any cup of tea ever could.

"Good morning, Perry," he said.

"Good morning, my Nutcracker Prince. Please, don't stop on my account."

But it was too late. He'd already made it over to her and gathered her in his arms for a kiss and...

They both pulled away.

"Morning breath," they said in unison.

Pauline looked at the clock in his kitchen. "I have to go see Mom, anyway. We had...a bit of a fight Saturday night."

"A bit" more accurately described the length of the fight as opposed to its effect on her. Pauline had summoned every ounce of mental strength she possessed the day before to push it out of her mind so she could perform. But now she needed to clear the air with her mother.

She pulled Perry out of the bag, and Todd laughed.

"He's starting to become real to me, too, so now it feels like you carry a dead body around."

Pauline tossed Perry's head on and parked her hands on her hips in discontent.

"Sorry, Perry."

Pauline lifted the head off, sprayed the inside with a diluted mouthwash spray, and asked Todd where she could set up her small fan to dry it out. He also pointed her to the laundry machine. She popped Perry's body in, added detergent, turned on the machine, and asked if Todd didn't mind hanging the costume up and brushing out the fleece before he came to the shop. She'd cover for him.

Fifteen minutes later, after her shower, they were sitting at the breakfast counter eating, and Pauline asked about the metal bar.

"That's barre as in b-a-r-r-e, not b-a-r as you would've had in gymnastics," Todd explained. "All terminology in ballet is French. We use it for warm-up. Austin pulled it out yesterday to get me off my sorry butt."

Pauline laughed. "Once he broke out of his shell, he couldn't stop breaking us out."

"He told me I was supposed to be his idol, not an idiot."

Pauline snorted and covered her mouth. "I'm glad he didn't have to tell me that."

"You got it easy."

"I was trapped inside Perry, wanting to have sex with you for over an hour!"

Todd took her hand in his. "Over an hour, eh?" He kissed it.

"Mmm. A whole hour." Their lips came closer. "It was utter torture." Pauline pulled back. "But I don't have time for that now. I have to go talk to Mom."

Todd planted his chin in his hand. "That's really not fair. I love you and this is how you treat me? By teasing me when you know you don't have time?"

"Yup!"

But Pauline was on a high again, because she knew she'd have all the time in the world with Todd soon. She just wanted to show Claire the respect she deserved by not only asking for forgiveness but permission for the next stage in Pauline's life. Now that she understood the trajectory her life had taken,

Pauline knew she wasn't giving up her dream: she was fulfilling her destiny. She knew who she was at last.

She wolfed down her food and grabbed her bag. "I'll see you in maybe an hour at the shop?"

Todd sighed. "I guess…"

She gave him a quick peck on the cheek. "I love you, too. With my whole heart." At that, Todd jumped off his chair, did a jumpy, switchy thing, and Pauline tried to copy him. All she accomplished was a burst of laughter from Todd but that was a good thing.

Because if they were going to spend a lot more time together, he'd better find her funny!

PAULINE WALKED around the back of the plaza, more nervous than she had been the previous night. She had stood up to Ben, survived the impromptu unmasking, reunited with Todd, and appropriately answered dozens of questions from the press, but to ask forgiveness from the woman who had made her dreams come true…that required a different kind of courage.

Courage that needed the right kind of tea.

Of course, the only way to get that tea was to step inside. She pulled her key out of her bag, took a deep breath, and unlocked the back door.

"Oh," Claire said, surprised. "I was expecting Todd. I thought you were staying in Toronto."

Pauline stared at the floor. "He'll come by in an hour or so. Mind if I make myself some Wuyi rock oolong?"

"Of course not, honey."

"Would you like anything?"

Claire smiled. "The usual."

Pauline was grateful for the task; it gave her longer to figure out what to say.

But by the time she served them both tea, she still didn't know where to begin. Everything Pauline wanted to say was jumbled in a ball in her throat. However, as she sipped on the tea, its aroma of the forest floor grounded her, and she knew she needed to start at the beginning.

"I'm sorry, Mom. I was so scared at how you'd react to the fact that I'd withheld my job from you for three years that I kept...I kept lying to you about it. It was easier to tell Tracy, because I wasn't as close to her."

The same reason Austin had opened up to her before his own mother, she realized.

Claire inhaled the aroma of her Earl Claire several times before responding. "Learning that hurt me deeply, Pauline. But it wasn't just the lies. It was also because I couldn't share in your *joy*. For three whole years, you couldn't tell me all your happy stories of working with kids. I know you love entertaining large crowds and that you need their energy to lift your spirits, but to not hear your stories about community skates and hospital visits and baseball games..." Claire laughed. "I still don't know how you hit a baseball in those costumes."

Pauline laughed with her. "Next time I do it, watch how I do a few 'practice hits' first to show the pitcher where I need the ball to come."

Claire smiled as she took a sip and nodded. "That's why I thought you weren't happy. There were no stories."

It always came back to stories.

"So," Claire said, a twinkle in her eye, "I take it you were at Todd's last night?"

Pauline blushed.

"He's wonderful," Claire said. "A very special, wonderful man."

"I know, and I almost lost him."

Claire tilted her head. "Tell me what happened."

When Pauline finished, she was happy: she had finally opened up to her mother about everything. But there was one thing more.

"I'm glad Mondays are quiet," Pauline said, "at least today, because there's something else I want to talk to you about."

Claire raised her eyebrows. "You mean there's more?"

"I'd like to take over the tea shop, Mom, if the offer's still open."

TODD GOT the distinct impression that mother and daughter weren't telling him something, but he knew better than to ask. At any rate, they seemed to have reconciled, and he was happy for both of them: he understood that feeling. His father had called before the flight. Michael would even make a sizable donation to a ballet company in Vancouver.

"I have to admit," Pauline said as she scooped some Darjeeling into a jar, "I would've thought after all the attention last night, somebody would've showed up by now."

"Nah," Todd said. "They got their questions answered last night. Articles ran in papers today, and that's it. I had a few calls, but I let them go to voicemail. They can check my social media for statements."

Pauline's jaw dropped. "You're back on social media?"

Claire walked in from the front of the café. "And if it remains this quiet, we'll close early." She smiled. "I understand you two have a lot to talk about."

Todd caught a look between mother and daughter, and daughter appeared not too pleased. Apparently, Claire and Richard weren't the only ones who spoke without words.

But when he thought back to the events of the last few days, especially the evening after the reopening, he and Pauline had also learned to speak without words, just differently—through movement. His body tingled at the hope of doing so again.

Just then came a jingle at the front door followed by the sound of a chorus of voices.

"What on earth is all that racket?" Claire went to check.

Todd knew.

"I told you to use the GPS, Russell."

"Those things never work. We tried that for our fortieth anniversary and almost landed in a lake."

"That was ten years ago!"

"Your fans from Toronto?" Pauline guessed.

Claire poked her head into the back room, a mischievous smile on her face. "I believe these customers would like to see you, Todd. Be sure to sell them some tea."

CHAPTER 37

Claire leaned wearily on her cane, and Pauline was astonished her mother had lasted this long.

"Mother, you really should go home."

Claire nodded. "I promise I will, honey. But I also promised myself that I would spend the Monday after reopening here as a way of celebrating everything you've done for me." She flipped the sign on the door to "Closed" and smiled at Pauline. "Plus, I wanted to do that. There. It's done."

A shiny red Porsche pulled up to the tea shop.

"You must be kidding me," Pauline said. "What's Ben doing here?"

Out of the expensive car stepped her manager, dressed in his usual expensive suit, shoes, and sunglasses, with his black leather briefcase that probably cost more than his entire wardrobe.

Todd joined Claire and Pauline. "I never did get introduced to him last night."

"I wanted to save you the headache." Pauline took his hand in hers and gave him a peck on the cheek.

Pauline let Ben in and locked the door behind him. "I thought we were going to video call tomorrow about the tour?" she asked.

Not bothering to acknowledge anyone else in the shop, he replied, "I'm meeting Tracy for supper, so I figured I'd kill two birds with one stone. No pun intended."

"Tracy? For supper?" He didn't need to drive to town in the evening to talk to Tracy.

He tucked his glasses into a case and the case into his jacket pocket. "Her idea to unmask you was brilliant even if it did make me look stupid. I'm thinking of hiring her to replace former me now that I've been promoted. She can't meet while she's working."

"So that requires dinner in a city you can't stand?"

"My business, not yours. Can we talk somewhere private?"

Claire sized up Ben with her gaze. "I'm Claire Robinson, Pauline's mother."

"Hi."

"I'd like to speak with you."

"I don't have time."

Todd held out his hand. "Todd Parsons. We never met yesterday. Thanks for the fun evening."

Ben shook hands, then checked the time on his watch. "I need to get going. Pauline?"

Pauline messaged Tracy. "I'm already texting Tracy that you'll be a bit late."

Ben clenched his jaw. "I don't have time for this. I need to get back to Toronto tonight."

Claire pointed to a table. "Please. Have a seat."

"I don't have the time."

Claire slammed her cane on the floor, and Ben jumped. "It's impolite to reject an invitation, especially from your elders."

Ben finally realized he wasn't in charge. His eyes darting between all three, he sat down.

"Todd," Claire said, "would you be so kind as to make Ben a cup of Earl Claire? I won't be staying much longer, so I'll be fine."

"Pauline, a Belmont Blizzard for you?" Todd asked.

So this was what it felt like to be supported by the people she loved.

Claire and Pauline sat down at the table with Ben but said nothing while Todd made the tea. Ben drummed his fingers, shifted in his chair, adjusted his collar.

"Are you going to say something?" he asked.

"Tea is about taking time to relax and enjoy your company," Claire said, "even if it means sitting in silence for a few minutes."

Pauline marvelled at how her mother could keep eye contact with Ben. The more she thought about it, the more she realized Ben rarely held eye contact with anyone: he was always talking while texting or shifting to the next conversation. To underscore her point, his hand moved to his phone.

"Ben!" Claire scolded. "We're here to have a conversation. Leave that phone where it is."

Ben squirmed. A minute later, Todd carried over two teas.

"So, this is what's become of the great Todd Parsons? You make tea?"

Where were ice-cold water balloons when you needed them?

"Some people actually find this job really hard. You have to respect people to do well at it," Todd said.

Pauline fought hard not to smile. "Thank you, Todd." She meant it as much for his support as for the tea.

Ben said nothing to Todd. But a moment later, he remarked, "Yours smells familiar."

"It's the tea I use to get pumped up for appearances,"

Pauline said. "Mom blended it for me ten years ago. You probably smelled it in the change rooms whenever you came in. What do you think of yours?"

Although Ben didn't make any special effort to inhale the aroma of his Earl Claire, Pauline knew he couldn't help but smell it, too. He nodded. That was the best response she could hope for.

"That's my signature tea," Claire said. "It's for when I'm feeling angry, sad, depressed, and hopeful all at once."

"I'm feeling just fine."

"Are you? Because you're acting like someone whose heart is encased in stone. You stole my daughter from me for three years. Do you know what that does to a mother? And do you know that in order for her to do her best work, she needs the support of her *family* behind her? How did you expect her to have that support if she couldn't be honest with us?"

Ben pinched the bridge of his nose as he squeezed his eyes shut.

"Well, Ben?" she said. "I don't know about you, but I was raised to answer my elders."

Pauline hated to think of what her mother had gone through in that first marriage. But whatever it was, it made her the woman she was today. If Claire ever wanted to talk to Pauline about it, she would be ready to listen.

"Sports marketing is a dog-eats-dog world. I had to protect the brand and deal with the PR issue Nate's actions had caused."

"Ballet's sometimes not much different," Todd said. "And not having my family's support made it even harder." He sat next to Pauline and held her hand.

"Ben," Pauline said, "the reason Nate got drunk that night was because a boy died in his arms that afternoon. The rush from performing at the game overpowered him while he was grieving. Nate was too young, too proud, and too inexperienced to understand what was going on inside him, and he drank in costume."

Ben looked as shocked as he probably had when the team won the cup. "I didn't know that..." he stammered.

"My guess is you probably weren't listening," Claire said.

Ben raked his fingers through his hair. "It was a PR crisis. I had to fix it."

"Had you listened," Pauline continued, "and compared Nate's background with mine, you would've known that wouldn't have happened with me, because I was psychologically capable of taking on that work. From volunteer placements in the pediatric ward at a local hospital in university to my work in Florida, all the way through my career, I'd already been in that situation dozens of times. I still grieve when a child dies in my arms while I'm in costume, but it doesn't shock me. Nate was traumatized, and drinking was how he dealt with it."

Ben looked at everyone at the table. "But you signed your contract."

"Because you offered me my dream. And I'll always be grateful for that. But the price you asked turned out to be too high."

He blew on his tea and took a sip. "Now can we talk privately, Pauline?"

"You're not going to apologize, are you?" Claire asked.

"I don't apologize for something I did with the best of intentions."

Pauline touched her mother on the shoulder and gave her a knowing look. Ben squirmed again, probably uncomfortable that words had been silently exchanged. But she told her mother that she'd been heard, despite Ben's lack of an apology.

Todd offered to walk Claire home and come back afterwards, and the two left.

Pauline's palms began to sweat. Her life was about to change course. She only hoped Ben wouldn't fire her on the spot, because the proposal she had wouldn't only bring him the most positive publicity he'd ever seen, it would let her live out her dream the way she had never dreamed possible.

CHAPTER 38

*P*auline's talk with Ben had gone well. He still hadn't apologized and probably never would—he'd even managed to take full credit for Pauline's ideas by the time their meeting had ended. But he did explain that his own tiny changes of heart had been related to something that had happened in his family. What it was he wouldn't say. But he had accepted Pauline's resignation: her contract with the Peregrines would end in ninety days.

Todd returned through the back door. Pauline wanted to run and jump into his arms, but she didn't want to break his back either.

So she jumped onto the counter, and Todd laughed as he entered. "You look happier than a Peregrines player who's finally won the NAHA cup." He hoisted himself up to join her, wrapped his arms around her, and pulled her in. As his lips neared hers, Pauline found herself caught in a dilemma: the good news, or a long, deep kiss?

A knock on the front door saved her from making a decision.

She dropped her arms. "Really?"

They were in clear view of the giggling teenagers staring at them.

Most of them girls with their hair in a bun.

"Dance students." Todd jumped down. "I should…"

"Yeah…"

Pauline jumped down, too, and disinfected the countertop while she waited. Using warming packs on her hip had done wonders, and although she knew hip replacement surgery was still in her future, with her new plans, she was no longer as concerned.

She glanced over her shoulder, and the teens giggled as they took photos with Todd and got his autograph on their dance shoes and T-shirts. He was in his element, enjoying the spotlight.

Guessing he'd be a few minutes, Pauline headed into the back room to put the cleaning supplies away and saw a small tin of tea labelled Todd's Travels. Was she allowed to open it?

"He shouldn't have left it where I could find it," she told herself. She touched the lid but then thought the better of it. He'd obviously blended this himself. Would he really want her to open it without him there?

As if in answer to her question, an arm reached around her shoulders while a hand pulled the tin away.

"Oh, no you don't," Todd teased. He spun her around and planted a kiss on her lips. "Am I going to have to hide Christmas gifts from you every year?"

Her eyes sparkled with mischief. "Maybe."

He turned off the lights in the front of the shop. Then he opened the tin. Enough light still shone through the storefront window that Pauline could see inside, and the most striking blend of tea greeted her eyes and nose: cornflower and calendula petals, mint, cinnamon, ginger, and dried mango all popped against black tea leaves. She inhaled deeply.

"Your mom helped me blend it. It's a collection of spices and fruit from some of the places I've travelled to. You tried my world of dance, and since I can't exactly try your world of mascots, I thought I'd try your world of tea."

Pauline's heart did a double-flip slam dunk.

Todd measured the tea into bags and poured hot water into mugs, setting the time to three minutes after filling the second cup.

"The first time I made you tea, I had no idea what kind of woman I was opening my soul to." He turned around and gathered her in his arms. "I promise to do everything I can to make us work."

She traced the contours of his face with her finger, starting at one grey temple. "You know, I don't think I've ever told you how seductive I find your hair."

Todd smiled, and Pauline's finger touched where his eyes crinkled. "And when your eyes do this."

He kissed one of her shoulders. "I tried to write a poem about how alluring your shoulders are." He kissed the other. "But let's just say it's better I stick to dance."

Pauline ran her hands through his hair. The aroma of his tea steeping in their cups wafted around them like morning mist as they pressed their lips together. When the timer beeped, they parted, breathless. Todd pulled the bags out.

Now was as good a time as any to share the major news with him. "You should know I'm going to be your employer soon."

Todd's eyes practically did a Patrick Swayze Jump. "What?"

Pauline reached for Todd's hand. "It's true. When I was getting ready for the fundraiser, I found the tin you had packed for me, despite what we were going through that night. I was so depressed that I hadn't even brewed any. But then I remembered what it meant to you: Belmont Blizzard was about transformation." She picked up her mug of Todd's Travels and inhaled its aroma. "Todd, this is magical."

Todd picked up his mug, too, and they headed to the lounge area, set their teas on the table, and snuggled into one another.

"My dream was to get a job like Perry and do that until my body fell apart, but that's not what I was actually *meant* to do.

"I've only ever stayed in any character for a few years because what I love is getting things started. I help transform a mascot program that could be maintained by someone with perhaps less experience but lots of endurance. It was like that with the national women's basketball team and in LA. With Perry, my job was to help them recover from a PR disaster but it wasn't that different. I love it but it's not everyone's..." She smiled. "It's not everyone's cup of tea."

Todd groaned at her pun, but then he shook his head in amazement. "The more I get to know you, the more you amaze me."

IT WAS TRUE. And that his fall from grace had dropped him into the arms of this bold woman...it was the metaphorical silver lining in a horrible twist of fate.

"But how do you find the strength to deal with so much sadness?"

"Those boxes of letters you found: I spend time before and after those visits reading them. They remind me of the difference I make in others' lives."

"Your version of dusting the photos." Todd caressed her cheek. That warm smile that was so often hidden inside the mask…he'd get to see it so much more now. "So when do you take over?"

Pauline's smile got even bigger. "After the tour."

So soon? Had Ben fired her? Had Claire convinced her to do this? Pauline had a gift. Just because she was developing arthritis didn't mean she had to give up her dream career. She wasn't giving it up for him, was she? That wasn't the woman he'd fallen in love with.

~

TODD'S REACTION was not what she expected. He sat up straight and drilled his gaze into her eyes.

"Pauline, that's your dream job. How can I be happy about that? After what I saw last night, and now that I know that was you at Austin's school, you *belong* in that costume. How can you help more people like him?"

"I do love my job. But I spend every game night in an ice bath afterwards, and…and my doctor suspects arthritis in my hip."

"That's what I thought, too, to be honest. Happens a lot to women in ballet. But you could probably manage it and still enjoy several years as Perry."

Pauline set her tea down. "I *love* performing, but at what cost? You saw what happened when we met Mom and Dad in the other unit. Right now, I'm looking at a daily physio regime on top of my usual workouts, and I'm guessing a more elaborate cool-down routine after games. That's to ward off surgery. Or…" She smiled. "Or I can accept my new choreography."

Todd took her hand in his. "But how are you going to handle working in such a confined space? And what will you do after a few years here? Won't you want to move on again?"

"A few years? Are you kidding? With a small business,

things change so fast, there's always something to fix and build up. I mean, there's that empty neighbouring unit, and Dad's pretty sure the owner would let us knock a hole in the wall. Would make for a wonderful bookstore..."

Todd raised his eyebrows. "Really?"

Pauline shrugged her shoulders. "Something to consider."

"So I take it that's what you talked to Ben about? What does he think of all this?"

She explained her idea to him: she would run a family-friendly, reality-show-style talent contest throughout the tour, plus workshops for high school and varsity mascots and for businesses to show them how to create a successful character. The Peregrines would announce the winner of the contest at the season opener.

"And this time," she finished, "Ben wants to try what that Indiana football team is doing: the actor unmasks as part of the high school rallies but still performs in full costume at games. He'll see if it works north of the border."

Todd shook his head in wonder. "Sounds like an amazing idea. But I wouldn't expect any less from an amazing woman."

"Then for here, I'll create a mascot, and I can still do community appearances, maybe even sponsor some minor league teams...it won't be the big crowds I'm used to, but I'll still get to have my fun, especially with the Thanksgiving Day parade and the Santa Claus parade. But at the end of the day, Mom taught me how to act as a conduit for emotions by listening. As a mascot, it's simply on a bigger scale. What I didn't want to acknowledge is that I can't keep up with that level anymore. But I can still help someone move from one emotion to another, or I can help them make an emotion stronger. If I have too many emotions bottled up inside me, I can go for a run, do parkour in Victoria Park, jump the counter—because it'll be my store. I can talk to my family, or talk to Tracy, but when I need to connect soul to soul…"

She set both their mugs on the coffee table, stood up, and offered him her hand. He accepted as he joined her. She pressed her hand to his and let the energy guide their bodies closer together until their faces were an inch apart.

"You can trust me," Todd whispered.

"I do."

Pauline entwined her fingers in his, hooked her other hand around his neck, and brushed her lips against Todd's. She pulled back, wanting to get another look at his grey temples and the wrinkles at the corners of his eyes. She could trust him with her heart, and after her two-month tour, she would see this remarkable man every day of her life.

After her heart did a jumpy, switchy thing, she led Todd to the back room, where they let their love for one another steep into their souls.

EPILOGUE

ustin was in the back room of Claire's Tea Shop packaging tea. It was his first week of Grade 11. Pauline had returned from the NAHA cup tour last night and was in town for two days before she had to return to Toronto to continue with the Perry auditions for the next actor. She and Todd were out front helping customers.

Austin had begun new medication immediately after school had finished in June. Side effects included a diminished appetite, tingling in his hands and feet, and forgetting words and sometimes faces, but he enjoyed having fewer seizures. The side effects were worse on some days, like today, than others, and he was still figuring out how to minimize them. His brain felt sluggish, like he was dragging his feet while pushing a wall. He, his mother, and his guidance counsellor had chosen to limit his workload to three courses this semester to give him time to get used to the medication. He was sort of grateful for the time and sort of not. It had meant summer school, which sucked, but that was part of his new choreography with epilepsy: experimenting to figure out what would work and if it was even worth it.

Although the bullying at school had stopped, still being in the hallways brought back those horrible memories. He was seeing a psychotherapist, and the hardest choreography that summer was accepting that those kids had traumatized him.

But the best part of this school year? He'd re-started ballet training, minus the lifts. Even if he gained full control of his seizures, he could never trust himself again after what had happened at his ballet school. Austin studied twice a week at a local studio and had private lessons at the tea shop on Sundays with Todd to see if Austin had what it took to compete in the Youth America Grand Prix in a year or two. It was one of the most prestigious ballet competitions in the world. Pauline had allowed them to move the furniture out of the way and to store a portable ballet floor in the back room. Todd brought his portable barre. They just had to reset the café, and Austin had to wash the floors before he went home and work one afternoon a week packaging tea.

He was good with that.

He sealed up the bag, then placed it on a tray with a bunch of others he'd already finished, and carried the tray to the serving area behind the counter.

"Here you go." He handed the tray to Todd. Life-altering diagnosis one year, work with your idol the next? It was like a fairy tale.

"Thanks, Austin."

Todd Parsons said my name. It'd been three months, and Austin still hadn't gotten over that.

Todd squatted below the counter and sorted the teas into their cubby holes. Over the summer, he had reorganized the service space so that customers wouldn't spend as much time waiting. A set of pincers hanging on a hook near the cash let Claire reach bags without having to bend.

Pauline returned to the service area carrying dirty dishes and gave Todd the one hundredth "I love you" look since Austin had arrived after school two hours before. He'd have liked it if they kept their lovey-dovey stuff a little more private.

The front door opened, and an entourage, complete with TV crew, entered. Was there news about Todd that Austin wasn't aware of? But he read all the latest ballet news every morning before school.

No. Upon closer examination, Austin realized the camera was focused on the man in the centre, who was dressed in a pressed white shirt, black slacks, and a brightly coloured tie. His black shoes shone as brightly as the sun. On one side followed a woman equally smartly dressed. Around them was a team of men in black: black trench coats, pants, shoes, even sunglasses.

This guy did look familiar… Was Austin's medication interfering with his memory, or did this man simply resemble someone Austin knew? It was moments like these that Austin hated the meds and wondered if he preferred uncontrolled seizures. Unlike other forms of epilepsy, his seizures didn't cause brain damage over time, nor were they life-threatening, so long as he didn't drive.

The smartly dressed man held out his hand to Pauline. "You must be Pauline Robinson. I understand we met at the Peregrines parade, though you were dressed a little differently." He meant it as a joke, referring to Pauline as Perry, and Austin laughed, but when he looked at Pauline, she was frozen like a mannequin.

I thought only Todd had that effect on her.

Austin nudged her. Still seemingly in shock, she shook the

man's hand but said nothing. Okay. So he was someone important.

The man extended a hand to Todd. "And you're Todd Parsons, one of Canada's greatest ballet dancers. I'm glad you've come back to us. I saw videos of you and this young gentleman here online. Very moving choreography."

"Thank you," Austin said.

When Todd didn't react, Austin pinched him. That woke him up.

"Oh, thank you," Todd said.

"I'm sorry," Austin said to the man. "They're usually much more talkative than this. Can I help you with something?"

The smartly dressed woman was evidently losing her patience. "We're here for an order for Susan Sanders."

He poked each one again. "You two? An order for Susan Sanders?"

They finally came to. What on earth was wrong with them? And now that Austin looked around the shop, everyone was staring.

"Sorry," Pauline said. "Just a little star-struck. We'll get it right away."

"Not a worry," the man said.

Nice guy, whoever he was.

"He's being too polite," the woman said. "This is the prime minister of Canada. He has an important announcement to make in thirty minutes."

The prime minister of Canada? What was more embarrassing: Austin's meds suppressing his brain so much that he didn't recognize the leader of his country? Or having seizures at inopportune times?

But if the camera was trained on the prime minister, and Austin was trying to raise awareness for epilepsy, and the prime minister had seen the video...

"So, Mr. Prime Minister, you said you saw the video of me and Todd?"

"I did. Spectacular dancing."

Someone in the prime minister's entourage signalled to the cameraman to point the camera at Austin. He was going to milk this.

"I did it first actually with Pauline at my school when she was still Perry. I was being bullied for loving ballet, being gay, and having epilepsy. I wanted the bullies to stop."

The prime minister looked sad. Austin hoped it was genuine. "I'm sorry to hear that. Sounds like you were very courageous."

"I just want other youth like me to know that they shouldn't be embarrassed by who they are. The LGBTQ group introduced themselves to me right away afterwards, and I've started an epilepsy support group at school, too. Did you know that about one in a hundred people in Canada get an epilepsy diagnosis in their lifetime?"

The prime minister shook his head.

"I figure that means about fifteen kids at my school. So, I started the group."

"That's very commendable."

"Thank you."

Austin looked at his watch, which he wore because he had programmed it to remind himself to take his medication. How long did it take to grab an order from the back room? Oh, wait…even though Pauline now lived with Todd, they had gone to the back room together after not having seen each other for two months…

"Excuse me, Mr. Prime Minister. I'll see where your tea order is."

The entire country was waiting on the prime minister for his important announcement, and they chose now to not keep their hands off each other?

"Todd? Pauline? Teenaged employee coming in. Keep it rated G."

A moment later, a man's leg, its foot fully pointed, extended into the doorway, a large paper bag dangling from his shoe.

"Ah," Austin said. *"Developpé* delivery. Got it. Not rated G back there."

Not even the prime minister of Canada could distract those two from their love for each other.

Austin took the bag off the foot and carried it to the front.

"The note here says it's all paid up, so you're good to go, Mr. Prime Minister."

"Thank you. And good luck to you," the prime minister said, and the entourage left.

Austin sighed. Hopefully he'd find his true love someday. But for now, he was happy with where his life was at: the bullying had stopped, he and his mom—who hadn't taken that job with the Peregrines—were talking, and he was dancing again.

He was going to ask Claire to create a new tea blend for that for this year's Christmas sale. He already had a name for it: Nutcracker Prince tea. Caffeine-free, of course.

SETTING THE RECORD STRAIGHT

Love on Belmont mixes real locations and situations with fictional ones. Here are some of the facts.

ARE TODD'S DANCE COMPANY AND AUSTIN'S BALLET SCHOOL REAL?

No. Because Todd was treated so horribly, the company that fired him isn't based on any existing dance company. I also didn't give it a name, because Canada has so many dance companies that I didn't want to risk duplicating one and implying any connection.

Although Austin's school didn't ask him to leave, I didn't want any existing ballet school in Canada to worry about negative associations with his story, so his school is fictional, too.

DOES 'SWINE LAKE' EXIST?

Absolutely! Search for "Swine Lake Muppets" on YouTube and you should find it.

EPILEPSY

Austin's form of epilepsy is similar to my own, but my eyes flicker. Other than that, our life stories are very different. For example, I was eleven and wasn't even aware I was having seizures when I was diagnosed: my parents had noticed my symptoms and had them investigated before I was old enough to drive. As such, my seizures feel more just a part of me, like your right arm feels a part of you. They also never affected my dancing, to my knowledge. I only began regularly drinking caffeinated tea in my forties. Before then, I rarely drank anything with caffeine.

For more information about epilepsy, visit epilepsy.ca.

BULLYING

Bullying is sadly still alive and well in our schools, often targeting LGBTQ students, disabled students, and male ballet dancers (regardless of sexual orientation). If you suspect your child is being bullied, don't be afraid to reach out for help. You can try BullyingCanada.ca or StopBullying.gov for resources.

Canada's Ballet Jörgen, who allowed me to use their rendition of *The Nutcracker* as Austin's inspiration for getting into ballet in the third short-story prequel, *Oh, Christmas Tea*, has begun a mentorship program for young male ballet dancers in response to bullying. It's called Böys who Dance: Abolishing Stereotypes. You can find more information at CanadasBallet Jorgen.ca.

MASCOTS AND COSTUMED CHARACTERS

I loved costumed characters as a kid. (But not Darth Vader. I apparently screamed that we leave Burger King when Darth

Vader entered as part of a promotion when I was a child.) By the time I'd reached my twenties, though, I'd become cynical and steered clear of any walking stuffed toy. When I travelled to a theme park in Florida in 2015 with my family, my curiosity got the better of me: as a Canadian, I wondered who in their right mind would voluntarily dress in a head-to-toe snowsuit in hot and humid conditions.

When we returned home, I searched the Internet for my answers and found myself following a rabbit trail of fascinating Reddit threads and blog posts. The idea for this novel baked in my subconscious for another five years until research began afresh in 2020.

Many of the professional actors inside those costumes do become as emotional as Pauline does. When I listened to *Between the Fur* and *Mascot Diaries* podcast episodes, I also started tearing up as these actors shared their stories. (The Indiana team referred to in the novel is real, though I don't know if the years match up. Listen to the *Between the Fur* episode from May 5, 2020, for the interview with Trey Mock.) I watched YouTube videos of stunts gone wrong and Mascot All-Star Games, too. Along with interviews with actors and a mascot costume designer, I discovered a career certainly not meant for me, but one for which I've developed a deep respect.

Unfortunately, the actors do get groped. But most enjoy their work and take it seriously despite either volunteering their time or being paid minimum wage. Mascots in the major leagues usually get paid more, but from the bit I could learn about salaries, it varies considerably.

I tried hard to get some experience in a costume, but it never worked out. So, if your brand ever needs a mascot actor, is open to a novice, and I'm in town, let me know. I'm 5'9", about 150 pounds, have about 20 years' experience in the performing arts, and can tap dance and do a cartwheel. Just please make sure the costume is clean.

CLAIRE'S SYSTEM OF TEA

Claire's system of tea is a combination of character development, research, and my own experiences with tea. Wuyi rock oolong, for example, does remind me of the forest floor, and I do find it grounding. The blends in the book, though, may or may not exist.

Tea can be very personal or communal. You can have six people over and each person can enjoy a different flavour of tea, or you can make one pot for all six. It's beautiful that way. Do you have a favourite tea? Drop me a line at author@loriwolfh effner.com or visit me on social media. I'd love to hear from you.

BELMONT VILLAGE

Belmont Village does indeed exist and is a wonderful, quaint shopping and eating strip on Belmont Avenue in Kitchener, Ontario, Canada. You can learn more about it at TheBelmontVil lage.ca.

Although the stores and businesses I use in *Love on Belmont* are fictional, there may be overlap with a real store, in which case I speak with the owner(s) first to ensure they're comfortable with me moving forward with my idea.

For *Tea Shop for Two* and its prequel short stories, that store is All Things Tea (AllThingsTea.ca), owned and run by George Broughton.

I'll be honest: I never liked black tea before starting this series, so I was a bit nervous about writing a book about a tea shop. But tea and books go together like Lois Lane and Clark Kent, music and dance, winter and snow. I had to open *Love on Belmont* with a book about a tea shop. So, if I was going to write about the world of tea, I had to step out of my herbal/rooibos comfort zone, and I'm so glad I did.

George and his wife Susan Broughton-Parks have been

extremely supportive in helping me learn about the world of tea. I placed my first order of black tea with George in the summer of 2020, and in the fall of 2021 as I write this, I still drink it almost daily. I'm very surprised that, depending on the day, my palate wants Ceylon or Darjeeling, because I can actually taste the difference. I have so many teas in my collection now that I have them sorted by baskets: herbals; black teas and pu-erhs; green, white, and oolongs; and rooibos. I drink two to four cups every day.

And it's no secret: the tea I drink when I write in the evenings is predominantly Spiced Chocolate Rooibos. (I enjoy a green tea for early morning writing sessions.)

Thank you, George and Susan, for a wonderful year and a half of tea education and for answering all my questions. I know that publishing this book does not mean the end of my tea journey, just the beginning.

All Things Tea's participation in this book was not a paid sponsorship. George and Susan volunteered their time, and I paid for a lot of tea. Just ask my bookkeeper.

ENJOY ALL THE LOVE ON BELMONT BOOKS

Join Pauline, Claire, and all your other friends on Belmont Avenue, where love and tea create a magical blend 🩶.

THE LOVE ON BELMONT PREQUEL SHORT STORIES

1. Claire's Tea Shop
2. Trick or Tea
3. Oh, Christmas Tea

THE LOVE ON BELMONT NOVELS

1. Tea Shop for Two
2. Oh, What the Fudge
3. Teas of Joy (*fall 2023*)

Read on for Chapter 1 of *Oh, What the Fudge*.

OH, WHAT THE FUDGE:
CHAPTER 1

*O*h, fudge.

Tracy stormed into Claire's Tea Shop, the door closing off the brisk fall wind behind her. She beelined for the counter and dispensed with the niceties to her best friend, Pauline, the owner. She needed something chocolatey.

Now.

How was she going to tell Pauline what had just happened? And that was on top of everything else that had happened to Tracy this morning, which was on top of everything already happening this month.

But *this* was the cherry truffle, and Tracy absolutely despised cherry truffles.

"I need the best you've got from David's chocolate shop. And a cup of Earl Claire. Pronto."

Pauline and Todd—Pauline's employee-turned-romantic-partner—put Tracy's order together. Tracy dropped a twenty on the counter while Pauline pulled a brownie from the display case below. The instant Pauline set a fork on the plate, Tracy dug in. She closed her eyes as the layers of flavour she so savoured in David's chocolate danced in her mouth.

"Oh, Pauline, this is perfect." She took another bite and let the crumbs carry the sweetness and hints of cocoa bitterness to her tastebuds. "Get me a second piece right away. I'm going to need it." The news was that bad.

Pauline did as requested. "I'm going to assume this means you're not okay," she said. "I know it's quarter-end and that Eric's going to start as the new CFO next week, but this much chocolate is out of character even for you."

Tracy answered with a full mouth. "If only you knew."

Todd brought over Tracy's tea, a blend of black tea, lavender, bergamot, vanilla, and rose petals. The scent of the lavender alone helped relax Tracy a smidge.

But just a smidge.

"I've got the counter," Todd said to Pauline.

Tracy was grateful. Usually not one to shy away from difficult subjects—as an executive assistant, her job was to get things done, no matter how great the challenge—she couldn't bring herself to address this one straight on. After she and Pauline had lost touch with each other for the better part of twenty-some-odd years, they had rekindled their old friendship this past summer. Pauline had returned to town, where she had simultaneously taken over her mother's tea shop and helped heal the rift that had grown between Tracy and her teenaged son. Now Pauline was taking time out of her busy day to invite Tracy to talk. She truly was the embodiment of the words "best friend."

Pauline carried Tracy's tea and second brownie to a table in a quiet corner of the café half of the cozy tea shop. Tracy followed. After they sat down, Tracy pulled out her phone to check that Austin was still in school. Good. If his medication was going to send him home, it would've done so by now. She put the phone away and continued chowing down on the brownie.

"Talk to me," Pauline said. "When you come over lunch hour, you usually start with lunch. That's a super-rich brownie, and you're…"

Tracy scooped up the last crumbs with her finger.

"Okay, you're done the first one."

Tracy sighed. "It's not only work. David's caught pneumonia and can't do the rest of the marketing for the Belmont Village Autumn Festival."

Pauline nodded. "Mom called this morning to let me know. I didn't want to start your Monday morning off by telling you."

"Cecilia called me from the hospital to tell me hubby wasn't doing so well. But to top off my Monday morning…" Here came the big news. "My car's in the garage because of a—wait for it—peregrine falcon."

Pauline's final full-time mascot job had been as Perry the Peregrine for the Toronto Peregrines, a major league men's hockey team.

"I'd laugh if your story didn't involve a car accident," Pauline said. "Not to mention everything else going on in your life."

The rest of the car story got stuck in Tracy's throat. She needed more chocolate. She dove into the second brownie. "Tell me about it!" she said, her mouth full.

"Are you okay? Was anyone else involved? Are they okay?"

Tracy nodded as she took another sip of tea. *Tell her now in case he comes here.*

He being Pauline's former manager, a control freak who'd forced her to sign a million-dollar non-disclosure agreement to play Perry. Pauline had signed—it had been her dream job. But when she'd had to quit after only three years, she never wanted to see him again. Her last day had only been a few weeks ago. Pauline's anger was still fresh.

Tracy had to break it to her. Chocolate coursing through her veins, she blurted it out. "I was driving by the TV station on King Street where that peregrine family lives, and I guess one was diving for food or something. Anyway, it spooked me. I got disoriented for a moment because of all the new light-rail tracks, and I slammed on the brakes. But the car behind me was going too fast to stop and he nicked me as he swerved to avoid hitting me. Then he hit the LRT platform, causing a bunch of damage to his oh-so-beautiful red Porsche, which is now also being repaired at the Belmont garage."

There. She'd said *red Porsche* with a drip of sarcasm. That should give Pauline a hint.

Instead, Pauline wrapped an arm around Tracy's shoulder and softly squeezed. Despite being a ball of energy and a six-foot-tall wall of muscle from weightlifting, Pauline could also be incredibly quiet and gentle. All those years in costume had taught her to listen. David's chocolate had been comforting Tracy for most of her forty-eight years, but Pauline's friendship was even more soothing.

"No wonder you're diving straight into the chocolate and tea. The accident, no marketing coordinator on the committee you're chairing, *and* you're going to have to work with your ex-husband. But you're sure you're okay? Do you need anything? Now I feel bad for charging you." Pauline stood up. "Let me get you a refund."

Tracy pulled her back down onto her chair. "I'd never expect a refund for something like this. And yes, I'm fine. My car's just getting inspected to make sure it's safe to drive, and Mayumi has to do a quick touch-up on the bumper." She took another bite of chocolate. "It's almost been a year since the separation but I still hear Eric in my head: 'You don't want to take any risks.' This time, though, he'd be right."

"Then what's worrying you? Are you concerned the other driver is going to sue you?"

Tracy almost choked. She *had* to tell her. Although Pauline wasn't the type to kill the messenger, with this kind of message, she couldn't be too sure. "How many people do you know who drive a red Porsche?"

Pauline's eyes popped open and darted in the direction of the garage. "He's not across the street, is he?"

A LAUGH CAME out of his phone. "Of course that would happen to you! Just watch your language when you go in there. This isn't the Toronto Peregrines' locker room."

Just his luck. The moment Ben wanted to cross the street, cars of myriad makes and models crawled past. Kitchener drivers. But where had all this traffic come from?

He pressed his phone closer to his ear so he could better hear his younger sister as he continued down the sidewalk. "This is a post-industrial, stick-in-the-mud town. Besides, Pauline doesn't run a hoity-toity tea shop. It's near some old factory. So, it's not like I'm in an upscale Toronto neighbourhood or anything."

"Ben! I hope you're not planning on saying that when you walk in there!" Susie cautioned.

"It's been a rough day already. I'm so f—"

"Benjamin!"

Ben groaned. "Don't call me that. You know I hate it."

"Someone has to since Mom and Dad passed away. You keep telling me about how important context is in business, so let me offer you some: you'll be in Pauline's business. Watch your language."

More cars? The world was rubbing in the fact that he'd have no wheels for at least a week. Because apparently life wasn't bad enough already.

"Things were rocky between me and Pauline but they ended on a good note."

"Things were rocky between you for *three years*. Just because they ended well doesn't mean she's going to put in a good word for you with her best friend, *who you were tailgating*!"

Ben groaned. "I didn't know it was her until after. I mean, what are the chances? Besides. It wasn't *exactly* tailgating. I was just kind of close. Tracy was going too slow."

"Too slow? Or the speed limit?"

"You can go ten over without getting a ticket."

Susie let out a sigh of frustration. "Change your attitude before you go in there. Based on everything you've told me, I'm pretty sure Pauline's not going to be happy to see you."

Ben pushed up his sunglasses as he rubbed his eyes. He'd had a job to do, so he did it. It wasn't his fault that Pauline's contract obligated her to never tell her family and friends that she played Perry. A video of the previous actor completely drunk with Perry's mask off had gone viral. *Perry the Pissed Peregrine*. Ben had kept his job by having the team's lawyers create an ironclad contract to ensure the incident wouldn't repeat itself.

Besides, he was certain he and Pauline had patched things up at the end. She'd told him he'd given her the best job of her ten-year career as a sports mascot. Why wouldn't she help him this once and convince Tracy to be his reference for the chief marketing officer position at her company? That idea had also seemed ironclad—or it had until Tracy slammed on her brakes.

He looked both ways along Belmont Avenue. "Does

everyone in Kitchener drive this road on their lunch?" He shifted his laptop bag to his other shoulder.

"Isn't there a crosswalk?"

"Sure. Ten steps back or so."

"Ben! Sometimes you're impossible." But Susie was laughing. "I still think you should take a break for a bit and think things over."

"I need a job, Suse. I can't do nothing."

Susie sighed. "I know." But there was doubt in her voice. "That's why we decided on your drive to New Hamburg that this was probably your strongest first step on your job hunt. But are you sure you don't want to just ask Tracy directly? Might not rock the boat as much."

Ben was sure. Back in the summer, Tracy had convinced him to publicly unmask Pauline at a major hospital fundraiser to show that a woman was underneath all that fleece. It had been a tremendous success. Only later that night did Ben understand he'd been tricked: the publicity stunt had essentially released Pauline from her non-disclosure agreement.

If things had stopped there, then yes, it would've made sense to ask Tracy first.

Except very few people could outsmart Ben. When that quality appeared in a woman in business attire...he found that very attractive. He wouldn't have acted on his attraction—he was a professional. But...he remembered it now with a smile... as he approached Pauline's change room that night, he had passed Tracy, and a gear shifted between them. Before he knew it, he was pinned against a wall as she murmured something about his hazel eyes. His smile grew as he recalled that intense kiss.

He had been less happy when he drove all the way to Kitchener only for her to turn down his offer to work under him— professionally!—after his promotion to marketing director.

She'd said something about the drive being too much. He had been disappointed: she would've made the perfect PR manager with her administrative background, understanding of public sentiment, attention to detail, knowledge of messaging, and ability to outsmart even him. Not that they would have worked together for that long, as it turned out.

A Maserati drove by, as if to add insult to injury that his beloved Porsche Panamera was being repaired. He dragged his feet back to push the crosswalk button. "Pauline smiled when she shook my hand on her last day. We're fine."

"Probably because she was looking forward to moving on."

Ben groaned. "You've been my rock for so long, Suse, and I appreciate it, but the last thing I need today is more honesty."

Her voice softened. "I'm sorry. You've got a good heart, but it doesn't help if I'm the only person who sees it. Just don't be…harsh."

The crosswalk signals flashed, and traffic finally stopped. Ben crossed the street, feeling again Tracy's soft, curvy body pressed against him that night. And her enticing lips desiring his.

But he'd stood next to her as the garage shop owner wrote down her contact info. Her silence toward him had told Ben where he stood now: in the mud.

No. She was Pauline's best friend. Tracy probably envisioned him more in a quicksand pit while she cursed him with a slow death.

Susie was right. He needed to prepare himself for the eventuality that Pauline wouldn't be too welcoming.

After working in marketing and public relations for a major league franchise for several years, Ben knew a lot of people in high places but he wasn't about to approach them for help: word of his firing would travel faster than a Formula 1 race car.

That left him with no other connections to help him than Tracy and Pauline.

He just hoped that Tracy hadn't gone to Claire's Tea Shop: that would thwart his plans even more. She'd probably taken a cab back to work, anyway.

As he passed the cars parked in front of the plaza and the store façades that covered the plaza's original red brick, he looked around him at the Belmont neighbourhood with a few brown-bricked apartment buildings and a mixture of small houses built long before cookie-cutter houses became the norm. The tall buildings of downtown Toronto felt like a fortress. Protective. Kitchener's much lower skyline and open neighbour-hoods left him feeling exposed. Vulnerable.

"I wish I could come home earlier so you wouldn't be alone right now," Susie said. "But Genny's mom's coming around to accepting the two of us together. We really need this time with her parents."

Ben could hear the regret in her voice. "No, no. Stay there. You're home in a few days. I'm glad things are looking up for the two of you. I can't believe I didn't know you're in Quebec City this weekend."

"You'll get through this."

He stared at the sign over Claire's Tea Shop again, the reality of his situation finally sinking in. "I'm not so sure. I worked for the Peregrines for ten years. I wasn't expecting to get fired this morning."

Ben ran his hand through his hair. Maybe his sister was right. Maybe he should continue to New Hamburg.

And do what? Mope? That wasn't what Ben Landry did. He sighed.

"I heard that," Susie said. "What is it?"

"Nothing."

"Benjamin…"

Seeing Claire's Tea Shop reminded Ben of nothing good. Only Earl Claire, lots of despair, and an attraction that had ended in rejection.

Great. His marketing mind was still working, only it was using his current situation to create sad jingles about his life.

Cue depressing music.

"Ben? Are you okay? You're going to be nice to Pauline, right? And you're not going to swear, especially in front of her customers?"

But Ben wouldn't have a chance to talk to Pauline first because Tracy was staring right at him through the front door of the tea shop.

"Oh, f—udge," he said aloud.

Buy *Oh, What the Fudge* now.

STAY IN TOUCH

Did you enjoy the book? You can stay in touch with Lori by visiting LoveOnBelmont.com and signing up for Lori's newsletter. She writes each one herself, so it's her words to you. You'll receive updates on Lori's next writing projects, be the first to hear about specials, and get deleted scenes. Plus, if you haven't read the short story prequels to *Tea Shop for Two*, they're included as part of your subscription.

ACKNOWLEDGEMENTS

Tea Shop for Two tackles a few stereotypes, and here I'd like to tackle another one: the lonely author. This book was certainly not written alone; I have a lot of people to thank.

Thank you to the following for their help with researching mascots:

- The management and staff of BAM Mascots;
- Russell Kovshoff, sports entertainment professional;
- Sandro Portanova, Wilfrid Laurier University alumnus and former mascot performer;
- Brittany Russell, Alumni Relations and Development Officer at Wilfrid Laurier University.

Thank you to the retired male ballet dancers who gave me insight into their careers, injuries, and transitions:

- Michel Faigaux, who retired in his 30s and opened a construction company;
- Michael James, who retired at age 25 and spent the next 15 years studying to become an orthopaedic surgeon to help dancers;
- Scott Maybank, DC, who retired at age 29 and became a chiropractor six years later.

Also thank you to Rob Jensen for his insights in teaching

boys, and Laura Murray of the Murray Patterson Marketing Group for helping me connect to some of the dancers.

(Quick note: the idea for DIY Home grew out of the plot; it didn't come from the interviews. Two of the three short-story prequels included updates to Claire's store, so it was natural to include another renovation here. As I developed the story, it became clear that I could involve Todd's family in the story in a more meaningful way by creating a national home improvement company run by Todd's father and brothers.)

Thank you to my writing team:

- Heather Wright, consulting editor and mentor;
- ali macgee, consulting editor and mentor;
- Susan Fish, editor;
- Jennifer Dinsmore, proofreader;
- Michelle Fairbanks, book cover designer;
- ZG Stories, marketing consultants;
- Anita Woodard, virtual administrator and bookkeeper;
- my street team for their feedback on early drafts of *Claire's Tea Shop*: Heather, Brenda Leavitt, Katrin Spence, Tracey, Gregg Simmons, Maria N., Sylvia B., Brittany Russell, Lois Raats, B. Mathies, and Dani Baker. They helped me shape *Claire's Tea Shop* and therefore the subsequent short stories and this novel.

I have a fabulous team. Any remaining errors in the novel are mine. (And yes, I've come to accept that "bicep" is becoming a singular noun.)

Thank you to the Writers' Union of Canada for a micro-grant to help with the outline of this book.

Thank you to Dani Baker, author of the *Hansel & Pretzel*

Mystery series, for loaning me the Kitchener Blizzard. Check out her books at DaniBakerBooks.com.

Thank you to my family for their support: to Mom and Dad for enrolling me in dance; to Kristin for answering some of my dance questions; and to Corey, Khristopher, and Jonnathan, for tolerating the insane hours I've been working this year.

Thank you to the producers of *The Masked Singer* for giving me and my family a show we all enjoy viewing.

Thank you to my dance teachers: to Deardra King-Leslie for teaching me tap and jazz (and a little baton), guiding me through over a decade of competition, and giving me so many opportunities to teach. Without you, this and many other books would have never been written.

Thank you to my ballet teachers: Beth Krug and Sharon Laramie for supporting my RAD exams in my youth, April March for supporting the later years of my competitive dance career, and Rosemarie Harris for re-introducing me to ballet in my adult years.

ABOUT LORI

Lori's first memory of Belmont neighbourhood is of her falling out of her bed at her grandparents' home when she was perhaps three. Opa, her grandfather, sadly passed away in his mid-60s, but that didn't stop Oma, her grandmother, from creating many, many happy memories in her home for her family.

Across the tracks and up a set of cement stairs was Belmont Village, a quaint shopping strip. Oma always bought her lottery tickets there and often took Lori and her sister to the convenience store to buy them a sugary treat.

But at the time, Lori had no idea Belmont neighbourhood and Belmont Village would be the source of the most wonderful romance in her life: her future husband.

When she met her future in-laws about 20 years later, they learned they had already met: Lori's in-laws had run that small convenience store until the mid-80s. Moreover, their paths had crossed often with those of Lori's mom's family before Lori was even a thought.

Happy memories, shared fates, love…

And shopping.

How could Belmont Village *not* be the perfect place to set a sweet romance series about different couples in different stages of a relationship?

Lori lives in Waterloo, Ontario, with her husband and two sons and visits Belmont Village whenever she can.

facebook.com/loriwolfheffner

twitter.com/LoriWolfHeffner

instagram.com/loriwolfheffner

goodreads.com/lori_wolf-heffner

bookbub.com/author/lori-wolf-heffner

pinterest.com/loriwolfheffner

amazon.com/author/loriwolfheffner